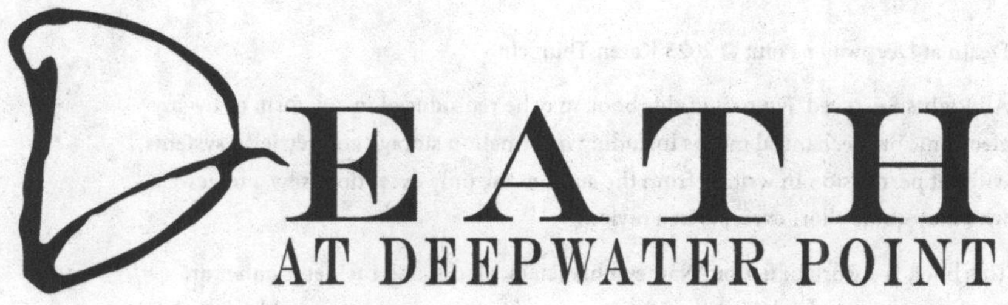

DEATH
AT DEEPWATER POINT

DR HAMISH HART MYSTERIES
BOOK FOUR

Printed in Australia
Cover and internal design by Shawline Publishing Group Pty Ltd
First Printing: June 2023

Shawline Publishing Group Pty Ltd
www.shawlinepublishing.com.au

Paperback ISBN 978-1-9229-9331-1
eBook ISBN 978-1-9229-9336-6

Distributed by Shawline Distribution and Lightningsource Global

 A catalogue record for this work is available from the National Library of Australia

More great Shawline titles can be found by scanning the QR code below.
New titles also available through Books@Home Pty Ltd.
Subscribe today at www.booksathome.com.au or scan the QR code below.

DEATH AT DEEPWATER POINT

DR HAMISH HART MYSTERIES
BOOK FOUR

KAREN THURECHT

Also by Karen Thurecht

The *Dr Hamish Hart Mysteries* series
Book One: *Murder at the Dunwich Asylum*
Book Two: *Plantation Murders*
Book Three: *Murder at Frog's Hollow*

*In celebration of strong, intelligent women:
my daughters-in-law Lozen, Bec and Yoori.*

CONTENTS

ACKNOWLEDGMENTS

I acknowledge and pay respects to the people of the Yugambeh language region of the Gold Coast and all their descendants both past and present. I also acknowledge the many Aboriginal people from other regions as well as Torres Strait and South Sea Islander people who now live in the Southport area and have made an important contribution to the community.

CHAPTER ONE

A Marine Board enquiry into the circumstances attending the collision between the Southport Steam Shipping Company's steamer Natone, and the Moreton Bay Oyster Company's steamer The President, which occurred off the jetty at Southport on the 5th instant, concluded yesterday. The first witness examined gave evidence to the effect that the Natone had been at the Labrador Jetty at about the same time as The President and was following in the wake of the vessel. After leaving the Labrador Jetty the Natone came out into mid-channel, being then about two lengths astern of The President. When abreast of the crossing mark on Stradbroke Island, the Natone's bow was just a little behind the port quarter of The President. There was a strong ebb tide and in crossing toward the Southport Jetty, the Natone did not follow its proper course but took a sweep towards the mainland. The next moment, the Natone struck The President a little above the midship section nearly at right angles.

The Brisbane Courier. Wednesday 26 May, 1886

"Good Lord! Why is there such a crowd at the wharf?" Dr Hamish Hart struggled to tuck his own case under his arm while simultaneously juggling Rita's luggage from one hand to the other.

Rita ignored the question.

"Which way do we go?" he said.

Hamish stood alongside his friend Rita to consider the options while their fellow travellers pushed past, impatient to join the throng. The humidity in the air tugged at his skin, exaggerated by the stifling proximity of the crowd. Brightly coloured hats fluttered like strange birds against the dull sky. Tugging at his collar, he felt the sweat drip down his neck.

"I don't understand why I'm wearing a woollen coat on a trip to the seaside," he said.

Rita feigned a look of shock. "Dr Hamish Hart," she said, "did you really expect to travel on the steamer in your bathing suit?" She stifled a laugh. Hamish was used to her teasing. They had been friends a long time. That they sounded to others like a married couple was a source of amusement to them. Hamish knew Rita would never marry him. Nonetheless, he found it difficult to love any other woman.

He was looking forward to the weekend at The Deepwater Point Hotel, as it would be a pleasant break from his general practice. While he loved his work, the monotony of the chronic illnesses of the middle-classes sometimes bored him. When Rita suggested they catch the steamer to Southport to see an exhibition by the famous balloonist, Celestine Dupont, he agreed enthusiastically. Now that they were on the wharf, hemmed in by a crowd of fellow travellers, he wondered if he'd made the right decision. He disliked crowds. And he was hot in his coat.

As they finally inched their way to the front of the mob, Hamish was able to gain a decent view of the two grand steamers that waited at the wharf. The President was berthed to the left, and the Natone, a much larger and more impressive vessel, to the right. The promenade deck appeared to lean towards the crowd, perched as it was above the roof of the saloon.

"Six hundred passengers can fit on the main deck and another two hundred on the promenade," said Hamish, unable to suppress his admiration.

"And here they all are," Rita said, looking around at the crowd.

Hamish's eye was drawn to the wheel reaching from the river to the full height of the main deck. "She should be quick with that double wheel," he murmured. He was startled by a man in a starched uniform who silently took his and Rita's bags and created a path to the back of the Natone where a ramp led into the steamer's lower section.

"I see we're booked on the Natone," said Rita. "I like the little steamer, The President."

Hamish noted the crowd thinning in the direction of The President. Passengers were already boarding the smaller steamer. "The Natone is said to be faster," he pointed out.

"They're not faster at boarding," said Rita.

"We'll get to Southport more quickly on the larger vessel," said Hamish. "I'm certain of it."

"I've heard The President provides the faster trip," said Rita, not looking at him.

Hamish stopped. "Really?" he said. "Would you care to make a wager?"

Rita looked up at him, a small tuck upward at the corner of her lips. "Certainly," she said. "What can you afford to lose?" Hamish immediately regretted his challenge. His friend was tiny, but relentless. Whatever wager he made now, he would be held to, should he lose.

He decided to make the stakes high. "If The President reaches Southport before the Natone, I get your Harriet Martineau translation of Comte. To keep," he added.

Rita's eyes grew large. She hesitated. Hamish knew well enough that was her favourite book. "Fine," she said at last. "If the Natone reaches Southport first, I get your first edition Darwin."

"What?" cried Hamish. "That book is worth a fortune."

"So, you are not so sure the Natone is the faster vessel, after all?"

"I agree to the wager," said Hamish. "I will not need to give up my Darwin."

They shook hands vigorously.

By the time the wager had been set, they had inched their way onto the gangway.

The substantial iron saloon steamer bustled with life as they and the other passengers filed on board and made their way onto the promenade deck. Rita slipped her arm behind Hamish's elbow and held tight. The agitation of the wait in the crowd fell away when Hamish felt her closeness. They climbed a narrow staircase to the upper deck and manoeuvred their way to the edge, where they gripped the rail, passengers pressing against them from behind. All the seats on the upper deck were occupied, but many of the passengers were crushed against the rails, gazing back at the wharf. The last passengers were still making their way onto The President when Hamish felt the Natone paddle turn in the river.

"We'll see who gets there faster," said Hamish over the noise. The Natone edged out into the river and passed the other steamer.

"Early days yet," said Rita. "Come downstairs with me. I need tea."

There were two saloons below. Hamish and Rita entered the one reserved for first-class passengers. They admired the maple lined walls and the tiny landscapes of Tasmanian scenery in the panels between the windows. As they took seats by one of the windows, they looked out at a view of bustles and waistcoats.

"You'd think we'd have a clear view in first class," said Rita.

Hamish was looking around for a waiter. "I believe the only difference between first and second class is the washbasin in the ladies retiring room." He waved towards a man in a white uniform.

Rita laughed. "Useful," she said.

The man in white placed tea and cake on their table and Rita tucked in.

"You're beaming," said Hamish.

"I love an adventure," said Rita over a creamed scone.

"I'm not sure how much adventure there'll be," said Hamish. "Southport is a sleepy place by all accounts. Unless you are excited by fishing."

Rita put down the scone almost knocking her tea over. Hamish reached over and put it right just in time.

"Of course, there'll be excitement," cried Rita. "There's the ballooning exhibition tomorrow. A lady balloonist! Who would have thought Celestine Dupont would come here to Queensland. It must feel like the end of the world to her."

"The owners of the Grand would have paid a fortune to get her here. Imagine the cost involved in securing someone of her celebrity and bringing her all the way from Paris to Southport."

Rita smiled. "Perhaps she was up for an adventure as well. People say she is tremendously attractive."

Hamish's eyebrows arched. "Do they now?"

By the time they had finished their second cup of tea, the crowd outside the window let out a collective gasp, and Hamish and Rita saw the tall chimney of The President steaming past. The passengers on deck waved enthusiastically at an equally excited crowd waving back at them from the deck opposite.

Rita thrust her slim arm in the air. "Yes!" she cried.

"That behaviour is un-lady-like," said Hamish.

"When have you known me to be lady-like? Besides, you're being sullen."

A gap appeared in the onlookers outside as The President disappeared and Hamish was able to see the bank of the river, the width of which had broadened significantly as they neared the mouth. A jolt made Hamish grab both cups of tea to steady them as the steamer made its way across the tidal currents into Moreton Bay. They turned the corner and were on their way through the Bay and along the coast toward Deepwater Point. There was a distinctly different smell in the air, the smell of the sea, and the air was cooler. Rita adjusted her shawl.

The steamers passed one another twice on the long trip south. Each time, Rita stood up to cheer on the object of her wager. The President was in the lead for two hours in the last half of the journey but in the end the Natone picked up speed in the final leg and came in view of the dock almost an hour ahead of The President. Hamish chose not to cheer out loud, though he was quietly relieved he could keep possession of his Darwin. He didn't really want Rita's translation of Comte. He decided not to mention the wager unless she did.

A rush of passengers pushed against one another to ascend the stairs and gain their first view of the seaside town. Hamish and Rita joined them and found themselves a spot three rows back from the rail where they balanced on their toes peering outward. Rita was too low to see anything, but Hamish realised the passengers at the front were pointing to something out to sea. He followed their outstretched arms upward to the object of their collective gaze. His eyes opened wide, and his lips parted.

"What is it?" shouted Rita. She was on the tips of her toes, but Hamish knew she wouldn't be able to see over the fluff, fur and flowers in front of her.

"She's majestic," cried Hamish.

"Who is?" screamed Rita.

"Look higher instead of trying to see ahead. Can't you see the top of the masts?"

Hamish joined the others and pointed toward a large schooner with a gleaming hull and tall masts. He was breathless. He'd always loved ships. At one stage, he had dreamt of work as a ship's surgeon. But when faced with the opportunity of such a position, the reality appeared to fall short of his imaginings and he decided to remain land based. Rita managed to wriggle her way into a front row position against the rail and cried out in delight at the sight of the massive ship aground on the bar. Everyone was awed by the sight of such a large ship trapped in the sand.

The Scottish Prince looked comfortable on her sandy perch, but the waves were beginning to rise and lick at her lower deck. "How did a ship that size come to be stuck on a sandbank?" Rita called back over her shoulder. "I'm sure the owners are asking the same question," laughed Hamish.

It was half-past six and a strong south-easterly wind had blown up during the trip. The passengers of the Natone made their way in single file toward the gangway and landed on dry ground in a single writhing mass. Rita struggled to hold on to her hat in the wind while Hamish placed his hand on her head. "It's an amazing hat," he commented. "I've never seen you wear anything like it." The hat had a low flat crown and a straight brim that increased in width at the front where the straw was turned up flat against the crown. "I'm not convinced it was a sound choice for a steamer ride, though," he added.

"It wasn't windy when we left Brisbane," quipped Rita.

A parade of men in the same starched uniforms were bringing the bags from the back of the steamer onto the jetty. They placed them unceremoniously on the promenade and a circle of people amassed around them. Passengers pushed past one another to identify and retrieve their bags.

Hamish was contemplating entering the fray when he heard a voice.

"Welcome Miss." The voice came from shoulder height. "I'll get *yer* bags *fer yer* Miss."

Both Hamish and Rita glanced down at the freckled face of a boy about twelve or thirteen.

"It's perfectly fine," said Rita, "the doctor can collect our bags." The boy lowered his head. Rita smiled. "Stay with us and I'll pay you anyway," she said.

"As soon as we clear ourselves from this mob," added Hamish, not sure why he had to navigate his way through the throng to collect the bags if they were paying the boy to do it.

By the time Hamish returned with their luggage, the crowd had dispersed into waiting carriages, or further along the promenade. Rita offered the boy a coin in her small, gloved hand. He took it gratefully and scampered away. Hamish looked to the left and right. "Up there," he said, pointing north along the road, "the Grand Hotel at Deepwater Point."

"It's certainly grand," said Rita, picking up the one bag she had packed for the weekend. They proceeded along the esplanade toward the hotel, the sound of the waves lapping against the seaway in their ears and the smell of salt in the air. Rita shifted her bag from one hand to the other and shook her wrist.

"Let me take it," said Hamish, wrenching the bag from her fingers.

"I don't understand why you didn't allow the boy to carry it," said Hamish. "I can't fathom your periodic bouts of fierce independence in relation to small matters."

"He's a child," said Rita.

"Yes, but now I'm carrying all the bags."

Rita smiled and her eyes danced. "Give mine back then," she said. "I didn't ask you to take it."

Hamish walked on. He and Rita had been friends since Hamish was fresh out of medical school. He knew her as well as anyone could, but she was still a mystery to him in many ways.

Ahead of them, the Grand Hotel towered over the esplanade.

"According to the Courier, it is the most glorious hotel in the colony," said Rita.

Hamish tilted his head to the side. "It looks like a miniature version of Parliament House. It has the same roof and gables."

"It's prettier than Parliament House," said Rita.

The pale green building stretched along the esplanade for one hundred and fifty feet, as if draped in brown lace as two balconies with ornate railings ran the entire length of the structure.

At the door, Hamish noticed a tall, slim man with impeccable style speaking with a shorter, somewhat gaunt Chinese man. They seemed to be in an earnest conversation when the tall man saw Hamish and Rita approaching. He immediately turned away from the Chinese man in a gesture of dismissal and looked Hamish and Rita up and down. The Chinese fellow scarpered away as though he was guilty of something.

"Why on earth are you carrying your own luggage?" said the tall man.

Hamish and Rita stopped in their tracks and Hamish dropped the bags. The man looked around for the bag boy, who was cowering behind him.

"I dismissed him," stated Rita. "I prefer to carry my own luggage."

The man looked at Hamish who had both his and Rita's luggage at his feet.

"Hmm," he said.

"I'll take them to your rooms, Sir," said the freckled boy, ducking around his boss to pick up the bags.

Hamish handed him another coin.

They followed the manager indoors and gazed around the interior of the entrance hall where a luxurious space unfolded and offered to hug them. It didn't seem possible to enter a space, the dimensions of which were difficult to comprehend, while at the same time feel the welcoming warmth of a beautiful home. Nonetheless, the sense of grandeur seemed incongruent with their expectations of a seaside village in this frontier colony. Hamish noticed an odour that filled him with warmth.

"What is that aroma?" he asked quietly. Rita was still taking in the scene with a sense of awe.

"Linseed oil and mahogany," she said.

Rita stared up at a glittering crystal chandelier that descended from the ceiling at the centre of the hall, overhanging an enormous staircase that swept elegantly up to the second floor.

A voice interrupted their thoughts.

"Campbell Charles," said the man, "hotel manager."

Hamish took his outstretched hand. "Doctor Hamish Hart and Doctor Rita Cartwright," he said.

Campbell Charles bowed slightly toward Rita. "A lady doctor. How very unusual."

"Isn't it?" said Rita. "And yet here we are."

"Dr Cartwright graduated from the London School of Medicine for Women," said Hamish. "She is very accomplished."

"Indeed," said Campbell Charles, still sounding doubtful.

"I work at the Lady Bowen Lying-In Hospital for Women," said Rita. "I am unable to register as a practicing physician in the colony at present, so I am employed as a pharmacist. I'm confident it will not be long before the restrictions are lifted."

The manager's lips curled upward only slightly as he handed them each a set of keys.

"Your rooms are upstairs and to the left," he said. "Dinner is at seven in the dining hall. It is said to be one of the finest examples in the colony."

He pointed to a large room to their left. Before the entrance to the larger room there was a small room with a bay window, two cosy armchairs and an occasional table.

"We call this the Reading Room," said Campbell proudly.

Hamish and Rita looked past the reading room into an expansive space set with large round tables and chairs. They were still trying to take in the enormity of the dining hall when Campbell Charles directed their attention to the right of the entrance hall.

"There are also some suites on this floor," he said. "Colonel Otis Winter and his nurse are permanent residents in one of them. In the others we accommodate families. As you can imagine, we are very busy over the Christmas season."

"I find myself grateful we have come in February," said Hamish. "I prefer a more relaxing atmosphere. Dr Cartwright, on the other hand, is seeking excitement."

Campbell Charles smiled condescendingly at Rita. "There'll be enough of that this weekend, my dear," he promised. "Celestine Dupont and her exhibition will satisfy your desires in that regard."

"I'm looking forward to it," said Rita.

Hamish was proud of her. She had shown uncharacteristic restraint in not bristling at the hotel manager's condescension. He held her arm lightly. "Shall we?" he said, gently guiding her toward the stairs before she had time to change her mind about letting the hotel manager off.

Rita followed him graciously. "I'll bring the book to you as soon as I have washed and changed," she said. Hamish smiled. "No need," he said.

They went into their adjoining rooms and Hamish stretched his aching arms.

"Come and look," Rita cried from the next room. "I have my own balcony."

Hamish joined her.

"I know," he said. "Every room has one."

Looking out over the sea wall, in one direction they could see a long stretch of ocean reaching to Burleigh Heads. In front of them, they could see across the passage to Stradbroke Island. They enjoyed the scene for a few moments before noticing the force of the wind on their skin.

Hamish brushed curly sand-coloured hair back from his face. His fringe was kept long to mask a scar down one side of his cheek, but at this moment it had been blown across his eyes and was caught in his mouth. "There is quite a blow," he said. Rita helped him push back his hair. The proximity of her hands to his face made him want to hold her, but he pulled away instead. "Leave it," he said, "I need to get inside out of the wind."

While Hamish secured the shutters, Rita discarded her shoes and tested the plush carpet with her stockinged toes.

Hamish dodged past her to the door. "I'll call for you in half an hour for dinner," he said. Within seconds, Rita was standing before him, her hands held out with the Comte translation as if it were a sacrificial offering. Hamish scanned the cover and looked into her eyes. "I don't want it," he said.

She pushed it further toward him. "You won the bet. You must take it."

Hamish took the book from her hands and turned toward the door. Then he turned back again and held out the book.

"I have this translation of Comte, you might like to read while we are on holiday," he said, "if you are interested."

Rita smiled and took the book back.

"It's only a loan," he said.

"Of course," grinned Rita.

CHAPTER TWO

The opening of the fine hotel which the directors of the Southport Land Company have erected at Deepwater Point, Southport, was celebrated on Saturday with an unpretentious little ceremony of a very enjoyable character. A party of gentlemen, thirty-five in number, including representations of the company and their friends, went to the spot in the steamer Natone, and were there entertained at a banquet in the evening, being thus enabled, not only to see the building itself, but also to test its cuisine and the contents of its cellar. The result was a triple success, each department coming in for its share of approval, the hotel itself and its magnificent dining hall, which is its principal feature coming in for the greatest amount of praise. The only fear that seemed to agitate the minds of the visitors was that the provisions made by the company would prove to be too much for the requirements of the locality.

The situation is a beautiful one for a seaside resort. The deep water from which the point takes its name was the delight of the old rafters, who here found a suitable place for shipping their timbers, which the sloping sandy flats of Southport and Labrador denied them, and the water is almost always within a few feet of the hotel door.

The Brisbane Courier. Tuesday 17 August, 1886.

Hamish and Rita were hungry after the trip and looking forward to meeting the other guests. Rita had quickly freshened up, but Hamish was still in the same coat and trousers he had worn on the steamer. Rita swept her hands down his coat and smiled at him affectionately. There were a lot of things Hamish worried about, many of them unnecessary in the view of others, but his appearance was not one of them. When Hamish and Rita entered the great dining hall, the fine proportions left them stunned. Hamish, who had an eye for geometry, noted it was easily sixty feet long, forty feet wide, with ceilings fifteen feet high. Two large bay windows and eight French doors meant the hall was flooded with light. At the far end, there was a card room.

Rita was taking in the grandeur when an elderly man in a wheelchair approached her.

"*Velcome* to Deepwater Point and the Palace of the Mosquito Swamp," said the man.

His German accent caught her off-guard. She turned around quickly and looked down on a mane of silver hair framing a tanned face with chiselled cheekbones and a square chin. He was peering at her through blue-white eyes, the colour of ice. The exchange had attracted Hamish's attention and he turned to face the man in the wheelchair. He could have been on a poster for a German travel company if it weren't for the chair. Despite the apparent disability, he looked lean and fit for his age. But age could be a deceptive measure of a man, Hamish knew. People were always mistaking Hamish's own age, taking him to be younger than his true years. It became a disadvantage in his profession when patients thought him young and inexperienced. Perhaps this man was less mature than was indicated by the silver hair, the wheelchair and the blanket on his knees. There was an oddness about him. He was too sure of himself, so much so that he felt bold enough to address a woman he had not met.

"Mosquito swamp?" Rita smiled.

"That's what they called this place before the hotel was built. It's known around here as the Palace of the Mosquito Swamp."

"But it's magnificent," cried Rita.

"*Ya-vol*, it is magnificent. Equal to such places in Europe. It is as if the population of Queensland is three million instead of three hundred thousand, and every man is a millionaire!"

Rita smiled.

"My apologies for not introducing myself," he said. "Colonel Otis Winter, retired. I live here at the hotel. I have a suite…" He pointed back over his head and inadvertently touched the woman behind his wheelchair on the arm.

"Hilda," he said dismissively, "my nurse."

"How do you do?" Rita and Hamish said simultaneously. Hilda barely nodded. Her face remained stern and unreadable.

Rita smiled again.

"I'm Doctor Hamish Hart and this is Doctor Rita Cartwright," said Hamish, holding out his hand. Hamish winced at the strength of the man's grip.

"A clever *frau* indeed," said the man, not shifting his gaze from Rita once, even while shaking Hamish's outstretched hand.

"Am I to take it you studied in Europe?"

"The London School of Medicine for Women," said Rita.

Just as they were wondering what to say next, the irrepressible hotel manager bounded over and addressed them.

"Wonderful," cried Campbell Charles. "I'm so glad you have already met. Follow me. I have you seated at the main table with Miss Dupont, Mr and Mrs Hembrow and Captain Black. Oh, and Mr Andrews, of course."

Hamish and Rita followed the manager to a large table at the centre of the room meticulously set with fine bone china, silver cutlery and crystal.

There was a setting without a corresponding seat, creating a space for the colonel's wheelchair. Hilda parked him neatly in his place before taking a seat herself beside him. Hamish and Rita sat together, opposite a young couple who looked to be oddly matched. She was beautiful, though overly made-up, the kind of young woman who catches the eye at any table, while he was distinct only in his ability to blend in. Hamish thought him pleasant looking, but without any notable features at all.

"Mr and Mrs Hembrow," said Campbell to the group.

"Good evening, Colonel," said Mrs Hembrow graciously.

"Dr Hamish Hart and Dr Rita Cartwright," said Campbell.

Though Hilda sat to one side of Mrs Hembrow, she was not introduced or acknowledged.

Next, a gentleman as broad as he was tall approached the table adorned in a long woollen coat that fell flush with his boots. Hamish was instantly struck by the aura of intrigue that surrounded him.

"Come, come Captain," said Campbell. "Here! Captain Murdo Black, Sea Captain."

"Retired," cut in Black.

"Indeed."

That single word resonated with a thick Scottish brogue that placed Black as Glaswegian, more forcefully than any lengthy introduction could. Whether it was his larger- than-life presence or Hamish's own romantic notions of a life at sea, Hamish liked him immediately.

Campbell proceeded to introduce Hamish and Rita.

Next to be introduced to the table was Mr Andrews, a consulting engineer from Sydney.

"Mr Andrews is here to look into the wreck of the Scottish Prince," explained Campbell.

The guests were happily exchanging pleasantries and commenting on the magnificence of the room when silence fell over the table. Hamish became aware of the most exquisite creature imaginable sweeping across the hall toward them. All the gentlemen stood and while doing so, Hamish knocked his crystal wineglass, managing to right it an instant before red wine spilled on the pristine damask tablecloth.

His mouth was dry as he took in the petite brunette gliding toward the table in a gown of mauve taffeta that rustled as she walked. Scroop. The sound embedded itself into his mind, like music one can't forget. The woman's eyes were hazel, pale. Mesmerising. When Campbell pulled out the chair beside Hamish for the wondrous creature to sit, Hamish felt the blood rushing up his neck and into his face. His heartbeat quickened. As she sat, a wave of perfume enveloped him. Was it Lavender? Patchouli? A combination of both?

"Miss Celestine Dupont," said Campbell, "let me present Dr Hamish Hart and Dr Rita Cartwright."

Hamish held the woman's tiny fingers gently and bowed, causing his fringe to fall forward. He looked up at her through his hair and his eyes met hers for a moment before he brushed his hair back with his free hand.

"A pleasure," said Miss Dupont, still holding his gaze. She gently drew her hand from his.

Rita then leaned across Hamish and held out her hand in greeting. Celestine Dupont smiled warmly at her as well. "A doctor?" she said. "I am privileged to meet such an outstanding woman."

Rita leaned in close to Hamish and whispered into his ear, "Change seats with you?"

Her eyes were dancing and she had a subtle cheeky smile.

"Not on your life," replied Hamish. He needed to focus. The presence of the magical French mademoiselle at his side unnerved him. It suddenly mattered to him how he presented himself. He decided to concentrate on the menu, a small work of art with gold lettering impressed into quality white paper. Hamish examined his closely.

"I understand *Potage Rachel*," he whispered to Rita, "but what is the next item?"

"Chef created a fresh menu, in honour of our guest Mademoiselle Dupont," said the colonel, watching Hamish struggle with the French offerings. "Not to my taste."

Hamish risked a glance sideways at the mademoiselle. She showed no sign of having taken offence at the colonel's remark.

Rita leaned over to look at the long description above Hamish's finger. *Toute de veau composee de longe de veau, leches de mignon de veau, de fole de veau rose etris de reau aux pistachios et aux truffes.*

"Veal pie with pistachios and truffles," she said.

"Right," said Hamish, relieved. He glanced sideways at Celestine, but she was in conversation with Mrs Hembrow and appeared oblivious to his linguistic limitations.

As steaming bowls of mushroom soup arrived before them, the colonel addressed Mr Andrews.

"How went the inspection today, sir?"

"It is my privilege to represent the owners of the vessel, the Scottish

Prince," Andrews explained to Hamish and Rita. "I hoped to carry out a close inspection of the barque today."

"Oh yes," said Rita. "We saw it on our way in. How long has it been there?"

Mr Andrews sipped his soup before answering.

"Since Thursday," he said, wiping each corner of his mouth carefully with a napkin.

"The third. The steamer ran afoul of a sandbank in the early hours of that morning. She's been stuck there ever since. The owner wants an assessment as to whether she can be floated."

"And what did you find?" asked the colonel. Hamish noted that he seemed annoyed at having to repeat his question.

"I went out on the Kate this morning, as you know. But these awful winds prevented us from getting close enough to board. We had to anchor inside Stradbroke Island, and the best I could do was to view the Scottish Prince through a glass from the end of the spit. I could get no closer."

"Inconvenient," said the colonel.

"What did you conclude?" asked Mrs Hembrow.

"In my opinion, she can be floated without much difficulty," he said. "She seems to be lying comfortably on the sandbar and since she has come to be, to a certain extent, embedded in the sand, the waves have not had too negative an effect on her. Tomorrow, I take a crew on the lifeboat to see if we can board her, weather permitting."

"The wind has picked up considerably this evening," said Murdo Black. "It'll not be clear on the morrow."

"How did the Scottish Prince get stuck?" asked Rita, genuinely interested.

"These things happen," said Mr Andrews. "It was no one's fault. A dark night and those shifting sands in the passage are treacherous."

Not a moment passed before Murdo Black shocked them all.

"*Shite,*" he declared.

Everyone stopped, soup spoons caught midway to their mouths. Hamish couldn't help an amused crook to the corner of his lips. He found himself fascinated as to what would come next from the giant Scotsman.

"*T'was Cap'n* Little *ta* blame," he said. "Navigating too close to shore, not keeping a proper watch. Should've used a lead string to test the depth and speed of the craft. Especially at night."

Curiosity piqued, Hamish asked, "how do you know that Captain… Little, is it? How do you know Captain Little was not taking the correct precautions?"

"I was on the ship," said Black. He tore a chunk of bread from the table in half and dunked one portion into his soup, spilling a good deal on the damask tablecloth as he did so.

The colonel turned his head in a gesture of disgust. He reached across with a napkin to soak up the spillage. Captain Black ignored him and carried on slopping his bread in the soup and popping it into his mouth without shame.

When it was obvious Captain Black was not inclined to provide further detail about his presence on the Scottish Prince, the colonel stepped in to clarify.

"The captain sailed from Glasgow on the Scottish Prince," he said. "When the passengers were taken off the ship and transported to Brisbane, Black came here to us instead. He states he has business in Southport."

The colonel motioned to a waiter to remove a soup-soaked napkin from the table.

"A couple of local fishermen sailed out to the steamer the night it stuck," said Black. "They warned Little, the tide was dangerously low and offered to pilot the vessel through the passage. Little dismissed them."

A murmur ran around the table. "He should have appreciated the value of local knowledge," agreed James Hembrow.

"Sounds like a case of *hubris*," suggested Hamish.

"Three tugs have tried to move her this week," pointed out the colonel, "to no avail."

"Nonetheless," said Mr Andrews watching the captain carefully, and clearly hoping to bring the conversation back from speculation to fact, "I am not engaged to assign blame, only to assess the condition of the vessel. I'm sure Captain Little will be required to answer to an enquiry."

"There must be a great deal of cargo on board," said Mrs Hembrow, changing the subject.

"At least ten thousand pounds worth, I should think," said Mr Andrews.

Mrs Hembrow's eyes lit up. "Imagine if the ship breaks up in the wind. All that would come ashore, wouldn't it?"

"Don't get your hopes up, darling," said her husband. "Mr Andrews says the ship is in great shape."

The mood had been lightened a little whether Mrs Hembrow intended it or not. By the time a full-figured waitress removed their empty soup bowls, Mrs Hembrow was beaming at the idea of treasure from the Scottish Prince washing ashore. Campbell Charles returned to the table to deliver the veal pie. Hamish was distracted by the enticing aroma, followed up by the delicious flavour, so he was taken aback when Black blurted out a further comment on the wreck of the schooner.

"The fact remains that Little is incompetent. His license should be removed."

Hamish almost dropped his fork.

Glances went back and forth around the table as the guests acknowledged the tension caused by the captain's outburst. No one wanted to look at Mr Andrews, at whom the comment was clearly addressed. Everyone was surprised when it was Hilda who broke the awkward silence.

"People in glass houses," she said, quietly.

CHAPTER THREE

We were ordered out the night before last to protect and escort a square of three regiments and 350 camels from Suakin to Zareba. We began at 9 in the evening and marched to the rendezvous, arriving at daybreak yesterday morning. It took us about an hour and a half to fill our balloon. At daybreak I sent Mackenzie up to a height of 400 feet and we worked at that altitude until he got all the outside country well searched. I then pulled down to 300 feet and worked him from the inside of the square for the seven mile march. We had no hitch of any sort. We could see everything and the COs of the different squares were both delighted as they asked me how far off the enemy were, so I kept them well advised, the result being that we did not lose a single man or camel.

The Argus, Melbourne. Tuesday 21 July, 1885

A tense silence gripped the table.

The nurse had not previously addressed the conversation, nor had she been acknowledged by the group. Hamish was ashamed to realise he had forgotten she was there.

"Are you addressing me?" asked Captain Black. His voice deep and his words coming slowly, a hint of threat implicit.

"As a sea captain, I am certain you would have had occasion to wish you'd made a different decision," said Hilda, carefully keeping her eyes down to show she was aware of her inferior status. At that point, Hamish wondered why she was seated at the table with them at all. The colonel had not appeared to him a man likely to treat a servant as an equal. As he pondered that thought, he noticed the sharp look the colonel shot at the young woman. Surely that would put an end to her impertinence.

"The sea is a dangerous place," Hilda Jenkins went on. "Can you say you have never been responsible for the death of any man… or woman… under your command, Captain?"

A shade of thunder descended over Murdo Black's face.

There was an uncomfortable silence while Hamish and the others waited to see what the captain would say in response.

"Be quiet," snapped the colonel. Hilda Jenkins was quiet, but she held her ground internally, her face bent over her soup, her mouth set and determined.

The comment seemed impudent to Hamish, coming from such a young woman, and addressed toward a man of the captain's age and rank, though he couldn't help thinking there was something deeply significant behind it, and wondered what that something might be. Black's rugged face was flushed. The rush of blood to his skin may have been an indicator of shame, but it may equally have been a sign of offence taken at such impudence. A flicker of confusion in the captain's eyes led Hamish to believe Murdo Black might be struggling to understand what the girl was referring to, or at least, how she knew about it. Black continued to fork pie into his mouth and chew slowly and deliberately. A ploy to calm his emotions.

The colonel glared at his young nurse for a few moments, then apparently decided the best course of action was to move the conversation on.

Turning his attention to Mademoiselle Dupont, he said, "the wind is blowing a gale outside. It seems the weather will not treat you kindly tomorrow. Will your equipment stand up to this force of nature?"

Celestine Dupont smiled confidently, her brown curls swept back on one side and held there by a shimmering diamond encrusted clip that caught the light and held Hamish's attention.

"*Oui, le vent souffle.* But I have flown in heavier weather," she said. "A bit of air behind the balloon can be exhilarating."

The colonel nodded in acknowledgement. "We had balloonists in the services," he said. "We sent them up to sail over the region and keep the officers informed as to the whereabouts of the enemy." He watched the aeronaut closely.

Hamish noticed Celestine hesitate. Her spoon stopped mid-air a few inches from her mouth. Her composure returned quickly, "Military experimentation has added *grande* value to the progress of aeronautics."

Hamish was impressed by her competent grasp of English. He imagined she travelled Europe with her exhibition, but it seemed an accomplishment to speak English so well. Perhaps it was becoming a universal language for those whose business took them across continents.

"There is talk in military circles about a new air balloon said to have been invented by one of your countrymen named De Villars," said the colonel.

The bright light that shone behind Miss Dupont's eyes went out and her neck stiffened.

Mrs Hembrow, on the other hand was intrigued. "A mysterious invention, Colonel? Do tell us about it."

"It seems that the problem of balloon travel has been pretty much solved," he said. "As you know, in the past, a balloon could only sail as far as the wind would carry it, and in the direction of the wind. But the direction of currents of air at different heights above earth can be used to steer a balloon if one has the capacity to send the balloon up higher, and lower, at will to make use of these currents." The colonel could see he had the attention of everyone at the table. "With an ordinary balloon, this is impossible because it would require too much gas and ballast. The inventor, De Villars, has found a way to raise and lower the height of a balloon without throwing out ballast, or depleting his supply of gas. It is said he sold the exclusive rights of his discovery to the French Government."

"What a boon that would be for the military," said Hamish.

"The French military," said Mrs Hembrow, then turning her attention to Celestine, she said, "surely, your father would have known this man De Villars. The ballooning community of France cannot be so large."

The colonel watched Celestine intently.

"My father may have known this man," she said quietly. "I did not."

The colonel continued watching her as a scientist might study an insect. "But you must," he said. "All of France must know of him. And what of Leon Gambetta? The man who escaped the besieged Paris in a balloon during the war. He must be a national hero in your country."

"The Franco-Prussian War?" asked Hamish. "That was seventeen years ago. Mademoiselle Dupont would have been a child."

Celestine sipped her soup, responding with no more than a slight twitch of her lips. She kept her eyes down.

"I read somewhere that your father was killed in a ballooning accident," continued Mrs Hembrow. "Are you not afraid when you go up after such a tragic turn?"

"*Nein*, that question is lacking tact," said Colonel Winter, feigning a look of shock. "Mademoiselle Dupont may prefer not to talk about her father's tragic accident at the table."

Celestine looked directly at Colonel Winter for the first time. She seemed defiant when she spoke.

"*C'est bon*," said the tiny brunette. "It is public knowledge, anyway. The story was in all the papers. A year ago, my father and I went up on a routine flight to test the equipment. We left from a village in rural France. Tragically, a change in the wind sent the balloon off course and then dangerous winds caused a tear in the fabric. We descended suddenly and landed in the Rhine. I was rescued from the river, but my father was not."

"My heavens," cried Mrs Hembrow, "was your father ever found?"

"*Non*," said Miss Dupont.

"He may not be dead," said Hilda.

Once again, everyone stared at her. Hamish wondered for a second time that evening why the young nurse would say such a thing. Before anyone else had a chance to voice their questions out loud, Glenda Hembrow made their reactions irrelevant.

"Yes," she cried, "he might be stranded on a deserted island, like… what's that book, dear?" She turned to her husband.

"Robinson Crusoe."

"Yes, that's it, Robinson Crusoe." Glenda Hembrow looked around the table triumphantly. Most at the table were trying to follow the connections.

"The Rhine is a river," said Murdo Black.

Mrs Hembrow looked confused and Hamish suppressed a chuckle.

But Celestine Dupont's face had darkened to a shade of fuchsia. She stood up in a rustle of fabric and said, "I have an early start." She nodded to each guest briefly before gliding rapidly from the dining hall. The remaining guests silently reflected on whose fault it may have been that their honoured company was troubled into leaving the table early. Suddenly, the shutters on the veranda crashed shut and those left at the table jumped.

Captain Murdo Black stood. "It's an ill storm that's brewing," he said. "I recommend an early night." With that, he strode from the hall, leaving the remaining guests looking nervously at one another.

"Well," said Mr Hembrow, "I imagine we are all getting up early for the exhibition in the morning, so it might be as well to take the captain's advice." He held his elbow out to Mrs Hembrow, who stood and hooked her arm through his. Her wrap slipped from the back of her chair and her husband bent over to pick it up for her. He placed it carefully around her shoulders. She looked frail in that moment. Like a woman carrying a burden beyond her years. Hamish was glad she had her husband to care for her. He laughed silently to himself at the notion that Rita should somehow hear his thoughts. She would dress him down thoroughly at the idea that a woman required a husband to take care of her.

As Mr and Mrs Hembrow were moving toward the great staircase, Mr Andrews also took his leave. Hamish looked at the colonel who said, "I'm going to retire to the smoking room," he said. Hamish picked up on the subtle invitation. "I think I'll join you."

Rita drank the last mouthful of wine in her glass. "Bed for me," she said. "You gentlemen enjoy your sherry and tobacco."

CHAPTER FOUR

At 11:34 a.m. our Southport correspondent telegraphed as follows:- The barque Scottish Prince missed stays at 3 o'clock this morning and ran aground in two fathoms of water off the bar at low water. Mr Buckley and a local crew boarded her at great risk, but the Captain, not apprehending danger, declined to land the passengers, who were numbered thirty-five. Three boats, however, are kept manned and lying alongside the ship, ready for an emergency. A tug-boat has been wired for and the vessel is expected to get off at high water with her assistance. A kedge anchor has been put out to hold the ship should she float. A light north-east wind is blowing, and the sea is moderate. The ship is lying to seaward.

Darling Downs Gazette. Saturday 5 February, 1887.

Hilda pushed the colonel and his wheelchair into the smoking room and placed him before the fireplace. There was no fire on this muggy summer evening. A large bunch of fresh flowers rested in the grate.

Hamish followed and sat down in one of the luxurious armchairs imported from America.

"Leave us, now," said the colonel. Hilda looked suspiciously at Hamish but left the room.

"A lovely meal," said Hamish, taking a cigarette from the ornate wooden case left open on the occasional table for their convenience.

The colonel tilted his head to one side and dropped one side of his mouth to indicate indifference. He also took a cigarette, lit it, and offered Hamish the use of his gold lighter. Hamish leant over to allow the colonel to light his cigarette for him, then drew in a long breath and blew out the smoke slowly.

This first draw was the most relaxing and he wanted to enjoy it. After that, the intake of the rest of the cigarette was mechanical.

"Mademoiselle Dupont seemed quite upset by the talk of her father," Hamish said when he was fully satisfied.

"Huh, the French are overly emotional," said the colonel.

"I don't know," said Hamish. "I think it was understandable. It was an insensitive question."

"Both Glenda Hembrow and my nurse Hilda, lack tact," said the colonel, "but while Mrs Hembrow is guileless, I'm afraid my nurse has quite a sting.

"What do you mean?" asked Hamish.

At that moment, the waiter brought in two glasses and a decanter of fine sherry on an exquisite silver tray. He placed the tray on the occasional table and left in silence. Hamish poured the sherry while enjoying the enticingly sweet aroma. The colonel took a long, appreciative puff of his cigarette. "I don't mean anything by it," he said. "Suffice to say, there is nothing naïve about Hilda. And her comments are not idle. There is bitterness behind them."

The colonel stubbed out his cigarette more forcefully than was necessary and sat back in his wheelchair, his sherry glass resting on his knees.

Hamish would have liked to pursue the subject, but something about the colonel's facial expression made it evident that he wanted to leave it at that.

"What do you make of this business with the Scottish Prince?" asked Hamish, deciding to pursue a different topic.

"I think the engineer Andrews is over-confident," he said. "That ship is going nowhere. These winds will cause havoc if they continue over the weekend. Captain Black is correct about that."

"Captain Black was disturbed about something Hilda said as well," said Hamish, returning to the topic the colonel apparently hoped to avoid. "He looked as though he wanted to kill her when she asked him if he'd been responsible for the death of anyone under his command. Do you think the captain has a dark secret?"

"I think most people have a secret, doctor. Something they would rather not have brought into the light."

Hamish thought about that as he sipped his sherry. Was there anything he didn't want others to know about him? He immediately thought about his feelings for Rita. But realistically, his feelings were no secret. Everyone who was acquainted with them knew. Even Rita knew, though she pretended she didn't out of kindness. And Rita was an open book. She had no secrets. She told everyone everything. She informed him of her preference for women on their first meeting, told him about her family's response and laughed about it. He knew it was hopeless, but he couldn't help it. Thoughts about Rita made him melancholy, especially when he was drinking. Who else did he know who might have a secret? Wallace, his cook? Now there is a man with secrets, he thought.

Hamish met Wallace during his time on Stradbroke Island two years prior. He was a cook at the Dunwich Benevolent Society at the time, but he had been a ship's cook most of his life. He was forthcoming with most aspects of his past. But he had enjoyed such a life of adventure that Hamish imagined he would not live long enough to hear all Wallace's stories. Perhaps certain categories of people held secrets. Like sea captains, and military men, and balloonists. Hamish felt himself nodding off in the chair.

When he woke with a jolt, he saw the colonel was already fast asleep. He pulled the woollen rug that lay over his knees further up and over his shoulders. The waiter came in at that moment.

"Don't worry," he said, "we take the colonel to bed most nights. He sits in here reading long after his nurse has retired." Hamish wondered why the colonel needed a nurse. He seemed to accomplish most things without her assistance.

Hamish mounted the great staircase and fell on his own bed, exhausted. He slept restlessly. In the early hours of the morning, he woke to the crash of torrential rain beating at the window of his room. He climbed out of bed to peer through the curtains and saw that the masts of the Scottish Prince were just visible through the rain, only now the main mast was jutting sideways at an odd angle to the ship. Though the ship was two miles distant, he could see the waves crash over the hull. Waves were also crashing over the seawall and onto the esplanade right in front of the hotel. The little beach sheds would be inundated. Hamish threw on a robe and ventured into the hall. He was making his way back from the storied suite of lavatories and bathrooms to the right of the main building when he stumbled into Celestine Dupont. Her hair hung wet over her shoulders and her face was as white as a sheet.

"What are you doing?" asked Hamish, shocked to run into her at the top of the stairs in the middle of the night, and even more startled to see that she had been outside.

"I was checking my equipment," she said. "We must inflate the balloon so we can fly at daybreak."

"Surely, you are not thinking of going ahead with the exhibition," said Hamish, "not in this weather."

"The conditions will settle. It is just a little rain."

"It's getting worse," cried Hamish, "not better. You must cancel."

"I won't cancel," said Celestine.

Hamish was startled by the abruptness of her reply. He put his hand on her arm to reassure her he meant no offence and was surprised by the coldness of her skin.

"Shoosh," he said quietly, "you'll wake everyone. I do think you should postpone the event."

Celestine's lips were firm, and her eyes determined. "I will not postpone. These people have come to see an exhibition by the great Celestine Dupont. They will not be disappointed."

Whether Celestine's determination had more to do with not wanting to disappoint her audience, or with her own determination to bend the world to her will, Hamish could not tell.

"Postpone until next weekend," he said. "People will come back."

Celestine caught his gaze in hers. Her face was still damp, and her eyes shone. "Will you return?" She asked, her lips barely parted.

Hamish felt himself caught off guard. Suddenly, she was no longer stubborn and determined, but small and vulnerable.

"Me?" he whispered.

"Yes, Doctor. Will you come?"

Hamish was completely disarmed. "Of course," he said, "if I can."

He immediately began planning how he might organise his return. Or should he stay? What appointments would need to be cancelled? He must see this exquisite creature fly.

"No reason why not," he said, catching his breath.

Celestine shifted her attention and Hamish felt as though a spell had been broken. He was confused by his emotions and embarrassed.

"I must make sure they have the balloon secured to the frame," she said. "The weather will have lifted by daybreak." She pecked Hamish on the cheek. It was the lightest touch, but it set his skin alight. "You still have two or three hours of sleep *mon ami*, go now." She hurried down the stairs and Hamish was left watching her, wondering what had just happened to him. When she was close, he lost all capacity to think clearly. Now that she was at a safe distance, he returned to wondering why she was running in and out of the building at such an odd time of night.

Hamish put his confusion aside and made his way along the corridor to his chamber. As he went, he noticed a light flickering under the door of Murdo Black's room. The carpet was wet outside his door. Had Celestine been visiting the captain's room? Hamish shook himself. The carpet was wet all along the corridor. A sea captain, he reasoned, would have a lifelong habit of interrupted sleep. It was no surprise he should be awake at an odd hour. For himself, Hamish knew he needed sleep. He let himself into his room and went to the window to draw the curtains. The rain was lighter than it had been earlier, but it still fell consistently.

Hamish was turning away from the window when a movement caught his eye. Someone had come to a standstill on the promenade directly in front of his window. It was a man in a thick coat with the collar up and his hat pulled down tight on his head. His shoulders were hunched to ward off the rain, but still he stood there. Why would anyone stand in the rain in the middle of the night? Hamish wondered if his presence may have something to do with the beautiful French aeronaut who was also wet at that time of the morning. He felt a pang of unreasonable jealousy. While Hamish was still watching him, the man began walking slowly toward town. Hamish lay on top of the covers on his bed, too hot to unrobe and listened to the rain. He imagined it was easing. Perhaps Celestine was right. Perhaps it was easing. Or was that wishful thinking? In a few moments, he was asleep.

CHAPTER FIVE

The balloon, which started on March 6 from Nice in the morning, rapidly rose to a height of six thousand feet. The view was at first magnificent. The Alps and a great part of Switzerland were distinctly visible, and the air was warm. But the clouds and a thick mist soon hid everything from view, and when by degrees, and in spite of every effort to prevent it, the balloon descended, the party found to their horror they were about nine miles out to sea, when they had all along believed themselves to be going in a north-easterly direction. Once or twice, Gabriel was induced to rise again for a short time, but it soon returned to the water; and although anchor, ballast, bags, boots and any article of any weight were thrown from the car; it remained obstinately wedded to the water. At times the balloon scudded along at a great rate, though the lower portion of the car was submerged, the water, which at first had been only ankle deep, finally rising sufficiently high to stop Mr. Allioth's watch in his pocket at 5:35 in the afternoon. Night found the unfortunate travellers in an even worse plight; and to add to their difficulties, the car began to rock with the waves, and although completely numb with the bitter cold, they were compelled to hold on tightly for dear life. At last, they spied, to their delight, the sail of an Italian craft bearing down upon them. A boat was speedily launched, and they were soon on board, in dry clothes and making a hearty supper.

Evening News, Sydney. Wednesday 8 June, 1881.

The next thing Hamish heard was a knock at his door. Before opening his eyes, he listened for the rain. He couldn't hear it anymore and light was streaming through his curtains, creating patterns on his eyelids. Reluctantly, he opened his eyes and forced his body to move. He climbed out of bed, stumbled to the door, and tripped over the untied sash from his robe as he went.

When he opened the door, he was surprised to see Rita there, pert, dressed immaculately and ready to go somewhere in a hurry. She looked surprised at his dishevelled state.

"Hurry up!" she said. "Why aren't you dressed? The exhibition begins in fifteen minutes."

Hamish stuttered while he tried to recall what she was talking about it.

"Good Lord, have I overslept?"

Rita laughed. "I'll meet you downstairs. You had better hurry if you don't want to miss Celestine go up in the balloon."

Hamish closed the door and rushed to dress. At the same time as he was climbing into his trousers, he hopped across to the window to look outside at the weather. The sea was grey and choppy, reflecting a silver sky punctuated by points at which the sun was attempting to shine through but not quite achieving it. Nonetheless, it wasn't raining and there was only a light breeze.

Five minutes later, Hamish joined Rita at the vantage point she had carefully chosen the day before. Record crowds were expected for the exhibition. The local hotels were at full capacity and hundreds of day trippers were expected from Brisbane and even Northern New South Wales. Rita made it clear to Hamish she was determined to gain the greatest advantage to see the balloon as it ascended. He had to admit the spot she chose at the edge of the grassy rise, where the balloon was waiting like a captured animal, was perfect.

A considerable crowd had gathered on the esplanade in front of the Grand Hotel and there was standing room only. The crowd spilled onto the beach, the sand still wet and firm from the storm tides the night before. Hamish could see that crowds had gathered all along the route southward, the route Mademoiselle Dupont planned to take, if the calculations of air flow proved accurate. But they were at the front of a tight circle that had formed around the giant contraption.

There was an air of carnival about the scene. A brass band played lively tunes loudly, people in colourful costumes balanced precariously on stilts and there was a Punch and Judy show to entertain the children. A vendor near the puppet show was selling spun sugar to women and children. Hamish grimaced at the thought of spun sugar at daybreak. The pounding enthusiasm of the brass band was wearing on his newly awakened brain as well.

Celestine's balloon had swollen to its full size. Hamish took in the massive envelope of violet and blue calico trapped in place by hemp netting and tied down by sandbags. How on earth did she transport such a contraption around the world? He counted the team of men gripping the ropes to hold the balloon steady. The number of people travelling with her must have been vast. Or did she hire people locally? A woven car sat below the opening of the balloon, ordinary, insignificant beneath the splendour of the balloon itself. The whole scene created an extraordinary sight. Hamish had only seen etchings of balloons in books. He was thrilled to be so close to such a machine.

"How does it work?" asked a woman pressed uncomfortably close to Hamish in the crowd.

"It works on the principle that anything lighter than the air surrounding it will rise," said Rita. "Hot air and inflammable gas both rise because they are lighter than air. In the case of inflammable gas, they say it is at least ten times lighter than air."

The woman glanced quickly at Rita, then turned her attention back to Hamish. She stared at him, waiting for him to answer her question. Hamish glanced at Rita, then back at the woman. He wondered if the woman had not heard Rita speak, but that was impossible. She was standing next to them both. Not wanting to seem rude, he said, "A balloon rises because it is filled with a substance lighter than air."

Rita glared at him. "I believe that is what I just said."

"Balloons are made from airtight material filled with either hot air or hydrogen," Hamish added.

The woman ignored Rita and looked directly at Hamish. "Which is this?"

Hamish opened his mouth to answer but Rita cut in. "It's hydrogen. That's why that pipe is pumping gas into the globe. Celestine will regulate the gas when she wants to ascend or descend. She also has sand ballast she can discard to manage the descent. A barometer shows her, by the elevation or depression of the mercury, exactly how high she is. The air becomes thinner the further one travels from the land, so the balloon will only rise to a certain height before its weight is no longer less than the air around it."

Immediately Rita stopped talking the woman looked back at Hamish. He felt uncomfortably trapped in her gaze.

"It's such a delightful colour," she said, looking up at him from beneath fluttering eyelashes.

Rita rolled her eyes and let out a weak snort while Hamish put his arm around Rita's shoulder in a show of support. The woman pursed her lips and turned her attention to the balloon.

A moment later, Mademoiselle Dupont appeared beside the balloon car, looking resplendent in dark riding breeches and a white frilled blouse. White lace softened her neck and dropped in waterfalls from her sleeves. Her brown hair, long and loose, framed her face and kissed her shoulders. The crowd cheered. She looked like a tiny, glamorous pirate. She easily swung one leg, then the other, over the top of the car and climbed in. The buzz in the crowd was infectious and Hamish recalled the brief moment in the middle of the night when she kissed his cheek. A thoroughly continental thing to do, he thought. When he glanced at Rita, her eyes were fixed on the diminutive pilot.

Gradually, the team of men holding the colourful creature captive released their grip and both balloon and car with Celestine Dupont aboard rose slowly upward. Everyone screamed with delight. The great blue-mauve structure ascended into the sky, disappearing into the grey clouds, then reappearing a little higher. The pale backdrop of the dawn sky invoked a sense of magic behind the colourful balloon and Hamish understood why these exhibitions were carried out against the dawn sky. The crowd was captivated. Rita stared upward in wonder as she clung to Hamish. Celestine Dupont was waving a large silk flag toward the crowd below.

At around four hundred feet, the balloon stopped ascending and began to travel horizontally along the beach. Celestine climbed up the ropes and struck a decorative pose, one hand and both legs clinging to the rope while her other arm stretched outward as though ready to touch the sun. She posed that way for a few moments while the crowd below held their collective breath. Then Celestine faltered. As she was climbing back down, her foot missed the edge of the car. The crowd gasped. Celestine fell. One foot caught in the car and one scrambling to gain a foothold. Hamish felt the tension of the crowd as they watched breathlessly. Rita squeezed his arm. It was only seconds but seemed much longer until Celestine managed to use her upper body to haul herself fully back into the car.

A collective sigh of relief went through the crowd and Hamish wondered whether she had ever been in any danger, or if the incident had been manufactured purely for their entertainment. Once safely in the car, Celestine continued to wave her flag at the audience gathered along the route. The crowd cheered loudly. It was clear that every man, woman, and child was on her side. The beautiful, brave aeronaut had saved herself through her strength and skill. She was a hero, larger than life in a world that was too often bleak and challenging. Celestine Dupont could meet a challenge.

The balloon began to descend close to Elston. The whole display lasted only thirty minutes and the crowd remained enthralled throughout. The onlookers were both excited and exhausted. It was a sight to be seen only once in a lifetime, a story to tell one's friends. It was a memory to treasure. If a man could fly… if a woman could fly… what might be possible?

"Flight will change everything," commented Rita. "Imagine when one is able to fly from one place to another instead of travelling by train or by steamer. Do you think the people here today realise the importance of what we bear witness to in this age of aeronauts?"

Hamish shook his head. "I think these people enjoyed the spectacle," he said.

Gradually, gently, the balloon descended to the sand where a carriage was waiting for Mademoiselle Dupont.

CHAPTER SIX

The Steamer Kate, which had been chartered by the agents for the Scottish Prince, in order to give Mr. Andrews, consulting engineer from Sydney, an opportunity of inspecting the wreck, returned from Stradbroke yesterday morning. Owing to the fact that a gale was blowing at the time of the Kate's arrival, she could not get near the stranded vessel, but anchored inside Stradbroke Island where the party, including Mr Andrews, landed and viewed the wreck from the end of the sandpit. From what Mr Andrews could see of the vessel with the aid of powerful glasses, he is of the opinion she can be floated without very much difficulty. When he saw her, she was lying as comfortably on the bar as though she were in dock, and the fact that she has become to a certain extent embedded in the sand, is looked upon as favourable to the saving of the ship, as the action of the waves cannot have so much effect upon her now as they would have had before she settled down. Mr Andrews remained at Southport with a lifeboat and a crew at his disposal. As soon as the opportunity offers, he will board the vessel, and determine what means should be adopted to save this fine vessel and her freight.

The Brisbane Courier. Saturday 12 February, 1887.

Hamish and Rita made their way back to the hotel. To the left of the entrance, they saw Captain Black talking to the same gaunt Chinese man they had seen with Campbell Charles on their arrival. Black and the Chinese man both looked as though they were trying to blend into the building, tucked behind an ornate column which blocked the view from the doorway and an overly enthusiastic golden palm that blocked the view from the street. Hamish noticed them for a moment as he and Rita passed through the only gap that could reveal them, from an odd angle between the column and the plant. The captain was exchanging pound notes for a small square package, which he tucked into his coat pocket. The Chinese man scurried away quickly, as he had done the day before.

Captain Black, Hamish and Rita reached the door at the same time. Hamish greeted the captain warmly, but the old man didn't acknowledge him. He tucked his head down and strode past.

"What do you think is bothering him?" asked Rita.

Hamish had his own thoughts, but he didn't want to share them. "I don't know," he said.

As soon as they entered the dining hall, the aroma of freshly fried bacon overcame any thoughts either of them had for anything other than breakfast. They sat in the same seats they had been allocated the night before. Captain Murdo Black was already seated, though he seemed agitated, and Mr and Mrs Hembrow arrived a moment later. The room bustled with excitement as everyone looked forward to Celestine Dupont joining them. Hamish realised how hungry he was when a waiter arrived at the table balancing silver platters in each hand piled high with bacon, kidneys, eggs and toast. They helped themselves to healthy portions almost before the platters touched the table and they were enjoying the meal when Mr Andrews joined them.

"Where is the colonel?" he asked.

The captain's eyes were darting around the room as though the colonel's wheelchair might suddenly appear.

Hamish realised for the first time he had not seen the colonel in the crowd outside. "I don't remember seeing him this morning," he said. "Perhaps he watched the exhibition from his balcony."

Another waiter arrived with a silver pot of steaming tea, which he placed at the centre of the table. Hamish poured tea for himself and Rita. He held up the pot to Mr Andrews, who shook his head politely. All thoughts of the colonel had vanished when they were distracted by the well-rounded housemaid, who ran into the room crying, "Doctor, doctor."

Hamish and Rita both stood up.

The maid ran up to Hamish in a state of breathlessness. "He's calling for you, doctor. Something's not right."

"Wait. Slow down and take a breath," said Hamish. "Who is calling for me?"

"The colonel," she said, after taking two great heaving breaths.

"Is he ill?"

"I don't know, sir. He's making such an awful racket. I daren't go in. He keeps calling for the doctor."

Hamish and Rita followed the housemaid into the private wing.

"Do you have the key?" Hamish asked the housemaid.

"Yes, sir," she said, taking it from her pocket.

Hamish banged on the door. He placed his face close to the wood panelling and cried, "Colonel Winter, are you ill?"

"I need someone to help me up, damn you," he called back.

Hamish nodded to the housemaid to unlock the door. She did so with trembling hands and Hamish and Rita entered immediately to find the colonel struggling to get out of bed by himself.

"I told that woman to wake me at four," he said. "Here I am, still in bed. I can hear the breakfast noise going on. I've missed the exhibition and now I'm going to miss my breakfast."

Hamish retrieved the wheelchair from its spot by the window and brought it over to the bed, while Rita assisted the colonel from his bedclothes and into his day attire. "I have missed it, haven't I?"

"I'm afraid so," said Hamish.

"And the *servant frau* had a front row spot. She'll receive the lash of my tongue when I find her."

"We haven't seen Hilda, if that's who you mean," said Rita. She looked at Hamish for confirmation.

"No," said Hamish, "Hilda wasn't outside for the exhibition either, as far as I can tell. Unless she watched from her balcony. But she can't have. She would certainly have come for you."

Hamish and Rita worked as a team to assist the old man into his wheelchair. It wasn't easy. He remained a dead weight, and a man of solid muscle.

"Damn her," the colonel kept repeating.

"Do you think she's all right?" Rita whispered to Hamish.

Hamish didn't know what to think.

"Is it unlike Hilda to sleep in?" he asked the colonel.

"She never sleeps in. She knows I was looking forward to the aeronautical exhibition."

When the colonel was seated comfortably in his chair, Hamish walked across the room to the door that adjoined the colonel's room and that of his nurse. "Does she usually come in this way?"

"*Ja, Jawohl,* that is the only way in. She usually keeps it locked from her side. As if an old invalid like me is of any threat to her."

Hamish knocked on the door. Then he knocked harder. Nothing.

"Miss…," he called out, his ear against the polished Tasmanian oak.

"I can't hear her moving in there," he said.

The housemaid was hovering at the colonel's door. "Do you have a key?" asked Hamish, his hand on the door that separated the colonel's room from that of his nurse.

"What the devil is going on?" A voice called out from behind Hamish. He leaned around to look past the housemaid and saw Campbell Charles.

Hamish stood up to his full height. "Hilda didn't come to assist Colonel Winter from bed this morning," he said. "No one has seen her, and she's not answering when I knock."

"She's probably sleeping," said Campbell. He pushed past Hamish and placed out his hand to the housemaid.

"Key, Beryl," he said. The housemaid Beryl produced the key from her apron.

The door opened slowly, and four heads leaned into the opening around him.

They saw Hilda in her bed, her bedclothes neatly pulled up to her waist, her hands clasped at her chest.

"There. Sleeping, as I said."

But Hamish noticed a water jug had been knocked off the side table and water had soaked into the carpet. "Something's wrong," he said.

Hamish stepped past Campbell and strode to the side of the bed, where he peered down at the peaceful face of Hilda Jenkins. He placed his hand gently on top of hers and found it cold and thick. A creeping sensation worked its way up his neck. He knew she was lifeless, but he searched for a pulse, anyway.

"She's dead," he said, looking at the four incredulous faces staring back at him.

"What? No!" cried Colonel Winter. "She can't be… she's a young woman… healthy as an ox…" His voice was faltering.

"I'd like everyone to leave," said Hamish.

Rita put one arm each around Campbell and Beryl and began to usher them out of the room.

"No," cried the colonel again. "I'm not leaving. I pay for this room. I'll not be sent out of it!"

He glared at Hamish, eyes bulging.

"By God, what happened to her?" he said.

"I don't know," said Hamish. "I need to examine her. Did she have a regular doctor?"

"No. She is… was young and healthy. In any case, how would she afford a doctor?"

Hamish felt the sting of his profession. He tended to those who could afford his services, while the people most in need of his help could not afford to pay for it. If he provided more services for the poor than he already did, he would not be able to sustain his practice.

He forced himself to focus on the person on the bed before him, though she was beyond his help now.

He said, "If you all go back to the dining hall, or to the waiting room, if you prefer, I'll see what I can find out. Mr Charles, you'll need to contact the local police."

"Police? Why?" Campbell Charles was red in the face.

"Because it is unclear how Miss Jenkins came to be deceased," said Hamish.

"You don't think it's foul play? Not in the Grand?"

"I don't think anything yet, Mr Charles. I can't examine the body until you all leave."

Reluctantly, they began edging out the way they came in.

"Not you, Doctor Cartwright. I need you in here," said Hamish.

Rita stepped away from the wheelchair and allowed Beryl to take over. She joined Hamish in Hilda's room and let the door close behind her.

Hamish was bent in half, his head close to the carpet examining the upturned water jug and the empty glass. Closer to the bed, he noticed a small package, the type medicines came in. The package had been opened and the paper was torn. He took a pair of tweezers from his pocket and moved the paper only as much as necessary to see the label. It read, *Hilda Jenkins. Dover's Powder. Take one powder before bed.* There was the name of the dispensing pharmacist after that, but the paper had been torn and the name could no longer be read.

"A common enough sleeping draught," said Hamish.

"On the face of it," agreed Rita. "Dover's powder has some opium in it. It wouldn't take much more than the prescribed dose to make it lethal."

Hamish pulled himself up and looked down at the body, still tucked snugly under the sheets and blanket.

"She looks for all the world like she's sleeping," he said. "There are no signs of disturbance."

Hamish gently lifted one eyelid. "Her pupils appear normal," he said. "An overdose of morphine would result in constricted pupils, would it not?"

"Yes, it would. There's nothing obvious by looking at her," agreed Rita. "No sign of struggle – no sign of an aggressive poison."

Rita brushed Hilda's hair back with her hand. As she did so, Hamish noticed a few strands of hair caught under the pillow.

"Look at this," he said.

Rita leaned in closer to look.

"How'd her hair get underneath the pillow?" asked Hamish.

"It's only a strand or two. Perhaps she turned the pillow over at some point."

Hamish stood back. "Does she look a bit too comfortable to you?"

Rita frowned.

"She's perfectly arranged," Hamish went on. "Her head centre to the pillow, her hands clasped across her chest, almost as though an undertaker has staged her."

"I see what you mean," said Rita.

"It was a hot night last night." Hamish felt the blood rising in his face. "I slept on top of the bedcovers."

"That's right," said Rita, "I threw the blanket to the floor."

"There is no possibility of her having slept tucked under these blankets," said Hamish. He noticed his hands were trembling as the realisation became inescapable.

"What do you think happened?"

Hamish put his head to one side and brushed back his fringe with his quivering hands.

"What if she took her sleeping powder and was in a deep sleep when someone came into her room? She might not wake. Then the intruder might have held the pillow over her face and suffocated her. She wouldn't resist if she was in a deep sleep. They could arrange her to look like this, place the pillow back under her head, smooth the sheets and covers. There would be no sign of a struggle."

Rita's eyes widened.

"You might be right," she whispered.

A knock at the door made them both jump. Campbell entered with another gentleman, who was as dishevelled as Campbell was impeccably neat. "This is Sergeant Cooper," said Campbell. "Dr Hamish Hart and Dr Rita Cartwright."

Sergeant Cooper neglected to greet them. "You haven't shifted anything have you, doctor?"

"I have not," said Hamish. "We know better than to tamper with the scene of a crime."

"Crime scene? Who said anything about a crime scene? At this point, all I have is a young woman who has died in her sleep." He turned to Campbell. "I've notified Brisbane. I expect they'll arrange for the body to be transported on the returning steamer."

Hamish felt a little relieved that the medical examiner in Brisbane would be taking over the investigation. He was used to being called in on occasion to act as medical examiner before the arrival of the new man. He didn't have a lot of respect for the fellow's methods, finding him less than thorough, but Hamish did not want to do the job himself.

He leant over and pointed at the torn packaging on the floor. "This must have been on the bedside table with the jug and glass," he said. "The medical examiner will need to see it."

Cooper leant over Hamish and stared at the packaging. After a moment, he reached down and picked it up, screwed it into a ball in his fist and threw it into the fire grate.

"That's evidence," cried Hamish. "It needs to be treated with care! It should go to the medical examiner with the body, and anything else you find in here."

Cooper moved so close to Hamish that he could feel the warmth of his breath on his skin.

"I'll decide what's evidence," he sneered. He turned to Campbell. "Keep these two out of this room. Lock it. Don't let anyone in before the authorities come for the body in the morning."

CHAPTER SEVEN

This pretty little town seems to be going ahead despite the bad times. There are about a dozen buildings in the course of construction. The English church in Nerang Street is nearly finished and will soon be of use. It is a fine building, high and dry, with a good view of the sea at the front. There is a new splendid drive along the esplanade — a fine hard road, well-drained and miles in length. The Divisional Board has made a long sea wall to keep back high tides. The beach opposite the Broadwater is the best I have seen in the colony for safe and pleasant bathing.

The railway here is now all the talk. A good deal of growling takes place about the station being put in a swamp or more properly, in the wide bed of a creek, and so far away from the centre of town, which will cause the storekeepers to have to travel an extra mile to collect their goods.

All the boarding houses and hotels report they are full. In fact, I know of some that have been taken into private homes for they could not, during the holidays, get lodging at a reasonable distance from the sea.

A voice from Southport, Queensland Times. Saturday 22 January, 1887

Hamish marched from the room, indignation coursing through his veins. Rita tucked her arm into his and his blood stabilised a little. "He's incompetent," he whispered so that only Rita could hear.

"I agree," she whispered back, "but it isn't your problem."

Hamish was about to object that the death of a young woman in the hotel was surely a problem for them all, but they reached the dining hall before he could say it. They found Colonel Winter, Mr and Mrs Hembrow and Captain

Black still there. Beryl was assisting two waiters clear away the remains of the breakfast buffet. As Hamish and Rita arrived, Celestine Dupont joined them.

She had changed into a day dress that Hamish thought was somewhere between blue and purple, her hair arranged in loose coils at the back of her neck. She sat and Hamish and Rita took seats either side of her. She smiled sweetly at each of them.

Colonel Winter was visibly shaken. "Do you know any more about poor Hilda's demise?" he asked Hamish.

Hamish shook his head. "Sergeant Cooper of the Southport Police has taken over. He's having the body transported to Brisbane this afternoon. The medical examiner will decide on the cause of death after examining the body."

Celestine's eyes were wide. "I've heard only rumours," she said. "It is true then that the colonel's nurse is dead?"

The colonel took out a large handkerchief and blew his nose.

"It is true," said Rita.

A thought then occurred to the colonel. "You're not suggesting the body is to stay where it lies in the meantime, are you? I'm not spending the day in there with a corpse in the next room."

"I'm sure Campbell will find you another room," said Hamish, "or you can relax in the reading room until dinner. The steamer will depart this evening and the body with it."

Celestine leant forward, her curls slipping softly over her shoulders. "Do the police suspect foul play?" she whispered.

"If we suggest the death might be suspicious, how would an intruder have gained entry to Hilda's room?" said Rita. "If Hilda had one key and the hotel the other. I saw the key still in the lock in the room when we went in. And Campbell used the other one to open the door."

"What about the door from the corridor?" asked Hamish. "That would be the obvious entrance to use."

The colonel seemed calmer now. "No one has used that entrance since we moved in. There's a dresser in front of it, in fact. Everyone enters through the door into my sitting room, then proceeds through my bedroom and on to Hilda's. Of course, in reality, only the house staff go into Hilda's room. Hilda did not entertain." Colonel Winter coughed into his handkerchief.

"You mean she had no friends at all?" said Rita.

The colonel took a couple of rapid, shaky breaths into his handkerchief. "Certainly not."

Rita was not discouraged by his manner. "You mean she had no one in her life and no role apart from taking care of you?"

Colonel Winter put his very wet handkerchief in his pocket. "She was a serious young woman," he said. "Devoted to her work."

"She mentioned she had a mother," broke in Mrs Hembrow, happy to have something to add to the conversation.

Hamish and Rita looked at the colonel.

"Yes," he said, "her mother lives in Nerang. Elderly. Unwell. Hilda spends some weekends with her," he said.

"No wonder Hilda came across as bitter," said Rita. "She looked after you all week and her mother at weekends."

Colonel Winter's eyes darkened. "I am no tyrant, Dr Cartwright," he said. "Hilda was well remunerated. I assure you, her social isolation was of her own choosing."

"The nurse has been murdered?" asked Murdo Black, as if he were only now walking in on the conversation. Hamish made a mental note of the way the captain's hands trembled on the table.

Hamish took a breath before speaking. "It's not really for me to say." He glanced at Rita. "But, yes. That is what I believe."

Silence fell around the table.

Celestine Dupont leant forward and plucked a carnation from the centrepiece and spun the stem between her fingers. Hamish watched her polished pink nails as the crimson carnation twirled.

"It's such a shame," she said, "this whole business has put a dampener on my exhibition. No one will be talking of anything else."

"Oh, no!" cried Mrs Hembrow, eager to reassure the aeronaut that the death of a servant had not diminished the wonder of her exhibition. "The exhibition was inspiring. I've never seen anything like it."

"Extraordinary," agreed Rita.

Celestine took Rita's hand in hers. "Do you really think so?" she said, holding Rita's eyes for a little longer than Hamish thought necessary. "*Merci bien*," she whispered.

Hamish noticed the pink flush in Rita's cheeks and a prickling discomfort in his own. Was he jealous because of the intimate moment Rita was sharing with someone other than him? Or was he jealous because Celestine, beautiful and fascinating creature that she was, was paying attention to Rita? He recalled the moment they had shared at the top of the staircase. He still felt the brush of her lips on his cheek. He tapped his fingers on the table to settle his emotions. As he looked down at his own hands, he noted the increased trembling in the larger hands of Captain Black.

"I must be going," Black burst out as he stood. "My apologies," he mumbled at the table in general as he turned toward the entrance hall and the imposing staircase. He moved away with quick purposeful strides, as though he wished he could run up the stairs, but felt he needed to control his movements. He gave the appearance of constraint, while getting away as quickly as possible.

"I must be going, also," Celestine said. "I should be supervising the workmen outside as they pack away my equipment."

The creature swept out of the room, leaving behind her a cloud of lavender. Mr and Mrs Hembrow and the colonel made their excuses and left the table after her.

"Come on," Rita said, taking Hamish by the arm. "I need some fresh air."

They went through the entrance hall and out onto the esplanade.

"Are we walking?" asked Hamish.

Rita pointed to the seat in front of the hotel entrance.

"Let's sit," she said.

Hamish and Rita made themselves comfortable on the seat facing the hotel, their backs to the sea. Couples strolled along the esplanade before them, animated by the balloon exhibition that morning.

"I'm concerned about Captain Black," said Hamish. "He was agitated this morning and he didn't sleep through the night."

"What are you thinking?" asked Rita.

"I'm not sure," he said, "there's something not quite right."

Rita took a few relaxing draughts of sea air.

"In any event, I'm glad the medical examiner will be taking over the investigation," Hamish said. "I don't feel confident in the role. It was never my intention to enter forensic medicine. I just seem to have fallen into it since the murders at Dunwich."

Rita scoffed. "I don't know why you would lack confidence. You're far more thorough than the actual medical examiner."

Hamish smiled a small thank you. He sighed, looking toward the horizon.

"I only wish that pharmacy packaging had stayed with the body," he said. "Cooper should have treated it more carefully. It's an important piece of evidence and I'm afraid it's lost."

"It's not lost," said Rita, pulling it out of her bodice.

"What?" cried Hamish. "You removed evidence?"

Rita considered the packaging. "Cooper didn't seem too interested in it. I thought I'd make sure it was safe. We can hand it over to the medical examiner ourselves. We'll be heading back to Brisbane tomorrow, I expect."

"Brilliant," cried Hamish. "When did you retrieve it? I didn't see anything."

Rita grinned. "Distraction," she said. "While the sergeant was threatening you, I took the opportunity to retrieve the package."

"Good on you. Now put it back… down there," Hamish pointed nervously at her bodice, "and keep it safe until we can hand it on."

Rita nodded toward the sea, creating yet another diversion while she tucked the powder wrapper between her breasts.

A boat packed with tourists, who had been enjoying the morning on Stradbroke Island, was sidling up to the wharf. Women lifted their skirts to disembark while gentlemen pretended to steady them by holding the tips of their fingers. They clambered along the wharf in a trembling, squealing mass. As Hamish sat transfixed, an image of squabbling seagulls taking the place of tourists in his mind, another larger boat sailed toward the wharf. It sat bobbing a short distance away, waiting for the Island Ferry to move. Hamish recognised the police boat from Brisbane. "They must have sent it to pick up the body," he said.

As a small group of passengers were making their way along the esplanade toward them Hamish wondered how many more guests would be joining them at the Grand. Campbell had told them the hotel was already at capacity.

Suddenly, Hamish stood up.

"What is it?" asked Rita.

Hamish stared as a tall man with a felt hat and tired eyes strode toward him.

"It's Sergeant Bellamy," cried Hamish.

Rita also stood up.

The sergeant put out his hand and Hamish shook it warmly. There was a familiarity between them that came as the result of having worked some difficult and dangerous cases together.

"What are you doing here?" asked Hamish.

"Look Hamish, Wallace is here too!" called Rita.

The ginger haired old cook stumbled up behind Bellamy and placed all their bags on the ground. Under one arm he was carrying a wiry terrier.

"Red!" Rita took the scruffy bundle into her arms.

The terrier wriggled and squirmed with delight, licking Rita all over her face.

"Come," cried Hamish, "sit down and tell us what's going on."

Sergeant Bellamy spoke first. "The Commissioner thinks that as you are already on the spot, you should act as medical examiner on this one."

Hamish's eyebrows shot up. "I thought Scratchley wasn't fond of me?" he said.

"He isn't," confirmed Bellamy, "he thinks you are a bleeding-heart liberal. But he also thinks you are a competent forensic doctor. Besides, the body is here – you are here. It's convenient."

"What about you then?"

"Scratchley doesn't trust Cooper. Thinks he's sloppy."

"There we agree," said Hamish.

"Wallace?" asked Rita, looking at him.

Wallace looked back with a cheeky grin.

"I wanted to see the Scottish Prince," he said. "The papers have been full of the story for a week. Red and I came down to see it for ourselves. We sent a telegram to the Grand this morning to book accommodation. We told them to add the price to your account," he said, looking at Hamish.

Rita laughed. "With all the excitement this morning, I suppose the manager hasn't had a chance to tell us." She hugged Red closer to her. "It's wonderful to see you both. I imagine this means we are staying longer than expected."

Wallace handed Hamish an envelope. "This came yesterday. It's from your mother."

Hamish took the envelope and stared at the handwriting. "She never writes. She leaves it to Father."

"I hope nothing is wrong," said Rita, looking over his shoulder at the envelope.

"It'll be nothing," said Hamish. He put the letter in his pocket. "I'll read it later."

CHAPTER EIGHT

Many important improvements are made in progress in this young and interesting seaside resort in Southern Queensland. The quiet passage from Brisbane, the cool sea breeze, the delectable bathing – both in the inner beaches and the ocean breakers – and the ample success in fishing in all weathers, have conspired to bring a number of wealthy families to choose Southport as their permanent home, and more recently the vice-regal summer residence has been completed here, in a charming spot looking down over the river, and out upon the ocean beyond with every incitement to moral repose and home enjoyments.

The esplanade is becoming a fine promenade and soon will give a drive of three miles along the beach to the retreat at Labrador. There is a project for erecting an hotel near Deepwater Point at central Southport, which will dwarf and shadow the largest and handsomest for many miles.

Some of the thoughtful gentlemen, to whose energy Southport is already indebted for its noble pier, its School of Arts, telegraph station, schools, police building, and churches are lobbying the powers that be into dredging the entrance to the bar, so that the intercolonial's mails may land here directly from the ocean and reach town several hours in advance of the steamer.

Evening News, Sydney. Tuesday 14 April ,1885.

Sergeant Bellamy and Wallace placed their luggage in their respective rooms, then Bellamy announced his intention to travel by cab to the police station to settle any hard feelings between himself and Sergeant Cooper. Wallace and Red set off on a sunset walk along the esplanade, from where they could gain a fine view of the Scottish Prince. Hamish and Rita returned to the colonel's suite, Bellamy, having finally convinced Campbell that Hamish had been instructed to act as medical examiner on the case. Campbell handed over the hotel's key to Hilda Jenkin's room with some reluctance.

Hamish entered the room and stood back to take in the scene. The empty water jug and glass still lay where they had fallen. The heavy drapes were closed to keep the room as cool as possible, but an odour of death was already pervasive. As she would no longer be travelling to Brisbane on the departing schooner, he would have to arrange for poor Hilda's body to be moved as soon as possible. Hamish noted the heavy sideboard against the alternative entrance to the room. There was no sign it had been moved and it would have been a heavy and noisy business to do so. That door had not been accessible for some time, as Colonel Winter said.

Hamish turned his attention to the door that was accessible. The key still clung to the lock on the inside, but was caught only by the collar, which on this key was close to the wards, meaning the shaft and bow were hanging at a forty-five-degree angle to the door.

"It must have been pushed through from the other side when Campbell first unlocked the door," said Rita.

"That is as expected," agreed Hamish.

Only when he was satisfied there was nothing more to see in the general environment of the room did he turn his attention to the body. He leant over Hilda's face and gently lifted her eyelids. Tiny pinpoints of blood dotted the whites of her eyes.

"I didn't notice this haemorrhaging in the eyes earlier," he said.

Rita peered over his shoulder.

Hamish examined Hilda's face closely.

"There are similar signs of haemorrhage around her nose and mouth," said Hamish.

Rita looked closely. "Yes, there are clear signs of asphyxiation."

"Do you agree there's no sign of contraction of the pupils as would be expected if morphine overdose was the cause of death?"

"Agreed," said Rita.

Hamish stood up to his full height again. He picked up the hairs that were beneath the pillow with his tweezers and placed them on his handkerchief, which he folded neatly and put in his pocket.

"Would you support her head while I examine the pillow?" Rita held the weight of Hilda's head as Hamish slipped the pillow from beneath her. He turned it over and saw a stain, still damp, indicating saliva on the fabric. There was also a slight tinge of pink. Hamish placed the pillow over Hilda's face gently and noted the stain was precisely in line with her mouth.

"Foam in the airway," said Rita. "It would have bubbled up and out of her mouth during suffocation."

"Death by suffocation," said Hamish. "I am certain of it. We could cut her open and observe further signs of haemorrhage in the lungs, but I don't think it necessary, do you?"

"No," said Rita, "the evidence is clear. This body needs to be buried as soon as possible."

Hamish conveyed the news to Campbell that the body could now be removed from his hotel. He was relieved to hear it and called the undertaker at once.

Hamish and Rita settled in the reading room where Hamish began writing his report. He listed the evidence clearly and methodically so that no reasonable person could dispute his conclusion of death by suffocation by a person or persons unknown. He was blotting his final sentence when Bellamy entered the room.

"How'd Sergeant Cooper take the news?" asked Hamish.

"As you'd expect," said Bellamy, who seemed disinclined to elaborate further. Hamish relayed his findings.

Sergeant Bellamy nodded.

"Who went into the young lady's room in the night and suffocated her – and why?" said Bellamy.

"And how did they get in?" added Rita.

Bellamy raised a single eyebrow at Hamish.

"The only accessible door was locked from the inside," said Hamish. "The assailant would have had to gain entry to the colonel's suite, then walk past him to enter through Hilda's internal door. The assailant then had to lock the door from the inside before leaving again through that same door."

"Windows?" asked Bellamy.

"Bolted on the inside," said Hamish.

"That is a mystery," said Bellamy, rubbing his brow. "How many keys are there to the room?"

"Two," said Hamish. "That is, according to Campbell Charles. He has one, the hotel key, and Hilda had one. Campbell says he has had his key in his possession since he retrieved it from Beryl when the body was found, and Hilda's key is still in the lock, on the inside of the room.

"Better round them all up for an interview then," said the sergeant.

Hamish was reluctant. "It's past dinnertime now," he said. "Couldn't it wait until morning? It's been a long day and everyone's tired. I think we'll get more from them if we leave it for the morning."

"It's murder," said Bellamy. "We must act immediately."

"They're not going anywhere. They can't leave until the next ferry tomorrow evening. Not unless they go by coach from Southport in the morning. The guests are tucked up in bed. Let's begin the interviews first thing in the morning."

Bellamy slumped into one of the armchairs. "As you say. I have a raging headache, anyway."

"We need to know more about Hilda," Rita said. "Why don't I visit her mother in the morning and offer my condolences? The local police will have informed her of the death of her daughter, so I can check she's doing well after the shock." Rita flashed Hamish a knowing glance.

"How thoughtful," he said, "if you accidentally find out anything about Hilda while you're there, so much the better. I believe she lives in Nerang," he added. "You'll need to take a carriage to the river and then cross on the barge."

"I'm looking forward to it," said Rita. "They say the scenery toward Nerang is breathtaking."

Bellamy stood up. "I'm for bed if there's no more to do tonight." He nodded at Hamish and Rita before leaving.

Rita stood also. "Sleep well," she said over her shoulder as she headed out into the dining hall.

Hamish watched her leave, then retrieved his mother's letter from his pocket. He carefully opened the envelope and slipped out the sheets of paper. There was no doubt it was his mother's handwriting, but it was wobbly. It was the hand of someone struggling with the task. It reminded him of some of his elderly patients who wrote notes to him listing their ailments. When had his mother become old? Hamish settled back in his chair to read the letter.

My Dearest Son,

I hope this correspondence finds you well. Please forgive me if the information herein appears jumbled. As you know, I am not accustomed to writing letters and I fear I am less organised in my thoughts of late. Nonetheless, I felt compelled to inform you that your father is unwell.

The exact nature of the condition is unclear. That is, he appears to be suffering from increasingly frequent bouts of memory loss. I wouldn't have worried you with such a minor development. Your father has, after all, passed his seventieth birthday and some forgetfulness is to be expected. I admit to it myself. At times I enter a room and wonder what my intention was in going there.

But your father's condition has regrettably become more serious of late. He was found by his friend Bert – you remember Bert; he spent a great deal of time at the house when you were studying. Anyway, Bert found your father sitting alone on a bench at the racetrack with his head in his hands. At first Bert wondered what could be the matter with him, but when he put his hand on his shoulder, to comfort him, you understand, your father leapt to his feet and knocked poor Bert flat.

Bert called out his name, but your father looked at him blankly. He didn't appear to recognise his own name. Nor did he recognise Bert. A police constable came to enquire about the scuffle and Bert told him it was an accident. He said he had startled his friend. Bert led your father to his carriage, and thank the Lord, he followed quietly. When he arrived home, he still didn't know who or where he was, but he allowed me to take him to his bed. He slept for ten hours. When he woke, he was quite himself, but he didn't remember the incident at all.

Dr Williams has examined him this afternoon and says he is physically healthy and articulate at the present time. But he warned me that we must consider the possibility of senility. I am to report to the Doctor if there are further incidents. If he creates a fuss in public, Dr Williams will surely send him to an asylum.

I tell you this not to worry you, my dearest. I know you have your own life in Queensland now. But I would be remiss if the condition worsens, and I had not told you anything.

Your loving mother.

The words on the page stared at Hamish while he tried to process them. There seemed little doubt that his father had senile dementia. There were so many questions to ask. How long had the symptoms been present? How frequent were his memory losses? Were there any associated signs of mood change?

There had never been much love lost between his father and himself, but he wouldn't wish this on him. Or his mother.

Good Lord. What if he became violent toward her?

Hamish immediately penned a response. He couldn't include all the questions he had in his head, anyway. By the time he received the answers, they were likely to be no longer the right questions. He concentrated on providing his mother with what advice he could, and asked her to let him know immediately, by telegram if need be, if there were any further incidents, and if she had to contact Dr Williams again.

Hamish folded the letter three times and placed it carefully into an envelope. He caught Beryl going by his door with clean laundry and handed her the envelope, asking if she would hand it on to be posted with the hotel mail. Beryl smiled and curtsied, almost dropping the sheets. Hamish then made every attempt to put the situation with his father out of his mind. There was nothing he could do. He would consider a trip to Melbourne to assess his father's condition himself as soon as he solved the mystery of who killed Hilda Jenkins.

CHAPTER NINE

The season at this rapidly rising and fashionable watering place is just commencing. Since the close of last season, great improvements have been made and many new buildings have been erected. The Police barracks are in course of erection and a new pier has been built by private subscription. The provisional school has been proclaimed a State School. Mr Fass, late of Toowoomba, has built a large and commodious boarding house with every requisite for the comfort of visitors, not omitting a very handsome and well-built boat of local construction, for the use of visiting families. Mr Andrews has just finished his new premises where you can get anything from a needle to an anchor and he says, at 'Brisbane prices'. There is a daily coach, daily mail, two or three steamers a week, a baker, two butchers and last but not least, a pharmaceutical chemist. The Divisional Board has sanctioned a ferry at Meyer's, about two miles from Southport, to the Main Beach. The Main Beach is always a great attraction and the drive, ride or walk to Burleigh Heads is magnificent.

The Telegraph. Thursday 13 October, 1881.

Hamish ran his fingers between his collar and his neck to allow some air to circulate. He was already sweating in the growing humidity, though they had only just eaten breakfast. Through the window, he could see the clouds building on the horizon. The steam rising from the esplanade was visible and the steady stream of strolling visitors had slowed to a trickle. Everyone would be looking for shade and a cool breeze if there was one to be had.

Bellamy joined Hamish in the reading room and sat down on the leather couch, creaking with newness. He had not been seated more than a minute when Campbell escorted the first of the guests to be interviewed into the room.

"Terrible," said Colonel Winter from his wheelchair.

"Can you tell us how you came to engage Miss Jenkins?" began Bellamy.

"A suspect, then? A common criminal?" barked the colonel.

"We need to talk to everyone who was close to Miss Jenkins," said Bellamy calmly, "and you were closer than most. It's a straightforward question. How did you come to engage Miss Jenkins as your nurse?"

"What has this to do with anything?" asked the colonel.

"Context," said Bellamy. "If you would humour us, sir."

The colonel shifted in his chair.

"I advertised," he said, "in the papers. She came for an interview. I offered her the position. No one else applied, in fact. Something wrong with the young today, afraid of hard work."

"Did she provide references?" asked Hamish.

"Of course, she did. She had a note from Mrs Whittleton. Said she'd worked for the family as a housemaid from seventeen. They had no complaints. Said she got on with her work."

"How did you find her work, colonel?"

Colonel Winter looked down at his hands in his lap. He examined one tobacco-stained finger.

"I found her efficient enough," he said. "She had a little too much to say at times, but a quiet word would soon bring her back."

"What do you mean?" asked Hamish.

"She was always listening when you didn't expect it. Then she'd blurt out a comment later, so you'd realise what she'd heard. It was disconcerting that was all. I spoke to her about it."

"Did Hilda have any friends?" asked Bellamy. "Was there anyone she talked about? Perhaps someone visited her here at the hotel? We'd appreciate it if you take a moment to think about it. Maybe there is an incident that has slipped your mind."

"I don't think the girl had any friends her own age," said the colonel. "As I said, no one visited her. She went to her mother on the weekend."

There was a break in the questioning while Bellamy overcame his frustration. Someone must have known the girl, thought Hamish, but he decided to believe the colonel was telling them the truth.

"What will you do now?" asked Hamish.

"I don't have any idea," said the colonel. "I suppose I'll have to start again. Advertise."

"Did you hear anything through the night of the murder?" Bellamy decided to change tack.

"No. Nothing."

"Was everything normal before you went to bed? Did Hilda seem anxious, or different in any way?"

"I didn't see her before bed. The hotel staff assist me into bed as I prefer to stay up later than the nurse. She tended to retire soon after the evening meal. She seemed normal at dinner."

"And you have never had a key to her room yourself?" asked Hamish.

"Never," confirmed the old man.

"Did Hilda take any medications?" asked Hamish.

"How would I know that?"

The colonel was evidently irritated by the questions being fired at him. Hamish thought it was an ideal time to end the interview. He doubted there was anything more the colonel was able, or ready, to tell them at that point.

Bellamy stood up. "Thank you for your time, Colonel," he said.

Hamish also stood and put out his hands to take hold of the chair, but the colonel swiped his hands away. "I'll manage myself," he said. "I'm going to have to manage now, anyway."

He threw his strength into mobilising the wheels. He coughed from the effort all the way through the door. Hamish watched on, thinking the coughing was more for effect than from any real weakness, as he hadn't had any trouble wheeling himself around earlier. When the colonel was out of hearing, he said, "do you think Colonel Winter can be eliminated from our list of suspects?"

"That depends," said Bellamy, "do you think he can get out of that chair?"

Hamish considered his response. "I can't be sure," he said, at last. "He would have to also have enough strength to suffocate the nurse. It's not as easily done as you might imagine."

Bellamy looked at him sideways. "How do you know? How many people have you suffocated?"

Hamish gave him a wry smile. "None," he said, "but I have the medical training to know that there needs to be some force on the pillow – or whatever other object is placed over the nose and mouth."

"Who is next, then?" asked Bellamy.

Mrs Hembrow appeared at the door. "Can we be interviewed next?" she asked. "Only Mr Hembrow and I are planning a trip to Stradbroke for lunch."

"I'd prefer everyone stay at the hotel for the time being," said Bellamy.

Glenda Hembrow dropped her bottom lip like a petulant child, then stomped into the room and slumped in a chair.

"When did you first meet Hilda Jenkins?" asked the sergeant.

Mrs Hembrow hesitated, fiddling with a fussy lace purse she had in her lap. She plucked at the stitching while Hamish noted her hands were quivering.

"When we arrived at the hotel," she said.

"When was that?"

"Wednesday," she said.

"Did you spend much time with the colonel and his nurse?" asked Bellamy.

"Only at dinner. And the occasional word in passing."

"What did you think of Miss Jenkins? What sort of woman was she?"

Mrs Hembrow's face went dark. It was only a flicker before she regained her composure. By the time she spoke again, she was sweetness and light.

"She was a funny one," she said. "She was mostly quiet, couldn't get a word out of her. But you got the feeling she was always listening. Always watching." Glenda Hembrow looked down at her hands and pulled at each of her fingers in turn.

"Did she say anything to you about family or friends?" asked Bellamy.

"Or enemies?" asked Hamish.

"No," said Mrs Hembrow, "I told you she didn't talk about anything."

"Do you know anything of her past?" asked Bellamy.

Glenda Hembrow's eyes widened and tears gathered at the rims.

"Certainly not." That is all she managed to get out before the tears fell freely.

Sergeant Bellamy and Hamish exchanged glances.

"Are you sure?" prompted Bellamy.

Glenda Hembrow sobbed loudly. "Why are you interrogating me like this" she cried.

"It's a simple question," said Bellamy.

Hamish placed his hand on her shoulder. "I know it can be overwhelming," he said, shooting a glance at Bellamy, who looked like he could throttle the woman. "A murder in one's midst. And then the questioning."

The sobbing became less violent.

"Am I a suspect?" she said through her tears.

Hamish handed her a handkerchief and she blew her nose.

"These questions are for everyone," he said. "Are you able to continue?"

"Yes," she sobbed through the handkerchief.

"Let us shift our attention to the night of the murder," said Bellamy.

"Did you see or hear anything that you can recall?"

"No. James and I left the dining room and I went to bed. It had been a long day and storms make me anxious, so I took a sleeping draught. James stayed up reading, I believe."

"What time did you rise in the morning?"

"We were both up early, just on daybreak, to see Celestine Dupont's exhibition."

"You didn't see or hear anything unusual?"

"Not at all."

At that moment, Campbell Charles came to the door and hovered. Bellamy glared at him.

"Sorry to interrupt, but morning tea is being served."

"Would it be possible to have sandwiches brought in for the doctor and myself?" asked Bellamy.

"Sandwiches, sir?" asked Campbell, as though he'd been asked to provide fried chicken feet in the reading room.

"Please?" asked Bellamy. "Mrs Hembrow may join the others in the dining hall."

"Naturally," said Campbell, turning on his well-polished heels. As Glenda Hembrow gathered her skirts to rise, she opened her mouth to speak, but closed it again.

"Don't leave the hotel until I give the word," said Bellamy. She dropped her eyes and left the room.

James Hembrow was now hovering in the doorway. "I'd like to join my wife," he said.

"We won't keep you long," said Bellamy. "Come in. Sit."

Mr Hembrow hesitated. "She seems upset…"

"Sit," repeated Bellamy.

James Hembrow sat.

"We asked your wife if she knew anything of Hilda Jenkins' past. She seemed upset by the question. Do you have any idea why?"

Mr Hembrow looked perplexed. "I don't see why that particular question should upset her," he said. "I know she is upset by the whole business,"

"Did she seem upset prior to our interview?" asked Hamish.

"She wasn't crying, if that's what you mean," he said. "She was looking forward to the boat trip to Stradbroke. A distraction. Of course, that's not possible now. The boat has left. Perhaps that's what upset her."

"When did you and Mrs Hembrow marry?" asked Bellamy.

Mr Hembrow blinked several times.

"What has that to do with anything?"

"Just answer the question, please."

"Five years ago," he said.

"No children?" asked Hamish.

James Hembrow turned to Hamish. "No. But I'm not sure what…"

Bellamy glared at him.

Hembrow looked from one of them to the other. "Mrs Hembrow," he began, "we have not been blessed."

"Can you tell us anything about your wife's past?" asked Bellamy.

James Hembrow's eyes darted about the room. "She doesn't like to talk about her past," he said. "She comes from a well-off family. They have property out west of Toowoomba. She has a brother in the army. They're a Christian family. That's really all I know. I've only met the family once."

"You have no reason to believe your wife knew Hilda Jenkins prior to your stay here at The Grand?"

"None at all," said Mr Hembrow.

"Did you see or hear anything unusual the night of the murder?"

James Hembrow narrowed his eyes. "I visited the amenities about midnight," he said. "Captain Black's light was on. That's it, I'm afraid."

Hamish was trying to anticipate the next question when Bellamy cut the interview short.

"Enjoy your lunch," he said, dismissing James Hembrow who, for his part, bolted from the room like a frightened rabbit.

"I saw Black's light on myself," said Hamish when he was gone. "That was about 3.30 in the morning. He seems to have been awake all night."

"Or he went to sleep with the gaslight on," said Bellamy.

"I also ran into Celestine. She was wet through from setting up the equipment."

"We'll get to her later," said Bellamy. "Do you think Hembrow was telling the truth about his wife not knowing Hilda Jenkins?"

"I think he was telling the truth as far as he was aware. I believe Glenda Hembrow did know something about Hilda Jenkin's past. But I believe that James is being truthful when he says he is unaware of any connection."

Just then, Captain Murdo Black strode into the room and sat in the leather chair. He leant back with his long legs spread wide, his hands on his thighs. He was too large for the chair, too large for the room. His presence seemed to fill the room beyond its capacity, while his ample black beard rested on his chest. He was calm and cool.

"When did you arrive at the Grand Hotel?" asked Bellamy.

"*Ya ken* when I arrived. I came on the Scottish Prince when she was grounded by that idiot Little a week ago."

Bellamy glanced at Hamish, who nodded.

"Captain Black was a passenger on the Scottish Prince," he confirmed.

"Did you spend much time with Colonel Winter and Hilda Jenkins during your stay?" Bellamy went on.

"Aye, I had long yarns with the colonel. He's an interesting man."

"What about Hilda Jenkins?"

"Had naught to do with the lassie," he said.

"Did Colonel Winter share any details about her family? Her friends or her past?"

"The colonel and I talked about other things," said the captain. "I don't recall him mention the lassie."

"You didn't see anyone unusual around the hotel the night of the murder?" asked Hamish.

"Depends what *ye* mean by unusual," he laughed. "That French lassie was wandering the corridors most of the night. In *an'* out. I opened the door twice when I heard a noise *'n' t'were* her each time. Wet like she'd been dragged out o' the sea."

"You seem to have been awake most of the night yourself," said Hamish.

"*Aye*, I've trouble sleeping. Too many years at sea. Too many years of night watch. I catch a couple of hours at a time. I *kin* survive on less than most."

Hamish lifted his head as a thought flashed into his mind. "That night at dinner, Hilda made a comment that seemed to jar you," he said. "She mentioned something about people in glass houses and went on to ask if you had never been responsible for the death of someone in your command. What was that about, do you think?"

Captain Murdo Black sat silent, staring at Hamish for a full thirty seconds. The carriage clock on the sideboard could be heard ticking.

"I *didnae ken*," he said. "The lassie was impertinent. She rarely spoke, but whenever she did, she was like a snapping fish. She listened in on people's conversations *'n'* made up half-truths from what she heard."

"Can you give us an example?" asked Bellamy.

"It was a general comment," said Black.

Bellamy and Hamish waited, but nothing more was coming. Captain Murdo Black was given leave to join the others in the dining room.

"The captain has me confused," said Hamish when he was gone. "I find that

I like him, but there is something about him that worries me."

"What?" asked Bellamy.

Hamish sighed. "He seemed overly agitated yesterday morning. Then, just now, he was as calm as can be."

"There was a murdered body discovered," cried Bellamy. "That would make all of them anxious."

"It's more than that," said Hamish. He decided not to pursue the topic. If his suspicions were correct, they would be confirmed in due course. Murdo Black's anxieties may or may not be linked to the murder of Hilda Jenkins. It was too soon to jump to conclusions.

"It seems to be a common theme that Miss Jenkins listened in on the conversations of others," said Hamish.

"And she enjoyed letting people know that she took in what she heard. Do you think she was compiling secrets?" asked Bellamy.

"She may have been. When I think about it, she also made Celestine uncomfortable at dinner. She seemed to suggest that Celestine's father was not, in fact, dead."

"Celestine?" asked Bellamy.

Hamish felt his face redden. "Mademoiselle Dupont," he corrected himself.

Bellamy shook his head. "Go and get her," he said. "We'll talk to her next."

CHAPTER TEN

Horse teams of five and six continue to bring down large quantities of sawn timber from the mills twelve miles up the Nerang River, to be shipped to Brisbane.
Australian Town and Country Journal. 30 August, 1884

Celestine didn't walk. She glided, her head held high like a proud pony with a thick mane the colour of chocolate. Hamish listened to the tap of her walk as she came toward the reading room. The first thing he noticed when she appeared, was the cream silk of her dress. He imagined how the cool silk would feel against his skin if he were to place his arms around that trim waist. Shaking himself free of that thought, he wondered instead how many times a woman could change her dress in a single day. It helped to cool his emotions by recalling that his mother was endlessly changing her costume, so much so it had made him giddy when he was young. Hamish, nonetheless, allowed his eyes to follow the two rows of perfectly shaped mother-of-pearl buttons that ran from Celestine's neck to her waist. The skirt was slim against her hips and remained narrow to her boots.

Hamish blinked as he realised Celestine was aware of his gaze. He gestured for her to sit, which she did with exceptional grace. He wondered that she could walk in such a skirt, much less sit. Hamish realised Celestine presented herself as a completely different woman as the day wore on. The changing gowns reflected changing personalities.

As Celestine began speaking, her voice sounded like treacle. Smooth and darkly sweet. Hamish even smelled treacle. Then, he realised both Celestine and the sergeant were staring at him.

"I'm sorry… what were you saying?"

"I was asking," said Bellamy, a touch of irritation in his voice, "what time it was that you ran into Mademoiselle Dupont the night of the murder?"

"Around half past three," said Hamish.

Celestine Dupont's large hazel eyes widened. She shifted her gaze slowly from Hamish to the sergeant.

"Mademoiselle Dupont claims she can recall no such meeting."

Hamish immediately defaulted to confusion. If there was a discrepancy in memory, it must surely be his. He concentrated.

"I can't be absolutely sure of the time, but we did meet at the top of the stairs. You were wet, your hair…"

The hazel eyes remained calm, unmoved.

"You said you were preparing the equipment." His brow wrinkled as he tried to judge the validity of his own memory. He couldn't have dreamt it. He still felt the brush of her lips on his skin. His brow furrowed further, and he became aware of an impending headache.

"I was preparing my equipment from about three o'clock," said Celestine. "And it rained, certainly. But I did not come indoors until I changed my clothes for the ascension at around five o'clock."

"You must have seen Mademoiselle Dupont, then?" Bellamy suggested.

"No. It was earlier than that."

"I assure you I saw no one when I came inside at five o'clock." Celestine Dupont looked concerned, but not nervous. She was either a credible liar or Hamish had dreamt the whole encounter.

"Let's move on," said Bellamy.

Hamish wasn't ready to move on, but he couldn't think of anything to say to further explore the issue. The woman was adamant they had not met during that night. What could he say without accusing her of lying? Why would she do that?

Celestine confirmed for the sergeant that she had heard nothing from the room of Colonel Winter during the night of the murder.

Hamish remembered the dinner conversation. "At dinner, Miss Jenkins made a comment about your father's disappearance that appeared to upset you. Why is that?"

Celestine stared at him with her large hazel eyes, lashes lowered so slightly, only Hamish noticed. "As I explained last night, my father and I were in a balloon at some height over the Rhine when the balloon unexpectedly made a rapid descent into the river. The balloon and I were recovered by fishermen, but my father was never found."

"Why did Hilda Jenkins appear to suggest that your father may not be dead?"

"This story received a lot of attention from journalists. Many have speculated about my father's fate. But I know that if he were alive, he would be in contact with me. Since he has not, I am convinced he is dead. I suppose the nurse developed her own opinion based on the articles in the newspapers." There was an edge to her voice when she referred to the nurse. Less treacle, more brittle, like burnt sugar.

"Did you find Hilda Jenkins unpleasant company?" asked Bellamy.

Celestine composed herself before she answered. She seemed to be searching for her meaning. "Not disagreeable... Perhaps *effronte*."

"Brash?" offered Hamish.

"*Oui.*"

Bellamy let Celestine go and he and Hamish spent two hours interviewing the staff. No one had seen or heard anything, and no one knew anything about Hilda Jenkins outside the confines of the hotel. The relationship between the colonel and his nurse was polite and professional, by all accounts. By the time the interviews were complete, Hamish and the sergeant were exhausted.

"Drink?" said Bellamy.

"Certainly," agreed Hamish.

Almost as though he had been listening outside the door, Campbell Charles arrived with a bottle of sherry and two glasses. He placed the tray silently on the table between them and turned to leave, before stopping short of the door and turning back. He seemed to have lost his voice.

"Is there something else?" asked Bellamy.

"I think I may have some information," he said. "Then again, it may be nothing at all."

"Come in and sit down," said Hamish.

Hamish and Bellamy waited while the manager found the words he needed.

"It might not be relevant…" he began.

"Get on with it," cried Bellamy.

"It involves breaking a confidence…"

"For pity's sake, a girl has been murdered," said Bellamy as though about to throttle him.

Bellamy's impatience only made Campbell more nervous.

"Hilda Jenkins was looking for someone," he said at last.

"Looking for who?"

"I'm not sure. I don't have a name. But she asked me a lot of questions about the sawmills on the Upper Nerang River. She wanted to know when the workers come down with the timber. She was looking for someone who she had word was working there. I told her which hotel the workers drink at and she said she was going to talk to them."

Hamish glanced at Bellamy and saw his brow had furrowed. "Do you know if she did talk to the timber workers?" he asked.

"Perhaps," said Campbell, "but it was less than a week ago that she made the enquiry."

"And you have no idea who she was looking for, or why?" said Hamish.

Campbell shook his head slowly.

Bellamy gestured that he could leave, and he did so without a word.

"What do you think of that?" asked Bellamy as soon as Campbell was out of earshot.

"It does seem odd that not a week after she was making enquiries about someone, she's killed. Who knows who else she asked about this timber cutter?"

Bellamy poured and Hamish held his glass high.

"To secrets," he said.

Bellamy shook his head. "To truth," he replied as they clicked glasses.

"To truth," repeated Hamish. "And its absence."

"That's the trick of it," said Bellamy. "It's up to the detective to work out which is which."

Hamish took a sip of the sweet liquid and enjoyed the burning warmth of it in his throat.

"Celestine Dupont is lying for a start," said Hamish.

"Yes. The captain's account matches with your own. He saw her at least twice in the corridor. And she was wet. She did come in and out."

"Why would she lie?"

CHAPTER ELEVEN

We experienced the full force of a violent storm on Friday and Saturday. It started raining on Thursday evening and continued without intermission until Sunday morning. The rain beat with great violence, forcing a way into almost every house and flooding the lower portions of the streets. A great deal of damage has been done to the roads and will require a large expenditure to restore them to their former condition. The whole beach is lined with debris carried down Broadwater and Nerang Creek. The creek on Saturday was a surging mass of discoloured water travelling about eight miles an hour and carrying down with it huge trees, logs and all descriptions of farm produce. Pumpkins, passionfruit, watermelons, two horses were seen, a calf or two and five or six boats. Mr Smith of Ashmore lost a punt, Myer's ferry punt was also washed away; and all the approaches to the ferry for thirty or forty yards on this side. The water rose at Nerang up to the back of the houses in the main street. The mouth of the creek has been altered forever.

The Queenslander. Saturday 29 January, 1887

Bellamy swallowed the remainder of his glass while Hamish pulled back the thick curtains at the window. The sky was bruised over a troubled sea. In the distance, white peaks reached up at the sides of the Scottish Prince.

"The wind is increasing," said Hamish, "and the sky is dark. I fear another storm is brewing. Rita left for Nerang immediately after breakfast. I hope she has returned."

They left the reading room together and found Campbell at the bottom of the staircase, giving instructions to Beryl. She was polishing the railing, but she tucked the polishing rag under her arm and scurried up the stairs when she saw Hamish and Bellamy approaching. Campbell stared after her until Hamish caught his attention.

"I was wondering if you've seen Dr Cartwright?" he said.

Campbell shook his head. "No. Dr Cartwright has not yet returned. Though I suspect she'll not be far away. The storm is close. She won't want to be caught in it."

"Indeed," said Hamish. He flashed a glance at Bellamy that he hoped relayed confidence.

"Come with me to the colonel's suite," Bellamy said. "It will keep you occupied until she shows up."

They let themselves in to the colonel's suite and proceeded to Hilda's room. It seemed like the murder had taken place weeks earlier. It was eerily quiet as they looked around once more. Hilda Jenkin's body was no longer there, and the colonel had been comfortably relocated to another suite. The jug and the glass remained on the floor, but the wet patch on the carpet had dried. Through the window Hamish watched the wind pound the waves one way and another. He couldn't see how the wrecked steamer could survive another storm, but others knew much more about ships than he.

He strolled over to the door between the colonel's sleeping chamber and Hilda's room. The assailant had to come through this door. But there was the key, still in the lock, just where it was when they first entered the room. The key hung loosely, the shaft down at an angle to the lock, presumably from the hotel master key pushing it from the other side. Hamish took it out and turned it over in his hand. There were only two keys, this one and the one that management held, the one he used just now to enter the room. Hamish slipped the key back into the lock and closed the door. He turned it, but it stuck. He couldn't make it turn all the way. He pulled it out and tried again. It still wouldn't turn. He took it out and tried the other side of the door. The key went all the way into the lock but wouldn't turn. Sergeant Bellamy joined him. "What are you up to?"

Hamish turned to him, his face pale. "This is not the key to this door."

"What?" Bellamy snatched the key from Hamish and tried it himself. It clanked against the mechanism inside.

"That explains how they got in," said Bellamy.

"They used the real key, then left this one in the door."

"But who? And why?" said Hamish. "And where's the real key?"

"When we find that, we find the killer," said Bellamy.

"We need to find out what door this key does open. It might not reveal the killer, but it will provide another avenue of enquiry."

As Hamish spoke, the freckle faced lad who had not carried their bags, and earned a penny for it, came scurrying down the corridor with two laundered suits for Mr Andrews.

Hamish had an idea. "I wonder if you could help us?" he said.

The boy stopped and looked suspicious.

"We want you to check this key with each of the rooms in the hotel." Hamish held up the offending key.

"That's evidence," whispered Bellamy.

"You'll be careful with it, won't you?" said Hamish.

The boy nodded vigorously. "Yes, sir."

Hamish held out the key and five shillings. The boy's eyes lit up.

"I'll be ever so careful, sir."

"Good lad. Bring us back the key and the information as soon as you can."

"I hope you know what you're doing," said Bellamy.

"It's perfect. No one will take notice of the lad turning a key in the doors. He can tell us which door it opens without anyone knowing we're investigating the key."

Hamish strolled down the wide staircase into the entrance hall and stood in the doorway looking out. He was hopelessly distracted. Small, heavy drops of rain began to fall. The smack of the waves crashing against the sea wall were beginning to encroach on the road. He stuck his head out far enough to peer down the street in the direction he expected to see Rita's carriage. An eerie green light pervaded the scene as the sky grew heavier and closed in on the deserted street. Sensible colonists knew to stay indoors when a sub-tropical storm was approaching from the sea. Hamish was absorbed by his anxiety and didn't notice Mr Andrews approach the hotel from the other

direction. Andrews was wet and harbouring anxieties of his own.

"Good day to you, doctor," he said.

"Good day," said Hamish, taking a step back. He tried to register to whom he was speaking, then realising, he spent another moment trying to think of something to say. It occurred to him that he and Bellamy had not yet interviewed the fellow, but it seemed inappropriate to do so on the doorstep.

"I'm afraid she becomes more damaged by the hour," the fellow said, staring out toward Stradbroke Island.

"Who?" asked Hamish.

"The Scottish Prince."

"Oh, yes." Hamish observed the great schooner, now tipped on a slight angle, but still with her masts intact.

"I sent a telegram to her owners this morning advising them she could be saved. They were going to place her on sale immediately after they heard from me. Another storm may change that assessment, I'm afraid."

Hamish continued to stare at the ship. It had seemed large and imposing when he first saw it. Now it looked frail.

Waves crashed against the hull on all sides. He could have sworn he heard the crack of splitting wood.

"I think Sergeant Bellamy wants a word with you," said Hamish, "about the incident."

It was Mr Andrews' turn to look confused. "Hilda Jenkins…" began Hamish.

"Yes. Yes. Naturally." Mr Andrews hurried into the entrance hall. "I'll change and find him," he called back without turning around.

Hamish stayed where he was, a clap of thunder curling his toes in his boots. Then sheets of lightning threw a ghostly glow across the sea. A gust of wind bent the palm trees sideways and sent a procession of tumbling leaves and sticks rolling down the esplanade. The smell of salt and the sting of sea spray mingled with the fresh chill drops of rain on his face.

Hamish returned indoors. He could worry about Rita as well from the warmth of the reading room. And there may still be a bottle of sherry in there. It occurred to Hamish that Bellamy would likely interview Mr

Andrews in that room, and he could think of no reason to be involved in that interview. He doubted the shipping engineer would have seen or heard anything anymore than the other guests had. Since he had only arrived a day prior to Hamish himself, he was unlikely to have made any particular acquaintance with the nurse.

When Hamish reached the end of the dining hall, he was surprised to see the door to the reading room open and the room empty. The bottle of sherry was still where he left it. He sank into one of the silk and wool embroidered chairs and poured himself a drink to settle his nerves. Another clap of thunder, closer this time, made his hand tremble. Campbell was scurrying along the dining hall, closing windows and shutters and drawing curtains. There was a sense of urgency in the building that conflicted with a similarly pervasive sense of stillness. The air felt heavy, swollen. Campbell bounded into the reading room and stopped, startled to see Hamish there. He was moving through the hotel, closing windows and drawing curtains as though he could ward off the effects of the storm by shutting it out.

"Please don't," said Hamish. "Don't close the shutters. I want to observe the storm."

Campbell stared at him as though he had taken leave of his senses, but he bowed and left the windows as they were in the reading room.

Another gust of wind, another crash of thunder and another flash of lightning almost immediately after it, then the rain began to pour. Not in single, heavy blobs of water, but in sheets, turned sideways by the wind and pounding directly at the building. The sound was terrifying. Rita could not possibly be out in this.

Hamish tore his gaze from the window to see Sergeant Bellamy standing in the doorway.

"Andrews had nothing to add," he said. Hamish was frozen in his anxiety. He barely registered the sergeant's words.

"There's no need to fret about Rita," said Bellamy.

He picked up the sherry and sat in one of the other chairs. "It's just a storm." Bellamy's face appeared more concerned than his words suggested.

Hamish poured himself a sherry and filled a glass for Bellamy. They listened to the distant crack of wood as the storm beat against the sides of the wrecked barque. The reading room was darker than they were used to. Hamish stared for a while at the bookcase that went from the floor to the ceiling behind Bellamy's chair. The owners of the hotel had stocked the shelves with titles from the classics to the modern, something to suit the tastes of every guest. The books looked new and untouched. There was a sense in the reading room, and throughout the hotel, that it was a place built before its time had come. It stood ready, in a landscape that had not yet caught up.

Hamish turned his attention to Bellamy and saw his body was slumped in the chair. His face looked pale and pinched. He must have sensed Hamish staring because he caught his eye, and the fear he conveyed stung Hamish like an arrow. Hamish wanted to voice his own fears out loud, but his throat wouldn't form the sounds. He wanted Bellamy to reassure him, but he could see in the sergeant's face, the reassurance wasn't there to give. A loud crash as a tree branch fell against the back of the building made them jump.

At the same time, the freckle-faced lad entered the room. Both Hamish and Bellamy were startled to see him suddenly appear. He was holding out the key. Bellamy took it from him. "I'm sorry, sirs, but the key doesn't fit any of the doors in this building," he said. "I even tried the scullery and the shed out the back." He looked afraid he had not completed the task to their satisfaction and would have to return the payment.

Hamish nodded. "Thank you for trying," he said.

"That's that then," said Bellamy. "No new information to follow up in regard to the key."

Hamish was pouring his second glass of sherry and breathing deeply to calm his nerves when he saw a shadow move past the window. The shape grew, but the rain was too heavy to let him see what it was. Then it stopped, blacking out his immediate view.

"A carriage!" he cried. Hamish ran through the dining hall to the entrance and out into the rain. A woman was climbing from the carriage and placing her shawl above her head as a shield against the beating rain. It wasn't working because the rain blew at an angle, came up underneath the shawl and wrenched it from her hands. Hamish threw himself at the woman.

"Rita!" he cried.

He shuffled her into the hotel while the soaked and bedraggled coachman led his horses toward the stable.

"I only just made it back," she said.

Campbell appeared from nowhere and began fussing about the amount of water dripping on his expensive carpet. Hamish and Rita moved on to the polished floor and Beryl appeared with a blanket to throw over Rita's shoulders. Rita held the blanket close to her skin, gratefully.

"The river is already high," she said. "If we hadn't come through when we did, we wouldn't have made it. We took the last run of the barge before he tied it up."

The rain continued to pound the building, so much that they had to shout to hear one another.

"Let's get you dry," said Hamish. "We can share information then."

"I have so much to tell you," said Rita as they climbed the stairs. "Your eyes will pop!"

Hamish was sorry he didn't have anything eye popping to share with Rita, but he was consumed with relief that she was safe.

Thirty minutes later, Hamish, Rita and Bellamy met in the dining hall. Campbell greeted them and proceeded to guide them to the table as usual. "Could we have the table in the corner this evening?" asked Hamish. "It will be more private."

Campbell raised an eyebrow to register his disapproval but led them anyway to the far end of the hall and a smaller, more intimate setting. "We'll need the table set for four," said Rita. "Wallace will be joining us."

Campbell looked as though it might be the last straw, that yet another servant might sit at the dining table in the hall. But he said nothing and strode off to give the appropriate instructions to the waiter.

They had only just settled when Wallace came in looking as pleased as punch. He had a scrag of red hair tucked under his arm. As he sat, he let it tumble to the floor. Red settled himself under the table at Rita's feet and prepared for the long wait until scraps of food came surreptitiously under the tablecloth in tiny, perfectly clean hands.

They quickly read the menu. Wallace's bushy eyebrows were raised critically while Rita translated the French for Hamish. Once they had ordered, they were eager to get on with the business of information sharing.

Bellamy began. "Really, we learned very little apart from the fact that Celestine Dupont is lying about being in and out of the building overnight."

Hamish nodded. "She said she went outside at 2:00 and did not come in until 5:00. But I saw her and indeed spoke with her at 3:30. And Captain Black saw her twice, both times she was wet from the rain."

"Interesting," said Rita.

"And the key in the lock of Hilda's door does not belong to that lock," added Hamish.

"That's one mystery solved," smiled Rita.

"And it doesn't belong to this building at all."

Rita blinked. "But wait until you hear this…," she said as she paused to take a drink of water. They all leaned in.

"Hilda Jenkins and Glenda Hembrow were already acquainted long before they met here a week ago."

"Now that is interesting," said Bellamy.

Rita returned to the beginning of her story.

Hamish noted how excited she was to have them all captivated.

"Firstly, can I share with you what a splendid trip it is to Nerang from here? The landscape is delightful. Ferns interspersed with lakes and lagoons. Green farmland in the distance and a range of magnificent purple mountains on the horizon. It is truly exhilarating. The Nerang River bordered with thick foliage and sandy beaches… earlier in the day, of course. There were no sandy beaches on the return trip. The river stretched well over the banks."

Bellamy fidgeted with his spoon as the waiter arrived and placed a dish of soup before each of them.

"The landscape is all very well," said Bellamy, "but I beg you to get to the point."

Wallace smiled as he tucked into his soup.

Hamish smiled too. He knew the more impatient the sergeant became, the longer Rita would take to tell her story.

Rita sipped her soup slowly from the spoon. "Well," she went on, "Mrs Jenkins has a small house a short walk from the river on the Nerang side. It's quite rustic, no more than a shed really, two rooms with a lean-to kitchen at the back. All timber. It would be leaking like a sieve now. I can't think what the poor woman is doing in this rain. I wouldn't be surprised if the whole thing hasn't blown down in the wind."

She turned to Hamish. "We must ask after her tomorrow. Make sure she is alright."

"Of course," said Hamish. "Does she have neighbours? Perhaps someone has taken her in."

Bellamy slammed his spoon loudly into his empty soup bowl. "Get on with it," he said.

Rita smiled sweetly. "Mrs Jenkins is a wily old thing. I'm certain not much escapes her."

She took a breath. "This is the important part," she leaned forward and her listeners did similarly.

"She told me that Hilda worked as a housekeeper for a well-off family in the region prior to her employment with the colonel. The family were fiercely Protestant, Baptist, she thinks. Anyway, they were very strict with their daughter, who was about the same age as Hilda. Hilda felt sorry for the daughter in some ways, according to her mother. Although she also resented her for the family's money and position. Still, Hilda kept her head down and worked hard. She never said anyone in the house had treated her cruelly."

"What has this to do with Glenda Hembrow?" Hamish asked.

Rita looked around at them all. "Glenda was the daughter of that family," she said.

Bellamy released a breath he appeared to have been holding through the whole story.

"Hilda worked in the household of Glenda Hembrow's family?" he cried.

"Why would Mrs Hembrow lie about that?" exclaimed Hamish.

"Because she had something to hide," said Wallace, looking behind him for the second course. Red was also becoming restless under the table. No morsels of food had yet made their way down to him.

"Did Mrs Jenkins know anything about that? asked Hamish.

"No," said Rita, "but she did think something odd must have occurred immediately prior to Hilda leaving the family's employment. Hilda accompanied the daughter, Glenda Hembrow, as she is now, on a stay at a friend's property in the hinterland. It was a grand house by all accounts and Hilda was excited about the change. There was only Miss… whatever her name was then, to care for, and the house had a full complement of staff. Hilda thought it would be a bit of a holiday. But when she returned, she was dismissed. They simply said they no longer had use for her services. Hilda had become more of a 'lady's maid' to Glenda, and in her absence, the family had employed a new housekeeper at Southport. Glenda said she no longer required a maid. As unfair as it was, Hilda was left without a job. Mrs Jenkins was certain her dark mood was about more than just losing her job, though. She became bitter."

The group at the table had been listening so intently they didn't notice the plate of steamed fish floating in a herb and cream sauce arrive at the table.

"I caught this fish," Wallace announced proudly as he examined the piece on his fork.

They all looked at him.

"At first I was catching small whiting from the beach," he said, "but this old fellow came up to me and offered to let me hire his boat. He was just returning from a night's fishing himself. *Why not?* I thought. So, I rowed to the mangroves near the river mouth and caught some small whiting. That'll be breakfast in the morning," he said.

"But this," he held his fork up proudly, "this is flathead. There was a hole – it must have been thirty feet deep. I waited for an hour or more before I felt that gentle tug on the line. You know, the one that excites all your senses. I let the line slip gently through my hands, so the creature thought he was dragging the prey through the weeds… then one jerk and he was hooked."

Wallace demonstrated the process with his hands, the flesh on the fork threatening to fly off across the table at any moment. "A thumping great flathead," he said. "And here he is, steamed and seeped in sauce for your enjoyment."

Wallace placed the creamy fish in his mouth and feigned an expression of ecstasy.

No one knew what to say for a moment. The shift from Rita's revelation to Wallace's story had been too sudden.

"Good for you," cried Rita at last and stuck her own fork into the fish. They all grunted some version of congratulations and appreciation of the catch.

"Getting back to the point," said Bellamy, "we must talk to Glenda Hembrow first thing in the morning."

Hamish, Rita and Bellamy looked toward the group at the large table and at Glenda Hembrow, in particular.

"They can't hear us, can they?" whispered Rita.

"No," said Bellamy, "they're too far away. Anyway, they're deeply engaged in their own conversation." Then, in the way people can so often sense the eyes of others on them, the guests at the centre table turned and caught Hamish, Rita and Bellamy staring at them. The conversation at both tables stopped. Hamish felt the blood rise in his face. Rita was the first to shift her gaze. She looked back down at her plate and speared another piece of fish. "Could I trouble you to pass the broccoli?" she asked Bellamy. He stopped staring to pass her a brimming porcelain tureen. The rest of the meal was punctuated with uneasy chatter about nothing important. They had all become acutely aware that someone at the centre table was almost certainly a murderer.

CHAPTER TWELVE

On those who follow the seas, nature has generally been kind enough to bestow a rugged constitution, capable of resisting all debilitating effects of the many varieties of climate they meet, the exposure and the terrific storms and hardships incident to their career. But those who go down to the sea in ships are only human and if the elements are unable to make the hardy mariner wince, time, that sure harbinger of fate, will eventually find some weak point in his armour through which to thrust its lance. Tales of their life have been woven in song and story, for folk yarns have fired the heart of many a boy and even made the pulse of old men beat faster. There is, and always will be, a halo of romance surrounding the lives of those who have kissed the sea-maiden and have been wedded to her broom; no lover is more true, and no knight ever fought more steadily than the sailor in defence of his love.

Eurora Advertiser. Friday 20 April, 1888.

"A drink?" said Hamish. "There's a decent sherry in the reading room if Campbell hasn't retrieved it."

"Aye, you don't need to ask me twice," said Wallace, plucking Red from his warm spot beneath the table. Rita had already excused herself after a long day, and Bellamy had also retired, saying he needed time alone in his room to think.

Hamish was looking forward to summing up the events of the day with his friend. Wallace had a way of seeing the truth of things. He could cut through social mores, individual psychologies and name the simple truth of a matter.

Hamish had to admit he was at risk of having too much information swirling around in his head and he could not tell what was relevant and what wasn't.

Wallace pushed back a chair to sit and, in doing so, placed it on the unfortunate foot of Captain Murdo Black, who had made his way to their table and was standing directly behind him.

"I was hoping to join you in that drink," he said.

The colonel wheeled himself alongside the table and said, "Me as well. What do you think?"

Hamish glanced past them, fearful the whole centre table intended to join them, but everyone else had left the hall.

"Wonderful," Hamish said through his teeth. "This way, gentlemen."

Wallace and Captain Murdo Black settled into the luxuriously embroidered chairs while Colonel Winter rolled up alongside and placed himself between them. Red curled into a ball at Wallace's feet.

The sherry bottle was still there, but there were only two glasses. In the magical way he had of doing so, Campbell appeared with additional glasses and another bottle.

"I will be retiring imminently," he said. "I thought the gentlemen might require an additional supply."

"Yes, the gentlemen would," Hamish said, taking the bottle. "Thank-you."

Campbell bowed and left them.

Outside, the storm was still raging, and while its force could be ignored or even forgotten in the great hall, it was unmistakable in the reading room. The shutter and drapes were still open as Hamish had requested. Hamish, Wallace, Colonel Winter and Captain Black were silent for a moment, gazing out at the wind and rain. Hamish went over to the window and peered out to sea where a faint outline of the Scottish Prince was still visible. The waves had almost completely engulfed the hull and all that could be seen were the masts. One had cracked and was hanging at a forty-five-degree angle to the deck.

"The Scottish Prince won't survive this," said Hamish.

"*Aye,* as I predicted," agreed the captain.

Hamish sat down and accepted the drink Wallace had poured him. While pouring the drinks, Wallace introduced himself to Colonel Winter and Captain Black.

"I apologise," said Hamish, "I'm not good with social protocols."

Winter and Black assured him there was no need to stand on ceremony. The colonel reached into his pocket and retrieved a small silver case bearing his initials. He snapped it open and offered slim cigars to anyone who wanted one, Hamish and Wallace each accepting with appreciation while the captain declined. The men lit their cigars and swallowed their sherry. They stretched back in comfortable companionship while the room filled with the pleasurable aroma of cigar smoke and alcohol.

Gradually, Hamish relaxed, putting aside his anxiety that his companions would probe for information about the case. The storm struggled and fought against itself outside, but all was calm within.

"The captain has a lifetime of experience at sea," said Colonel Winter. "When he said the ship would not sail again, I took him for his word. It seems poor Andrews will have to deal with a disgruntled owner."

"What happens to a ship when it can no longer be sailed?" asked Hamish.

Wallace let out a long breath of smoke that curled into a perfect ring in the air.

"The responsibility reverts to the captain to either salvage it or sell it in parts," Black said.

"The issue is *nae* the ship, but the cargo. Within the next few days, ten thousand tons o' cargo will be washing up on the shore."

"Who owns that?" asked Hamish.

"In theory, the folk that put it on the ship. Merchants, manufacturers. But they paid the company *tae* ship it, so they won't be happy at the loss."

"Nah, it's those that picks up the pieces from the shore, that's the owners," said Wallace.

Black chuckled. "True enough."

The colonel's face was stern. "Theft can be punished with a fine," he said.

"Nonetheless," said Wallace.

Hamish emptied his glass, poured another, and topped up the glasses of his companions.

"Exactly what is your role, Mr Wallace?" the colonel asked in the polite voice the privileged use when they are being offensive.

Hamish choked on his wine.

Wallace looked confidently at the colonel and smiled. "I'm currently in the employ of the doctor," he said. "But I have long worked as a ship's cook. In fact, I've travelled the world by sea since I was twelve years of age."

Hamish butted in. "Wallace is more friend than employee," he said. "We met at Dunwich, where he was running a kitchen. He was most helpful to me in an investigation I became involved in there. As I have no skills in the culinary arts myself, and Wallace has a remarkable talent in that sphere, I employed him. But to say he is my cook would be to vastly underestimate his value to me."

The colonel took a sip of his wine. "No offense intended," he said to Wallace in the tone privileged people use when they have been offensive and know it.

He went on, "we must always distinguish between right and wrong."

"Right 'n' wrong *dae nae* have clear distinctions," said Black, "regardless of how strongly we might wish they did."

The colonel sighed and sucked deeply on his cigar. "It is an observation of mine that there is no heroism these days," he said. "Men are given up to greed and self-seeking."

"I disagree," said the captain. "I *kin* tell a story o' my own experience that will demonstrate true heroism."

"Are you the hero of your story?" asked the colonel with a wry smile.

"I am not," said the captain.

Hamish was relieved that the conversation had moved far from the events of the day, and he was excited by the prospect of a good story. He liked this Captain Murdo Black in his long, black coat and boots to his knees. It was a perfect wild and stormy night for a story from a sea captain.

Murdo Black began.

"Donald McGill 'n' I were friends at school," he said, his head to one side and staring upward as if he might see his friend's image on the ceiling. "He was an odd sort. He had a peculiar way of looking at things and it seemed to rub folk up the wrong way. He questioned everything."

Black shifted his gaze back to his listeners.

"The thing that impressed me about him was that, even as a schoolboy, he had a passionate sense of justice. He was moved by the misery of folk who were suffering. If he perceived wrong-doing toward others, he had a pure burning desire to redress it."

"I like your friend already," said Hamish.

"A drink to Donald," said Wallace, holding up his glass and then swigging the contents.

Captain Black continued. "We parted ways after school, and I did *nae* see him for years. When I next heard of him, he was working in a merchant's office. I would now '*n*' then see him at intervals between voyages. Years passed '*n*' I heard that Donald had been transferred from Glasgow to manage his employer's business in Foochow. By this time, I was in command, and owner of a schooner called Liberty, trading between Calcutta, Singapore and China. I also transported cargo to Sydney on occasion. It just happened that I was in Foochow for a couple of weeks, obtaining a cargo of tea for Sydney. I ran into my friend, and we spent quite a bit of time together."

Black paused to take his sherry in one swallow. Colonel Winter looked sceptical that the story would provide any evidence of heroics as promised and Wallace appeared to have fallen asleep. But Hamish thought he could listen to the sea captain's Scottish lilt all night.

When Black spoke again, his voice was deep.

"One day, I persuaded him to accompany me back to my ship. *T'was* an exceptionally hot day, and though late in the afternoon, the sun had a sting. We struggled, walking through the narrow, noisy streets to the city gate in the heat. The lanes through the shambles between the gates '*n*' the river were worse. Passing down the main thoroughfare we happened *tae* glance up a narrow lane and saw a sight I shall *ne'er* forget."

Murdo Black poured himself another glass of sherry. Hamish could see him savour the warm liquid as it slipped down his throat. Colonel Winter was leaning forward in his chair now and Wallace's eyes had snapped open. They were hanging on the captain's every word.

Hamish waited desperately for him to swallow the sherry and continue his story.

A loud crack made them all jump. They turned toward the window. "That'll be the end o' the Scottish Prince," said Black.

"What did you see?" cried Hamish.

Foochow, 1877

Some half dozen men stood along one side of the street, each strapped into an individual cage of sorts. *T'was* brutal. An iron collar circled their necks, '*n*' they were tied into a wooden frame that kept their feet from touching the ground. Their hands were strapped to a crossbar attached to both the frame '*n*' the collar. Each man carried the entire weight of the contraption on his shoulders. Their bodies were emaciated. It looked as though they hadn't eaten in days '*n*' their lips were blistered from lack of water. I recall the stench even now. The men soiled themselves where they hung. Clouds of mosquitoes darted about every aspect o' their bodies left uncovered. As their clothes were falling off them, there was plenty o' bare flesh for the taking. The sun beat on my own head with such a bite, it made me dizzy. I could only imagine the agony o' their circumstance, hour after hour in the blinding heat.

We'd been staring a while when a passer-by stopped to gaze at us. He looked from us to the prisoners and back to us again. He had a wide grin with few teeth, and the drawn face o' a peasant.

"Been there for a week," he said in English.

"What possible crime…?" Donald wanted to know.

The Chinese peasant shrieked with laughter. He backed away from us, laughing and bowing until he almost fell. When he righted himself, he ran down the street '*n*' disappeared.

Donald's face had not moved a muscle. He was horrified by the plight of the devils.

I tried to make him see reason.

"*Ye* don't *ken* what the devils might have done," I told him. "They could be the worst kind *o'* men. Pirates, scoundrels. How do *ye ken* they don't deserve the treatment they get?"

But he was having none of it.

"They won't have done more than offend an official," he said. "I guarantee it."

Donald was full *o'* resolve. "Only the poor are punished this way. Anyone with money would simply bribe the authorities out of their trouble," he insisted.

"The lower classes are ground down in this region, I grant you," I said, "but they are desperate. They'll do anything to avoid starvation. They'll be thieves, I'm telling you."

I hoped that would be an end to it. I wanted to get away from the rancid scene. But Donald looked at me in such a way that I knew immediately he wouldn't be letting it go. We parted ways uncomfortably that day.

I was busy preparing the ship for the long voyage to Sydney for a few days after that and I didn't see Donald. The incident in the back streets of Foochow was far out *o'* my mind.

Then one morning Donald appeared at the boat. He told me he needed to talk to me privately, so we went directly down to my cabin. He was haggard and pale. I was anxious for his health.

"Have you contracted fever?" I asked him.

He walked restlessly from one side of the cabin *tae* the other, wringing his hands. Then he stopped at last and gripped the back of a chair so tightly his knuckles were white.

"I want *ye* to help me," he said.

"What do *ye* mean?" I asked. I was genuinely mystified.

He stared hard at me. The muscles *o'* his face were tense and his jaw clenched. But his eyes captured me. They looked at me as though he wanted me to read his meaning. In little more than a whisper, he said, "I have no right to ask this *o' ye.*"

"What are you talking about, Donald?" I demanded, oaf that I was.

He stopped wringing his hands.

"If I were to bring a passenger on board tonight, would *ye* take him to

Sydney? No questions asked."

I stared at him.

"I'll pay his passage," he added quickly.

"What foolishness have you been up to?" I wanted to know.

Then, don't ask me how it happened, but I began *tae* understand. The scene in the street rose before my eyes *'n'* I knew.

"You're not mad enough to think *ye* can save one *o'* those fellows we saw the other day?" I said. I couldn't believe it was true when I saw the look of confirmation in his eyes.

"I can't bear it," he said. "They haunt me day and night."

"Don't talk of it," I told him. I went to turn away, but he placed his hands on my shoulder. He said, "there's one man – he's done no wrong. I spoke to him last night when I took him water. I promised I would save him tonight or die for it."

I walked away from him. I needed to calm down and consider matters. I could see there was no way Donald was going to be diverted, so I needed time to think about what could be done.

Finally, I had a plan. I turned back to him and laid it out.

"The Liberty will set sail as expected this evening, then lie low along the river after dark," I told him. "Somewhere away from the town, I'll tell *ye* the exact spot. I'll send a boat ashore between two and three o'clock in the morning. You bring the prisoner to the boat and return to town by daylight."

Donald was enthusiastic about the plan. He showered me with praises of gratitude. I was less enthused. I believed a positive outcome unlikely, but I wouldn't allow myself *tae* ponder all the potential negative consequences. Such pondering on the seas leads to inaction and certain death. I took no money from Donald for all his attempts to pass his heavy pouch over *tae* me. I told him I owned my ship and need answer to no man. I only hoped the fugitive would reach the boat and Donald would return to town safely. If I were a God-fearing man, which I'm not, I would have prayed that night.

As soon as I had a few minutes spare, I spoke to my first mate, Johns. He'd sailed with me for years and though he was as shifty and silent as the grave, I trusted him as my right arm. Johns' grim face lit up when I told him the plan.

For him, danger was more intoxicating than the cheap wine he and the rest o' the crew drunk by the barrel.

That evening, just before sunset, the Liberty dropped down the Min River with all her sails set. Then after dark, we brought her up at the agreed spot and laid low. There was no moon at all that night, the blanket of darkness perfect for our need. The water swilled around the ship's hull as black as East India ink.

About one o'clock I dispatched Johns in a small boat to wait for Donald at the designated spot. I watched the boat disappear into the darkness and waited until I could no longer hear the splash of the oars. It crossed my mind that I should have gone to pick the fugitive up myself, but I was compelled to stay with the ship. I reasoned that if the authorities did chase Donald and the fugitive, they would catch them long before they reached the river. I convinced myself I had placed Johns in no danger.

It was the longest hour I ever spent.

At last, I heard a faint splash and ran to the side. Johns managed to get the boat alongside the hull and shouted, "Lower away! They can't get up themselves."

A crew member held up a lantern and, in the glow, I saw Donald lying white and helpless at the bottom of the boat. For a moment, I thought he was dead.

The tackle was soon rigged, and the fugitive was brought up first. A Chinese man was lifted to the deck, his eyes hollow, his lips shrivelled and his clothes hanging loose from his bones. I recognised them as Donald's clothes. I expected the man to fall into a heap on the deck, but he didn't. He shuffled to the side and gripped the rail, his head over the side, watching the crew as they next lifted Donald's limp body and placed it on the deck. The Chinese man fell to his knees beside him. Donald was near death, I could see that.

None of us knew the full story until much later. For many days, as the Liberty sped southward, Donald lay between life and death from fever. The Chinese fugitive never left his side."

Captain Murdo Black took another cigar from the box and tapped it between his fingers. His eyes were still back there, on that ship. Hamish waited, afraid that would be the end of the story. But the captain began again, in his own time.

"His name is Sing Wei. He told us days later that Donald came to him after dark with a knife and a file and set to work cutting through the bamboo and iron clamps to release him. This took some time. Then Donald gave him clothes and they escaped through the streets. Sing Wei could hardly walk, so Donald dragged him along as best he could. As soon as they were out of town, Donald packed him on his back and carried him for the greater part of the journey. By the time they reached the boat, Donald fell into a faint without saying a word. He was nearly dead from exhaustion, and he'd taken on a fever. Johns couldn't leave him there on the riverbank, so he brought him to the ship."

Murdo Black stopped talking and his companions waited.

"Did your friend recover?" asked Hamish.

"Yes, he recovered," said the captain. "He returned to health by the time we reached Sydney. As it happened, we obtained a commission to bring cargo to Brisbane and continued our journey. Donald and Sing Wei disembarked in Brisbane and now run a farm in the hinterland to the south of here. In fact, one of the reasons I wanted to stay in Southport was to visit with my old friends."

The colonel's brow was furrowed. "I can't decide whether your story is one of heroism or villainy," he said.

"That's the point," said Wallace, "judgement is so often a matter of perspective."

Hamish was thinking about something else. He said, "What do you think Hilda Jenkins was referring to when she asked if you had been responsible for any deaths?" he asked.

"That," said Black, "is a story for another day. Good night, gentlemen."

He downed his third glass of sherry and left them. Hamish watched the silhouette of his broad shoulders, the long hair that fell down his back, the heavy coat that he wore regardless of the heat and the thick leather of his boots. Everything about him was large. He was a man of presence.

Hamish noticed the colonel watching Murdo Black at the same time. His face did not reflect admiration or even awe. There was an upturned lip, fierce dislike. Or was it disdain? Colonel Winter clearly found nothing to admire about Captain Murdo Black.

The colonel excused himself and wheeled his chair out of the room.

Hamish and Wallace were left to stare at one another. "Winter travels remarkably well without the nurse," said Hamish. "I wonder that he needed her at all."

"One last?" asked Wallace, holding up the bottle.

Hamish pushed his glass forward.

"The captain can certainly tell a story," said Hamish. "I wonder if there is anything in it that relates to the death of Hilda Jenkins?"

"No. Black's too keen to talk. There'll be nothing he said that ties him to the murder. I do wonder if there's more to that story, though."

They drank the last of the sherry. "I'm interested in the story he didn't tell," said Hamish. "The one Hilda implied she knew."

Red scrambled up Wallace's legs and pulled at his beard with his teeth.

"Time for bed alright," he said. "We're going up. Red has had enough."

"He has a point," agreed Hamish. "It is late."

CHAPTER THIRTEEN

All hope of getting the barque Scottish Prince off the beach at Southport was abandoned after the heavy winds of Friday and Saturday last. On Friday afternoon, the main mast went about 20 feet from the deck and the ship's back was broken and the sea was washing through her. The Collector of Customs announced that all cargo, tackle etc. washed ashore from the barque must be handed over to customs officers at Southport. It may be mentioned that there is a penalty of one thousand pounds, or six months' imprisonment attached to any offence against the above. The ship is parted in two pieces. The foremast only is standing and the afterpart has drifted round, the stump of the mizzen mast being barely visible. The Stradbroke beach is strewn with wreckage; sewing machines, cases of beer and whiskey, mousetraps, sweets and blankets are washing about in the surf. Mr Andrews dispatched horses and drays to collect the cargo from along the coast. The first of the cargo saved from the wreck arrived in Brisbane on Tuesday.

The Queenslander. Saturday 19 February, 1887

Hamish entered the dining hall eager for breakfast and found the room buzzing. "What's the excitement?"

Wallace, who was piling his plate with buttered whiting, answered him. "The cargo from the Scottish Prince is washing up along the shore, here and on Stradbroke. People are out and about collecting treasure."

"Oh dear."

"They say the ship is broken in the middle and the sea's rushing in. The beaches are strewn with cargo – sewing machines, cases of whiskey, sweets, blankets, rat traps for heaven's sake, hundreds and hundreds of rat traps — all washing about in the surf. Mr Andrews despatched horses and drays to collect the loot from all along the coast. But I think he'll have to race the people of Southport to it." Wallace laughed mercilessly.

"What happens if people take things home?" asked Hamish.

Wallace stopped laughing long enough to answer.

"Andrews made clear this morning, to anyone who would listen, that the Collector of Customs instructed all cargo washed ashore from the barque is to be handed to the customs officers at Southport. There's a penalty of 1000 pounds or six months in prison for breaches. Sergeant Cooper is running around like a goose, trying to retrieve the stuff and charge the scavengers." Wallace continued to enjoy the public displays of larceny.

Hamish smiled.

"I'm glad the sergeant has something to occupy him," came a voice from behind. Hamish turned around. "I overheard the end of the conversation," Rita said. "All hope is lost for the Scottish Prince to sail again, I take it?"

"There is no hope," confirmed Wallace. "Andrews says the underwriter has abandoned the ship. It's up to Captain Little to sell the wreck and cargo for as much as he can get and distribute it among the creditors. Apparently, there have been bidders prepared to pay seven or eight hundred pounds. Still, she's a different proposition this morning than she was two days ago."

As they finished breakfast, Sergeant Bellamy appeared, looking flushed. It was obvious he had come in from outdoors.

"They haven't got you chasing sewing-machines, have they?" asked Hamish.

Bellamy rolled his eyes. "I was instructed to keep the local sergeant informed on the progress of our investigation," he said. "But he wasn't in his office, so I chased him halfway down the coast to Burleigh. All he could do was blather about the cargo from the Scottish Prince. I understand there is a lot of money at stake, to wealthy merchants on the other side of the world mind, but I'm investigating a murder, right here under our noses. I won't bother with him again."

"I still maintain it is a bonus for us that he is kept busy," said Rita.

Bellamy calmed down and sat. A waiter, ever at hand, brought him tea.

"Where is Red?" asked Rita.

"We took a walk along the esplanade this morning," said Wallace. "He's exhausted."

"What are your plans for today?"

"We'll catch the ferry across to Stradbroke, I think. Whiting is running off the beach there."

"This is quite the holiday for you and Red, isn't it?" said Rita, one eyebrow arched.

"It is at that," agreed Wallace. He smiled and left them with a swagger.

Hamish was too preoccupied to notice the exchange.

"I've arranged for an interview with Glenda Hembrow this morning," said Bellamy. He wiped his mouth with a napkin and stood up. "I would like you both there."

Hamish was already standing.

Rita gulped the last of her tea and followed them.

Five minutes later, the three of them sat in the reading room with Glenda Hembrow. She was immaculately dressed in a trim woollen skirt and bodice cut to accentuate the waist, but without the fashionable frills and fancies popular among many women. Hamish couldn't help making the comparison with Celestine's poise and presence. Glenda struck him as a woman who wanted to exhibit such poise but did not.

She looked at them with an expression of innocent wonder.

"I can't imagine what more I can tell you." Her eyes were open wide.

Hamish felt affronted by the feigned innocence, by the knowledge that she had been lying to them all along.

Bellamy leant back in his chair. "You can begin by telling us about your relationship with Hilda Jenkins."

Glenda Hembrow's eyes narrowed at the question.

Bellamy went on. "What we already know is that Miss Jenkins once worked for your family, during the time you were also residing at the family home."

A lip twitched.

Bellamy took a deep breath and leant low across the desk toward Glenda.

"Mrs Hembrow, is it true that Hilda Jenkins worked for your family during the time you lived in the family home?"

Glenda Hembrow swallowed. "Yes," she said quietly.

Bellamy leant back in his chair again and picked up a pencil. "You lied," he said, pointing the pencil in her direction.

Mrs Hembrow shuffled in her chair.

"We had a sort of silent agreement," she said. "Hilda and I. We were both shocked to run into one another here and neither of us wanted to bring up the past."

"What is it in your past that neither of you wanted to bring up?" asked Bellamy.

Glenda Hembrow paled but retained her composure.

"Nothing," she said, "nothing in particular. Hilda left under difficult circumstances, that's all. She was bitter."

"What circumstances?"

"Nothing really. Certainly nothing to do with her death." She looked around at all their faces. "You can't think…"

Bellamy cut her off. "Simply tell us about Hilda's time working for your family and the circumstances of her leaving."

Glenda shrugged her shoulders and appeared resigned to telling the story. "There's nothing to it," she said, "but if you must know, Hilda worked for us for four years. From when she was sixteen. She was a housemaid. When I was feeling poorly, mother decided I would benefit from time in the country, so she sent me to stay at a friend's house in the hinterland for a few months. Hilda was sent to take care of me. She was more of a lady's maid during that time. When we returned, I found that mother had hired a new housemaid for the Southport house in our absence, and there was no longer need of Hilda's services. Mother and father were going through a rough patch financially. Hilda was given the appropriate notice and dismissed. She was very upset about it. She thought it unfair, and it probably was," conceded Mrs Hembrow, "but it wasn't my fault. I was embarrassed. I didn't want to talk about it with her, and to my relief, she didn't seem to want to talk about it either."

"Why didn't you tell us this after her death?" asked Bellamy.

"It was fourteen years ago!" cried Mrs Hembrow. "What relevance could it possibly have?"

"Your past acquaintance with the murdered woman has every relevance," said Bellamy. "We know nothing of her interests, her friends, her enemies."

"She didn't have any friends or enemies," said Glenda. "She wasn't that sort of person. She was… a nothing sort of girl. One didn't notice her most of the time."

"Someone noticed her. Someone found her so noticeable they felt the need to eliminate her."

Mrs Hembrow shook her head. "That's what I don't understand. There was nothing about her to incite such strong feeling."

"We've heard she had a sharp tongue," suggested Hamish.

Glenda's eyes shone. "Yes, she did have that. But she couldn't say anything that *really* mattered. No one listened to her."

Hamish looked on as Bellamy examined the woman's face. "Do you have any idea who she might have been searching for?" said Bellamy quietly.

Hamish saw a flicker in Glenda's eyes. She managed to control it almost immediately, but he had seen it. He couldn't work out what it meant. Was it fear? Shock?

"Searching for?" repeated Glenda. Her eyelashes fluttered rapidly. Hamish knew enough to know she was buying time, time to control her emotions, time to steady her nerves.

"Yes," said Bellamy patiently, "we have information that Hilda Jenkins was looking for someone. Do you have any knowledge of that?"

Glenda's voice was strong and suggested she was in complete control by the time she spoke. "Certainly not," she said. "Why on earth would I?"

"If there is nothing more you can add, I'll let you go," said Bellamy. "Though I would caution you that obstructing the police in their investigations is an offence."

Glenda Hembrow put her head down and rose to leave them.

"Just quickly," said Hamish. She turned to him. "Is your husband aware that you knew Miss Jenkins?"

"He is not," she said and left the room.

"Do you think that is all there is to it?" asked Bellamy when she'd gone.

Hamish bit his lip. "I don't know," he said. "She reacted when you asked about who Hilda might be searching for."

Rita nodded her head. "Mrs Jenkins was certain there was more to Hilda's change than bitterness at an unfair dismissal."

Hamish's hand shot to his forehead. "Mrs Jenkins," he said, "we agreed we would check on her today. Ensure she is safe after the storm."

"I was planning to go there this morning," said Rita, "until the sergeant said he wanted me at the interview."

"My apologies for keeping you," said Bellamy. "You both go now. I want to write all this down and think about where we are with these interviews. It seems to me at this point that a lot of people here at the hotel are harbouring secrets."

CHAPTER FOURTEEN

Nerang. The now approaching Spring is a most glorious one. Everything that can grow is growing, and our farming class are having a busy time of it. The incoming crop of early potatoes looks well, and I hear good accounts on all sides. On the Upper Nerang, the cultivation of tobacco has been commenced chiefly in small patches; but there is little doubt that tobacco will be a product of the settlers on our back farms who find such difficulty in carriage with regard to maize. The Nerang Races fixed for New Year's Day are progressing well. Judge and stewards have been chosen and prices set. A proposal to amalgamate the Nerang and Coomera Races was knocked on the head at the Committee Meeting, those present being determined in having races at Nerang yearly and establishing Nerang as a sporting centre.

The Queenslander, Brisbane. Saturday 30 October, 1880.

Hamish and Rita organised a cab to take them to Nerang. As they rattled along, they were shocked at the debris lying on either side of the road. Workers had been through, clearing the carriage way but large trees, complete with root systems spanning a yard in diameter, lay along each side. Minor debris, branches and leaves, still lay in the path of the horses who were reluctant to walk over them. This made the going slow. Large potholes had been carved into the ground and the cab rocked from side to side as they dodged one hole only for the wheels to hit another. There were spots at which Hamish and Rita feared the cab would tip.

Expansive waterways and lagoons and the silver glint of water extended as far as the eye could see on either side of the carriageway. Trees, scrub and sky were reflected in the water, creating a mirrored effect. It was difficult to identify the horizon, and apart from the jolt of the carriage, it was impossible to orient oneself to land and sky, creating a sense of unreality.

Hamish thought it a miracle the road was sufficiently clear for them to pass. The closer they came to the river, the less clear the road became, with great stretches reduced to muddy sludge. It was a challenge for their driver to navigate. The line at which the river ended and the road began were blurred. The river itself, when they finally reached it, was swollen and brown, as though an almighty power had tipped it upside down. They were surprised to find the punt still in operation.

The operator stood on his flat deck, pole at the ready. "I saw a couple of cows floating down here yesterday," he said. "You'll find plenty of damage at Nerang."

Hamish and Rita stepped nervously onto the punt. It seemed to sit dangerously low in the swollen river, but the operator navigated seamlessly across, ducking and weaving between the floating branches and debris.

When they disembarked on the other side, they walked along a narrow path toward 'town'.

The narrow path along the river was eerily quiet apart from the chirp of the cicadas, all the louder for the silence around them. And mosquitoes. Hamish and Rita swatted left and right as they made their way through the long grass. The air was thick. This humidity in the height of summer was something Hamish had struggled with since his arrival in Queensland. Sometimes it felt too thick to breathe and this was one of those days. The water was being drawn upward to the sky where great grey clouds were forming, ready to pound the earth once more. What was that smell? It was sweet and sour at once. Decaying vegetation, swollen with moisture, and steaming in the sun. The combination of the humidity and the smell left him nauseated.

They had walked no more than a hundred yards when Rita stopped. Splintered and twisted timber sat piled high to the right of the path. The odour reached out to them. More than the sludge and the steaming mud, something like rotting flesh circulated around them and sent claw-like tendrils into their nostrils. Hamish placed his handkerchief to his face and turned away from the pile of corrugated iron that had fallen in on the timber. The iron reflected the heat of the sun, creating an oven beneath.

"This was her house," said Rita.

"Maybe she stayed somewhere else?" said Hamish, without confidence in the idea. He was holding the handkerchief to his face and looking around for another house when he heard a sound in the scrub behind. He stiffened.

"What's wrong?"

"Shh." Hamish remained still, peering in the direction of the sound. He thought he saw a movement, the shape of a man. But staring into the scrub, he could make out no sign of life.

"It's nothing," he said.

They picked their way through the debris to the main part of the shack, though there was very little left of it. The roof had collapsed into the interior. Between them, Hamish and Rita were able to lift one corner of the rusted iron sheeting and Hamish peered beneath it. A wave of putrid heat hit him in the face. He wanted to gag, but he kept straining to see what was inside. He waited for his eyes to adjust as everything merged into shades of grey and he struggled with the smell. There were some small shafts of light filtering through the collapsed timbers and gradually Hamish made out delicate patterns of light in the darkness. Then, all at once, he caught sight of two staring eyes. His heartbeat quickened. He made out the face of an elderly woman lying in a ghastly twist. Her terrified eyes turned toward the sheet of iron that had come from above to crush her. Hamish stood back.

"Is she in there?" asked Rita.

Hamish nodded.

"Dear God," said Rita, "I should never have left her there. I should have taken her back to the hotel. I knew the storm was going to be bad."

Hamish held her by the arm.

"It's not your fault. She wouldn't have come with you, anyway."

Rita looked at the rubble helplessly. "I don't believe she would have," she said, "but that doesn't make me feel any less responsible."

"We need to get back to Southport to notify the authorities," said Hamish, gently leading her away from the shambles.

As they walked back to the riverbank, Hamish couldn't shake the feeling they were being watched. He tried to keep his attention on any signs of movement or sound around them, without alarming Rita. When they reached the river, the punt was there waiting.

"Back so soon," said the operator as they stepped aboard. "Did you find the person you were looking for?"

Hamish and Rita glared at him.

"Oh," he said and quietly stuck his pole deep into the river to get the vessel moving. The barge slipped away from the bank.

"Can I ask who it was?" he said when they were half-way across the river.

"Mrs Jenkins," said Hamish.

"From the shack along the river?"

"Yes. The shack has collapsed."

"I'm sure it has," said the bargeman. "That shack wouldn't have survived the storm. I'm surprised my punt didn't get washed down the river. Why didn't the old woman get herself away to neighbours?"

Tears were welling in Rita's eyes.

"Can I ask you something?" said Hamish. "Did you take anyone back on the barge just now, after dropping us on this side?"

"No," said the bargeman, "not a soul."

Hamish stared hard back at the riverbank. Whoever had been following them, and he was sure there was someone, they were still on the Nerang side of the river.

"Have many been across this morning?" Hamish asked.

"Not many. A couple of gentlemen early on, and a man by himself after that."

"Can you tell me what the man looked like?"

"No, I can't say I could," said the bargeman. "Men come and go across this river. No time to make a note of appearances."

The next couple of hours were spent at the Southport Police Depot reporting the finding of what they were sure was Mrs Jenkin's body. By the time Hamish and Rita returned to the hotel, Bellamy and Wallace were waiting for them in the reading room.

"We were getting worried," said Wallace.

"Did you find anything out?" asked Bellamy.

"Yes," said Hamish, "we found out that Hilda Jenkins' mother is dead. Her shack collapsed in the storm."

"I'm sorry," said Bellamy.

"The colonel and Glenda Hembrow seem to be the only people left who know anything about Hilda Jenkins," said Wallace.

Hamish felt washed out. The sight of the old woman crushed under her own roof on top of the events of the past twenty-four hours left him emotionally drained. Hilda Jenkins and her mother were ordinary people, struggling to survive. They weren't wealthy or powerful, and they weren't considered of any great value to society. Hamish worried that if he and Bellamy were not able to identify Hilda's killer within a few days, the investigation would be dropped. She and her mother would be easily forgotten. He was on his way to sit on the bench outside the hotel when Campbell called out to him.

"A telegram came," he said, holding out the slip of paper. Telegrams were rarely good news and Hamish hesitated before taking it. "Thank you," he said finally. He took the telegram and made his way to the bench opposite the sea and settled down before reading it.

It was from his mother.

> *Don't worry. Situation stable. Albert organised everything. Track allows father to operate as usual, but no money changes hands. Bert manages all clients. Friends have rallied around and overlook minor inconsistencies. No noteworthy incidents at home.*

Hamish took a deep breath of relief. At least he wasn't betting away the family fortune. He laughed. He suspected that had already happened, given his latest information that his parents had moved into a smaller home. The nagging problem of his father's illness, and what was inevitably to come, was set aside again. Hamish was glad to be alone with his thoughts.

CHAPTER FIFTEEN

All visitors to the popular watering place of Southport will remember the glorious drive along the main beach to Burleigh Heads, where as the buggy travels smoothly along the firm sand, the rollers of the mighty Pacific Ocean break close to the horse's feet. Nowhere else, within such easy access of the Metropolis can such a ride be had; at whatever time of the day you start and however sweltering the heat may be elsewhere, here there is always an invigorating breeze.

Until quite lately it was impossible for a visitor to partake of one of the keenest enjoyments within reach of Southport, viz a gallop on a good horse along the beach to Burleigh, on account of two great drawbacks; one was the great difficulty of getting a horse, and the other, there were no means of satisfying the craving of the inner man on arrival at the destination. It is almost agony to go without dinner after such a trip.

But now things are altered. If you are staying at a hotel in Southport, you can telephone Echlin & Co., and in half an hour a first-class buggy will be at the door waiting for you to start. When one arrives at Burleigh, one is struck by the beauty of the scenery, the high, steep hill of basaltic formation, covered towards the top with a vine scrub and a beautifully sheltered valley behind, some distance up which will be found the Burleigh Heads Hotel.

Queensland Figaro and Punch. Saturday 13 February, 1886.

Hamish wasn't alone for long. The aroma of lavender and patchouli reached him before he saw her approaching.

"You work too hard," Celestine said as he moved along the bench to make space for her. "I wish you would take time to relax."

Hamish wondered at the emerald specks that appeared in her eyes in the sunlight.

"I'm relaxing, enjoying the sea and the sun."

"Surely you can have more fun than this while enjoying the sea and sun," she smiled.

"What do you suggest?"

"Campbell recommended a carriage ride down the sand to Burleigh this afternoon. Why don't you join me? It will do you good to get away from here."

"A horse and carriage can travel on this sand?" said Hamish, looking south along the shore in disbelief.

"Apparently, they frequently take visitors at low tide. Come along, Hamish. I don't want to go alone."

She pouted slightly, full pink lips accentuated, and her face as low as possible so she could look at him through long curled eyelashes.

"It doesn't seem appropriate," murmured Hamish. "Not without a chaperone."

Celestine threw her head back and laughed. It was a big laugh, honest and musical.

"Don't be ridiculous," she said. "I travel the world alone. I have long since passed the point of propriety. It's a carriage ride, that's all. It'll be fun."

Hamish felt awkward that she was laughing at him, but he couldn't deny his desire to accompany her.

"All right, when do we leave?"

"Now," laughed Celestine, jumping to her feet.

Hamish followed her gaze north and saw that a buggy pulled by two horses was making its way down Marine Parade toward the hotel. Celestine tugged at his hand and pulled him to his feet. They waited on the promenade for the carriage to reach them. "Campbell ordered the buggy from Echlin and Company," she said. "They come as arranged to take visitors to Burleigh Heads."

Hamish held the door open and assisted Celestine into the contraption, then he climbed in after her. The aroma of her perfume so close to him made him feel intoxicated. He felt his arm pressed against her white shoulders, covered only in a flimsy layer of the finest muslin. When she smiled with the joy of being close to him, he caught his breath. He couldn't stop himself from smiling back. The buggy rattled into motion, and they travelled along the road, past Government House. Hamish glimpsed the flag-pole through the trees. "The flag is not up," said Celestine.

"That means His Excellency is not in presence," Hamish smiled.

"I would have thought he would come to Southport to see my exhibition."

"His loss," said Hamish, still smiling.

Within a short distance, they approached the Nerang River and Meyer's Ferry took them across to the other side. They travelled down a decently formed road a short way until the ocean burst into view, and they saw an endless expanse of sea, deep and turquoise beyond the whitewash. The horses trotted onto the firm sand and headed toward Burleigh. The long stretch of sandy beach lay ahead of them, with Stradbroke Island disappearing behind. Occasionally, they saw the splash of a whale some distance out to sea and Celestine cried out. She seemed eager that Hamish see the whales, in the same way a child is eager to call a parent to look at something they find delight in. She seemed almost childlike away from the business of aeronautics. Hamish caught himself wondering how she could possibly be the same woman, the famous adventurer, Celestine Dupont.

On Hamish's side, they watched the township fade away to scrub land. Olive and silver grasses held the sand dunes together, where sea birds darted among yellow native flowers in search of tiny prey. The scenery forced everything from Hamish's mind. Celestine had been right. He needed to get away from the hotel. When they reached Broadbeach, she slipped her hand into her basket and pulled out a package wrapped in a thick towel. She carefully opened the package.

"Sandwiches," she announced. "Campbell told me you like them." She handed him small triangles of bread with ham and pickles made by the cook in the Grand Hotel kitchen.

"How did Campbell know I would be joining you?" Hamish asked.

Celestine smiled. "Just eat your sandwiches."

She also produced a silver flask and offered it to Hamish. He took a long sip of fruity wine and handed it back.

"My father would have loved Australia," sighed Celestine, staring out to sea.

The cheeky smile that had enticed him to join her had receded.

"Why?" he asked.

Celestine swung her head round to look at him. "The open spaces," she said, incredulous that he would have to ask. "The endless sky. What could an aeronaut love more?"

"Why did he not come south?" asked Hamish.

Celestine stared out her window at the sea for a few minutes.

"His work was in Europe."

"I suppose you can attract a much larger crowd to an exhibition in Europe than would be possible here," said Hamish.

Celestine looked confused. "Yes," she said, "that too."

They were both silent for a moment, then Celestine turned her face to him. "What about your father?"

"We don't get along," said Hamish.

"Why? What does he do?"

"He made his money on the goldfields. That's where I grew up. Running wild on the Ballarat Goldfields. That's how I got this." Hamish pointed to the scar on the right side of his face. "I fell down a mine shaft. I was there for hours before they found me."

Celestine ran two fingers gently down the scar.

Hamish swallowed.

"More recently, he was a Set Price Bookmaker." He hoped the statement would ease the tension he was feeling in his body.

Celestine placed her hands in her lap. "Has he retired?"

Hamish considered his response. "He has dementia," he said at last.

Celestine looked away. "I'm so sorry," she said. "That must be difficult for your mother."

"He isn't too bad at the present, as far as I can make out. Confused, memory loss. But the disease will progress. I fear what my mother will go through as it does."

Celestine looked thoughtful. "My countrymen have made great strides in the research of this disease, I believe."

"Yes, they have. As have the Germans," said Hamish. "But they are only identifying the characteristics of the condition, defining it. There is no sign of a cure. In fact, it is the French who have stated conclusively that there is no cure. The disease is degenerative and will only get worse as the patient progresses along the disease pathway."

Celestine spoke quietly, "we have both been losing our fathers gradually. My father disappeared, but it was a long time before I could accept that he was dead. Your father is disappearing also. Eventually, the body you are left with will only be a shell."

Salted water gathered at the brim of Hamish's eyes and the prickly sensation caused him to blink several times.

Celestine smiled at him and lowered her lashes. He thought for a moment she was going to lean in and kiss him and he panicked.

He instantly gathered his defences and asked a question that he knew would shut down the uncomfortable emotion of the moment.

"I sense that you distrust Colonel Winter," he said.

Celestine's demeanour changed. She leant back in her seat and looked ahead. Taking a slim cigarette from her purse, she held it out for Hamish to light.

"I distrust him," she said simply.

"But what is it about him that makes you uncomfortable?" asked Hamish.

She waved the cigarette as if to dismiss the question as pointless.

Hamish wasn't deterred. He had seen the effect the colonel had on her. He continued watching her and waiting for an answer. Finally, she said in exasperation, "He's German, isn't he?"

"So...," prompted Hamish.

Celestine made a theatrical flourish with her hands that almost caused the cigarette to burn a hole in his sleeve.

She stared out the window for several minutes before she finally spoke. "What are they, the Germans?" she said.

Hamish was at a loss. She turned back to look him directly in the eye. "A loose federation of states," she said.

"I don't think I understand," muttered Hamish. Was this the frail girl who spoke of her father only ten minutes ago? Celestine's personality changes were rapid and disarming.

"Germany has no soul," she said in the deep treacle voice he remembered from the evening before. "France - she has a soul. She has been a nation for one thousand years."

She looked away to blow smoke from her cigarette out the window. Hamish was trying to adjust to this version of Celestine.

"Tell me if I understand this correctly," began Hamish, "you distrust Colonel Winter because he is German, and for no other reason?"

Celestine turned back to him slowly and deliberately. "Of course, *mon ami*," she said. There was no hesitation or question in her eyes. Her voice lowered to little more than a whisper.

"My dear boy," she cooed, "there is no way you can understand this. Your own country is too young. There is no soul here, either."

Hamish immediately felt defensive, but he couldn't think of a single argument to validate the notion that the country of his birth had a soul. If Australia did have a soul, it belonged to the original inhabitants, he thought. A soul that was deeper and more mysterious than anything Europe could claim. But it was beyond his experience, this ancient soul.

He felt out of his depth in the present line the conversation was taking.

"I know you were in and out of the building the night we met on the stairs," said Hamish. "We met at around three. I am certain of it."

Celestine continued to stare out the window.

"What I don't understand is why you would lie about it."

Celestine turned back to him slowly. She licked her lips while considering her response.

"There are some things that must remain secret between us, *mon ami*," she said. "But I assure you my activities that evening had nothing to do with your investigation."

Hamish was recalling the man standing in the rain the night they met at the top of the staircase.

Suddenly, Celestine's cheeky smile returned, and she poked him in the ribs, becoming threatening in an entirely different way.

"What's going on with you and the lady doctor?" she said.

Hamish felt the flush rise in his neck. Soon his whole face would glow red.

How he wished he didn't wear his emotions on his skin in this way.

"Nothing is going on. Dr Cartwright and I are friends."

Celestine lowered her voice. "No, *monsieur*, that is not so."

Hamish wanted to protest, but he feared that would only make matters worse.

"You are in love with her, yes?"

Hamish reddened further.

"But I see that you are attracted to me. That is good," she said.

Hamish wondered how he had allowed himself to get into this situation alone with this woman.

"Don't worry," giggled Celestine. "I'm not going to eat you."

Hamish couldn't decide whether he was relieved or disappointed.

They had travelled seven miles along the sand by the time they could clearly see the headland. As they drew closer, they were struck by the beauty of the steep rise, a hill of basalt that reached proudly up from the sea as though aware of its ancient grandeur. The top was covered with viny scrub. As the horses climbed the hill, they saw a beautiful, sheltered valley behind the headland. Some distance up the hill was a house offering accommodation and light refreshment.

"What a magical place this would be to stay." Celestine placed her head on Hamish's shoulder. "Don't you wish we could disappear together in this valley?" she said quietly. "It's such a pretty place. And so private."

Hamish felt her warm skin against his shoulder and smelled the lavender in her hair. He didn't make any attempt to move away. For a moment, he shared her fantasy. It did seem like another world in the lush valley, with the sea lashing against the basalt on one side and the dark mountains on the other.

They sat on the headland together looking out to sea, while the driver took the horses to Fowler's to rest them. Celestine held Hamish's hand and he didn't dissuade her from doing so. When the horses returned fresh, they started back.

"I think I need another sip of that wine," said Hamish as the headland began to disappear behind them. Celestine handed him the flask, waited for him to swallow a long mouthful, then snuggled up close and spent the rest of the trip with her head on his shoulder, sleeping comfortably. Her breathing was quiet and shallow and reflected the rhythm of the horses. Hamish wished he could achieve such a trouble-free sleep. When they reached the Grand Hotel, Hamish gently woke her and moved her head off his shoulder so he could get out of the carriage, but she kept hold of his hand. He assisted her out and she stood on the sand with her head tucked under his chin. She looked up at him and whispered, "I trust you." With that, she kissed him on the lips.

Hamish felt the same tingle he had experienced before when she kissed him, but there was no longer the same yearning. There was something about her sudden and unpredictable changes in mood that made him guarded. She broke away and Hamish watched her climb the stairs up to the promenade. He wondered what he had done to earn her trust, and what he might be required to do to maintain it. As enchanting as she was, an instinct in him had been triggered. He would be wary.

CHAPTER SIXTEEN

The Germans have found out already that the policy of colonisation entered upon by them involves increased responsibilities, chief among them being the necessity of forming a colonial army. It used to be a standing objection years ago, when an abortive movement was set on foot to acquire colonies, that an overseas extension of Germany was contrary to her military institutions and opposed to the principle of general liability to military service. As complications similar to those on the West Coast of Africa may be expected in the Pacific, the question arises how to raise a force available for quelling disturbances and guarding the interests of the empire. Two facts must be looked in the face: one of which is that up to the present time, recent German colonial acquisitions have all been in the tropics; the other that the Germans have had to deal, not with the compact nations, but with tribes usually at variance with each other. The latter circumstance is rather in favour of colonial policy, as it enables the colonising power to play off one tribe against another, and thus employ only a small force in keeping them well in hand.

The Brisbane Courier. Thursday 25 June, 1885

The sun was low in the sky by the time Hamish returned to the hotel. He strode into the reading room to find Bellamy shrouded in yellow light, holding his teacup in both hands, the light contributing to a look of melancholy.

"Is anything wrong?" asked Hamish.

"Report writing all afternoon," said Bellamy. "And we are no closer to finding out who killed Hilda Jenkins."

Hamish nodded sympathetically while pouring himself a cup of tea.

"Where have you been while I was working?"

Hamish tucked at his collar. "Ride down to Burleigh."

Bellamy didn't bother to ask why or with whom. He wanted to get on with the case.

"We need to speak with James Hembrow. Find out if he did know anything about his wife's relationship with Hilda."

"I passed him on my way in," said Hamish. "He's sitting on the bench on the esplanade. He was alone when I saw him." Hamish put his cup down. "It might be better to talk to him informally. He might be less defensive. I'll go now, talk to him alone, if he's still out there."

Hamish was happy to put distance between himself and Bellamy in case he decided to ask questions about his beach ride.

Bellamy hesitated, then nodded. "Find out what he knew. It makes all the difference to whether we consider him a suspect or not."

James Hembrow was sitting with his knees wide apart, his elbows on his knees and his head in his hands. Hamish sat beside him on the bench, but James didn't acknowledge him.

"Is everything alright?" Hamish asked.

The man looked up as though he hadn't noticed Hamish sitting there. He straightened himself.

"Call me James."

Hamish held out his cigarette case.

James took a cigarette and Hamish lit one for each of them.

Then he waited. He wanted to give James time to regain his composure, gain his trust, and to speak. But there was nothing other than the sound of drawing tobacco and the sea. The tide was returning, leaving only a thin strip of bare sand. Patches of the wet sand shone pink, an exact mirror of the sky.

"Terrible business," Hamish said at last.

James nodded. "It has had an effect on Mrs Hembrow."

Hamish saw his opening. "Was Mrs Hembrow close to Hilda?"

James looked surprised. "Not at all. They barely spoke."

Hamish's question hung in the air.

"It's the whole business," James went on. "Someone murdered right in your midst."

Hamish reflected. As he could recall, Glenda Hembrow hadn't seemed upset the morning they found Hilda.

"How long have you been married?" he asked.

"Seven years."

"No children?"

James did not seem disturbed by the question. "Glenda doesn't want children. I must confess I thought when we married, they would come naturally... but no."

"How are the potential grandparents coping with that decision?" laughed Hamish. "My mother will be demanding grandchildren within the first year of marriage. Mind you, she's finding it a challenge to convince me to marry at all."

"Glenda's parents are very controlling," said Hembrow. "And controlled when it comes to their emotions. They have never mentioned it. My own parents are in England, so they wouldn't see their grandchildren, anyway."

Hamish continued to enjoy the view of the sea. He wondered how he could broach the subject of Glenda's past. Fearful that James would retreat at any moment, he decided to get right to the point. "Do you know much of your wife's past?" he asked.

James dropped his cigarette and stubbed it out with his shoe. "Why on earth would you ask that?"

Hamish's eyebrows shot up and his mouth twisted to one side. He knew he was on prickly ground. James hesitated a moment, then his frown faded. "You're investigating me," he said. "You're not being thoughtful, you're detecting!"

For a moment, Hamish expected him to get up and walk away. But James stayed.

"Glenda lived at home with her parents," he said. "The family is well off, but it doesn't matter. I have money of my own. I believe Glenda led a sheltered life, very much under the control of her mother, a formidable woman."

"Did she have any friendships, perhaps among neighbouring families?

Or the servants?"

"Do you mean male friendships?" snapped James.

"Not at all. I mean in general."

"No. I don't think she had any social life at all."

Hamish considered his next question carefully. He didn't want to cause discord between husband and wife, but Glenda was the strongest link they had to Hilda's past.

"Are you quite sure," he began, "that your wife did not know Hilda Jenkins before they met here at the Grand Hotel?"

James Hembrow tucked in his chin and looked incredulous.

"Good Lord. No!" he said.

He sat back. "She never mentioned it." He seemed a little less sure of himself.

Hamish stared at his eyes. Only questions were reflected back at him.

"Thank you for talking to me," said Hamish as he stood to leave.

"You can report back to Bellamy everything I told you," James called out.

Hamish stopped and turned back. "I will, of course," he said, and left James alone with his fears.

Bellamy was still alone in the reading room when Hamish returned.

"He says he knows nothing of any connection between Glenda and Hilda," said Hamish.

"Do you believe him?"

"Yes."

"Did you tell him what you know?"

"No!"

"Your questions should stir up some interesting conversations between husband and wife just the same. I think it's time to bring the colonel back in. He's the only other person with a direct link to Hilda."

"Agreed," said Hamish.

Campbell was dispatched to find the colonel and bring him to the reading room. Ten minutes later, Colonel Winter was wheeled in by Beryl and set before Hamish and Bellamy.

"Formal interview?" he said. "I wouldn't want to miss dinner."

The aroma of the evening's menu was already permeating from the kitchen.

"The problem is," said Bellamy, "there is little evidence to go on and we know so little about Hilda Jenkins. It is difficult to identify a motive for her murder."

"I don't know that I can help you," said the colonel. "I know nothing about her myself. Other than she made an efficient and competent nurse."

"Did you know she worked as a housemaid for Glenda Hembrow's family?"

"*Nein*, I did not!" said the colonel. He stared into the empty space between Hamish and Bellamy as if he were turning a thought over in his mind. "Hilda did not say this, and Mrs Hembrow said nothing of it." His eyes narrowed. "Mrs Hembrow is fond of her own importance. If I reflect on it, she's not the type to mix with servants."

"Yes, but you would expect her to admit to knowing the girl once she was murdered," said Hamish.

"Did she not?" asked the colonel.

"We found out from Hilda's mother," said Bellamy.

"There do seem to be secrets out there."

Bellamy was watching him closely. "Tell us about your own background."

Colonel Winter laughed. "I enjoy telling stories about my own past a little too much, I think.

"I was in the Imperial Army until I retired in 1877. I came to Australia at the request of my daughter. I was an absent father most of her life, but we were always close. I decided the warm sun in the colony was preferable to the endless, icy winter alone in Berlin. I found the weather and the wide skies very pleasant. Unfortunately, my daughter passed away three years ago. Nevertheless, I cherish the time we had together. Her husband returned to Holland, but I decided, since I had no one in Germany, to stay here and enjoy the warmth in my last years of life. I found this hotel owned by friends. We made an agreement that I could stay here, and I hired Hilda to help me. I have felt very comfortable at the Grand for six months."

"Did Hilda ever talk to you about her own life?" asked Hamish.

"Never," said the colonel. "I paid her to listen to my stories, not tell her own."

Hamish and Bellamy shared a glance.

"Hilda was a fine young woman. It was almost as though she might have been of German descent."

"What do you mean?" asked Hamish, intrigued.

"In Germany, the education of women makes her the queen of the home, not a weak imitation of what she is not. She is not the bad imitation of a boy, such as our French mademoiselle, who goes about piloting aircraft, nor is she a mere ornament for the saloon. The German woman is educated to elevate a man, to make him happy after his toil and to reward him. Hilda understood this. She expected nothing for herself. I grant it, her tongue was sharp at times. This was her small way of inserting herself into existence."

Hamish stumbled on his words. "Was this how your daughter was raised?"

"Of course," said the colonel as though the question was not worth asking.

Hamish caught himself saying a small prayer of thanks that Rita was not present to hear this diatribe concerning the education of German women. He acknowledged, if only to himself, the irony. In the colonel's mind, he was paying German women a compliment. He noted the colonel seemed to have as little regard for Celestine as she had for him.

Bellamy hadn't been listening to Hamish and Colonel Winter. He was thinking about the case.

"We keep coming to the same dead end," said Bellamy. "No one knows anything about Hilda Jenkins' past."

"Except for Glenda Hembrow, it would seem," said the colonel over the top of his glass.

"There is that missing three months," said Hamish. "That's when she changed, according to her mother."

"We need to press her for more detail about what happened during their time away."

Rita appeared in the doorway. "I don't know what you said to James Hembrow, but he is having a whopper of a row with his wife," she said.

"What about?" said Bellamy.

"He's saying she needs to tell the truth. That even if she won't tell him, she needs to tell the police. She's saying it has nothing to do with the case and it won't serve anyone to bring it up now. She will never tell."

"If she knew Hilda, she must tell us what she knows," said Bellamy. "I will find out."

Hamish nodded. "Perhaps it doesn't have anything to do with Hilda's death, but the fact that she seems to be the only one who knew Hilda previous to her time at the Grand, means that we need her to talk."

Campbell Charles appeared at the door with a white napkin draped over one arm. "Dinner is being served," he said. "I trust you will be joining the others in the dining room?"

Hamish thought about requesting something light in the reading room, but the look on Campbell's face led him to abandon the idea.

"We'll take the corner table again," said Bellamy.

Campbell pursed his lips. It was obvious that it was his preference the guests mingle over meals. Hamish was certain he considered it a personal insult that they preferred to stick to themselves.

CHAPTER SEVENTEEN

Lady students at the Melbourne University are permitted to graduate in the Arts course, and we have at least half a dozen feminine B.A.s and M.A.s but the medical school is strictly closed against them, under existing conditions they have no chance of developing into M.B.s or M.D.s. For the removal of this disability, they are now organising with a vengeance. The would-be lady doctors contend they have a legal right to enrol themselves in the medical classes if they see fit, and they deny that the mere passing of a resolution by the University Council is sufficient to shut them out from the medical education they desire. Accordingly, they mean to tender the prescribed fees and ask to be enrolled as medical students, and if the University officials hand them back their money and refuse to take their names, they will go to the Supreme Court, where Chief Justice Higinbotham is an earnest advocate of women's rights. The general anticipation is that the decision of the Supreme Court will be in favour of the audacious girls, and that the University will be compelled to enrol them as medical students. The reason for opposition, of course, is found in the influence of male doctors who are naturally nervous at the considerable loss of income they would suffer if lady doctors became available for lady patients.

Maryborough Chronicle, Wide Bay Burnett Advertiser. Friday 4 February, 1887.

Mrs Hembrow sat opposite Hamish and Sergeant Bellamy in the reading room once more. This time, she disappeared into the armchair. Either it had grown, or she had shrunk. The mask of innocent confidence was gone and one of frailty replaced it. Tears stained her cheeks, and her eyes were red and swollen from the argument with her husband. Hamish felt the first twinge of sorrow for her. He hadn't seen any emotion in their previous encounters and her coldness ensured his own feelings had not opened up to her. A fully developed tear slipped down her cheek. Hamish handed her his own handkerchief, and she wiped the corner of her left eye with it. Glenda Hembrow shook her head, fixed the pin holding back her tight curls and threw back her shoulders. Her face remained pale, but she had regained her composure. Rita sat alongside her, opposite Hamish and Bellamy with an air of protectiveness about her. Hamish hoped Mrs Hembrow would sense this.

"We know you and Hilda were acquainted prior to meeting here at the Grand," began Bellamy.

Glenda Hembrow looked at her hands in her lap, where she was pulling at the edges of Hamish's handkerchief. She bit her lip and turned her face towards the window.

"Tell us once more how you knew her," said Bellamy. Glenda glanced towards Rita, who smiled and nodded.

"I told you, Hilda worked for my family as a housemaid," she said. "It was some time ago."

"She accompanied you on a trip to the country for your health?" said Bellamy.

Glenda nodded.

"And then when you returned, she was dismissed?"

Glenda nodded.

"What happened during that time away from Southport?" asked Bellamy.

Glenda gripped her hands together, the handkerchief strangled between them. Her knuckles white, and her eyes darting about as though searching for a way out.

"You must tell us. This is a murder investigation. You must share everything you know about Hilda Jenkins' past. What is it that happened during your time away from home that would cause Hilda to return a different young woman?"

Glenda responded swiftly to the suggestion that there might be more to

Hilda's story than she had told. "Who says she was different? She was bitter, that's all. Angry about being dismissed."

She looked Bellamy directly in the eye for the first time since the interview began.

"Her mother," said Bellamy firmly.

Glenda looked from Bellamy to Hamish.

Suddenly, she broke into tears. They began slowly, but soon she was sobbing so hard it was difficult for Hamish and Bellamy to make out any intelligible words. Rita held Hilda's hand in hers and squeezed for a few minutes while she wept. Then Glenda Hembrow stopped crying, wiped her eyes with Hamish's handkerchief, threw back her shoulders and told her story.

Beaudesert, 1875

"The trip was difficult." She shook her head and took a deep breath. "It took two days. We stayed overnight with a family reluctant to call themselves into the business of providing accommodation, but willing to put travellers up for the night if required to do so. It was comfortable enough, but not *pleasant*." She checked the faces of her audience to ensure she had their attention. "I had to share a room with Hilda," she said with emphasis. "Needless to say, I didn't sleep well."

She glanced around at all three of them for assurances they understood. They didn't, but they nodded for her to go on.

"The passage to our destination was no more than a track. Rocky and treacherously pitted. It was fortunate father made good on his promise to send his best driver, or we might not have made it at all."

Tears began to fall again, and Glenda looked out the window. She no longer attempted to clear the tears away with the handkerchief. She wrung it between her fingers in her lap. After a few moments, she looked at Rita through weeping eyes and silently pleaded for the strength to continue. Rita placed her hand over the woman's fingers and the wet handkerchief. Glenda took another deep breath.

"Our spirits were low when we set out the second morning, but they dipped even further when we passed through the main street of Beaudesert after lunch. A row of timber buildings rose from the dust. They might have been whitewashed once, but when we saw them, they were the same colour as the road. Red dust everywhere. Even the trees were the colour of dust." She made a small click with her tongue at the memory and shook her head.

"That my parents would send me to such a place," she said and threw her head back. She looked to the ceiling for motivation to go on.

Hamish, Bellamy and Rita waited silently. They were terrified that any gesture from them would cause her to breakdown completely and they would never hear her story.

At last, Glenda looked directly at Hamish, though she seemed to see right through him.

"This is not where we imagined spending our exile," she said.

"Exile?" asked Hamish. "I thought you were unwell…"

Glenda went on as though she had not heard him speak. There was a glassiness to her eyes. She was lost in her memories. "At least twenty minutes' ride from town, the carriage stopped in front of a small square timber building in the middle of nowhere. There was nothing to see in any direction but sheep. Then a man appeared, looking as though he'd risen from the dirt. His skin was dark and we were frightened of him. He didn't look at us. He didn't speak. He just took our bags from the back of the carriage. What could he be doing? Was this black man robbing us? I didn't know what to think." Glenda motioned for the jug of water on the occasional table. Hamish poured her a glass and handed it to her. Without comment, she drank and then continued with her story.

"It wasn't until the man dumped our bags at the gaping black hole that stood for a door, that the full weight of realisation fell on me. The man opened the door to the carriage and waited without raising his eyes. We continued to sit there. I knew Hilda didn't understand. Finally, I summoned enough courage to step out onto the dirt and Hilda followed me. The coach rattled away and our only lifeline to home was gone."

Glenda held herself tightly, her arms crossed over her chest. She began to rock gently. When she spoke again, it was in a deeper register.

"The Big House, when we passed it, seemed closer to town than to this shed in a paddock. I thought we must have been circling around it. I was certain we were going to stay at the magnificent country home of my father's business associate. I had dreamt of wide verandas and grand rooms. Of rose gardens and fragrant herbaceous borders. Not this. Not *here*. Evidently, my father's friendship with the master of the house didn't extend to allowing his unmarried daughter to see out her confinement within the family home. I ought to have known."

Hamish felt his breathing miss a beat. *Confinement, did he hear that correctly?* He dared a quick glance at Bellamy, but his face had not changed. He recovered his own poker face and hoped Glenda had not registered his shock.

There was no sign that she had as she continued with her story.

"The black man stood tall by our bags. He kept his eyes down and seemed to be waiting for us to address him. I tried to speak, but my throat was hoarse.

'I'll be keeping an eye on *ya*,' said the black man, as soon as he realised we were not going to speak first. '*Yas* have no need to worry.'

I thought it ironic that he claimed himself our protector when it was his presence that caused our fear.

'But who will protect us from him?' I said loudly enough for him to hear. He took our bags inside and promised to bring fresh bread and cheese each morning. And lamb once a week. Then he strode toward the fences and disappeared among the sheep, where he blended in as though he were one of them."

Glenda's eyebrows dipped, as if a thought had only that moment occurred to her. "He did keep his word. Every day he came, like clockwork, in the mornings and sometimes in the evening as well. He brought us supplies, brought water from the river and he kept the fire lit. In all that time, we never asked anything about him."

Hamish and Rita exchanged a glance.

"Go on," said Bellamy.

Glenda began again. "Anyway, we were left alone with only the timber hut and the terrible heat for company. The hut was terribly primitive. I don't know the words to make you understand our initial impression. Thick slabs of iron bark, rough and undressed, just as they came split from the tree, stood vertical to the left and right of a slim opening as black as coal. A sharply angled roof fashioned from shingles sat precariously over the top. I couldn't imagine it keeping out the rain and cold for a minute.

I felt frozen to the spot, as though once I walked in, I was accepting a strange new reality. Hilda took the plunge first. She went through that dark hole as though it were nothing. It wasn't until it had swallowed her, I realised I had to move. The heat of the sun was burning my skin and my hair was limp and damp.

Inside, the hut was divided into two halves by a wall made from the same slabs as the outer shell. The front section had a large bed to the left, nicely made up with clean sheets and a quilted cover. To the right, there was a small dining table and a sideboard. In a nook added to the side of the square was a cooking area with firewood and an iron kettle suspended over wood from a tripod. In the back section of the hut, there was a small bed to the left and to the right was a copper sink for washing.

I had no idea how to cook on an open fire, but it seemed obvious that tea could be made without any fuss with the use of the kettle. I directed Hilda to light the fire and get the kettle boiling as a priority. I sat at the table and peered through the wooden slats. Hilda did as she was directed, but I could tell she was terrified. I could feel her shaking even when I couldn't see her. The truth of it is, I was too ashamed to look at her. She could only guess at why my parents had sent us to such a place."

Glenda rolled her eyes and pursed her lips. She seemed to be struggling still with her parents' actions. She slumped back in her chair before beginning again.

"To her credit, Hilda made tea without question, and we sat together at that table, as roughly assembled as the hut it sat in, and sipped quietly. The stitches of my dress were stretched to breaking point at the waist and I could hardly breathe. As soon as we'd finished our tea, I directed Hilda to help me out of the thing.

She unbuttoned the dozen covered buttons down the back of the gown without complaint and then peeled my arms out of the sleeves one by one. There was a lot of tugging and pulling before the dress fell to the floor. And the corset and heavy undergarments followed. My body was my shame, but there was no one to hide it from in this desolate place. Hilda looked at me, unable to conceal her shock. Then suddenly, as if a light had shone down from above, there was a flicker of recognition in her eyes. I knew, she knew in that instant, why we had been sent away and what our exile meant."

Glenda glared at her listeners, seeming to demand judgement.

Hamish wore his emotions on his sleeve, but it was not shame that Glenda could see. It was horror at the injustice. That these women, little more than children, had been placed in this situation, was abhorrent to him.

"Don't pity me," Glenda whispered when she registered the empathy in Hamish's eyes.

"Not that."

Hamish looked away silently.

"Hilda said nothing as she unpacked one of the looser gowns my mother had commissioned in Melbourne. She had forbidden me to wear them at home, believing my condition might be revealed to servants, friends, or neighbours. It was ridiculous, because no one ever saw me. Once I fell… ill, I didn't leave the house. I barely left my room."

Glenda dabbed her cheek with the handkerchief, well and truly wet by now.

She went on, "Hilda said nothing as she helped me into the larger new gown. Even to comment that I might be more comfortable would have been to put voice to the situation we were in. We created an unspoken pact of silence. I believed, at that time, that if something were not said aloud, it did not exist. We made that agreement then, and we have kept it ever since."

"This silent pact between the two of you is why you didn't reveal any of this after Hilda's death?" said Hamish.

Glenda nodded.

"The first night in the house was troubling," she resumed her story. "We were not used to the sound of sheep bleating and strange birds wailing. We felt so alone. Though the Aboriginal man had said he would watch over us, we wondered how that would work. Was he outside hovering? Were there more of them about?

"In the morning, the man told us his name was Jimbo. He brought supplies of sugar, flour, butter, oats and milk. There was also a slab of lamb.

'Best cook it today while it's fresh,' he told us. Hilda had never been a cook, but she did cook at home for her mother, so knew the basics. 'There's a *vege* patch out back,' Jimbo said. He told us to pick what we needed. The vegetable patch was a tangle of weeds to the eye, but Hilda assured me there was good food to be found in there, and that we could grow more. She set to work that day to clear the weeds and collect water in containers to encourage the vegetables and herbs to grow. She was surprisingly successful and managed to produce passable examples of spinach and tomatoes. Naturally, there was no point planting seeds that would take a season to grow to fruition, as we were not going to be there long enough to harvest them.

Hilda must have known more about cooking than she'd thought, as well, because she started creating lamb dinners in a cast iron pan with a lid, and stews with the vegetables from the garden.

The pregnancy wasn't mentioned in those first weeks in exile. I ate as little as I could, merely enough to stay alive, despite Hilda's efforts. The people from the Big House never visited and we both gave up expecting they would.

Because there was no mention of the pregnancy, there was also no mention of the father. I would never say who it was, not even on threat of death."

Glenda's eyes were as cold as stone. No one doubted her resolution.

"Hilda did everything in her power to care for me, to do the job she had been assigned, albeit unknowingly. I think she regretted I couldn't accept our circumstances as well as she had. She was worried when I wouldn't eat. She tried everything to entice me to nourishment.

We both knew the baby was too small. I didn't care. I didn't think of it as a child. I thought of it as some form of growth, something that my body would expel at some point. I couldn't wait to be rid of it, this invasion of my body.

Mostly, I detested my bloated breasts. They disgusted me. I was reminded of the milkmaids in the sheds pulling down on the soft pink nipples of the cows.

One night, when the thing inside me was squirming to the extent that it made sleep impossible, Hilda sat on my bed to distract me from my discomfort.

'Do you think it's a girl or a boy?' she asked innocently.

I couldn't believe she had spoken the words aloud.

'It's an affliction,' I cried, 'and the sooner it's resolved, the better!'

Her eyes were as wide as saucers.

I controlled my voice so that I could make her understand.

'When this affliction is at last dispelled from my body, it will be no more a child than the squirming mass that is inside me now,' I said.

Hilda's face took on a grotesque shape, her mouth open, as though ready to scream. 'It is not a child,' I tried to explain to her, 'it's an affliction, the horrible consequence of the devil's work.' I raised my voice then to drive the point home. 'It is the physical representation of my shame.'

Tears ran down my cheeks and Hilda took my hand. There was pity in her eyes. Pity! I didn't want her pity. I wasn't crying for my shame, I was crying out of frustration… and anger. I was so angry that she refused to understand.

'The shame must end,' I shouted. Then I lay back on the pillows and told her to leave.

'Get out,' I told her. 'Sleep.'"

Glenda coughed, a small noise at first, but it gained momentum, and she was soon gasping for air. Hamish poured another glass of water and handed it to her. She managed to swallow and settled.

"I didn't think much about the date this shame was to end, but by my rough calculations, there should have been about four weeks to endure when I fell ill. Hilda encouraged me to take short walks in the fresh air each morning. We never went far. I couldn't stand the emptiness of the place. I was sick of red dirt and yellow grass, and that relentless sky that reached almost to one's feet.

One day, we had barely taken a dozen steps outside when I was overtaken by an excruciating pain in my back. I grabbed my side and Hilda helped me return indoors. The smell of the bog where Hilda emptied the chamber pot stuck in my nostrils and I vomited. I yelled at her to make me tea. Jimbo had already delivered water and lit the fire, so Hilda ladled water into the kettle. She kept bringing me freshly brewed tea all day. But I didn't drink it. Hilda wanted to summon a doctor. She became more anxious as the day went on and my pain grew worse. How could I know if I was experiencing the usual pains prior to birth? How could Hilda know? I reckoned it was at least a forty-five-minute walk to the Big House, if Hilda went as fast as she could. She wanted to go, but I wouldn't let her. They hadn't wanted to know about us before, so why would they help when it came to the birth, the most shameful event of the whole sinful story? No. I didn't want anyone there to witness my shame. I wanted it over. I didn't care if I died.

Hilda tried to argue that she should at least find a midwife, that surely if she went into town, someone would guide her to someone local.

But again, I insisted that no one be summoned. It was backache, nothing more.

The pain continued to worsen. Then, at about four o'clock in the afternoon, Jimbo arrived with additional wood for the fire. Hilda must have spoken to him because I saw through the window, he was running across the paddock. I was too distressed to wonder what it meant. Half an hour later, he arrived with a black woman, no older than me. Her dress was European, though it was stained the colour of the sheep. Her hair was tangled. I don't think it had ever seen a brush.

'My wife can help,' said Jimbo.

'Don't bring that woman into my bed chamber,' I yelled.

They froze in the doorway while I shouted for them to get out. To go away. I was not having that woman anywhere near me.

Hilda stood near the table looking terrified and unable to decide what to do. The black woman and Hilda exchanged glances as though they were communicating about *me*. I screamed at them at the top of my lungs. Finally, Jimbo took his woman by the arm and led her away from the hut. I could hardly bear Hilda near me after that, but I needed moisture and she held a mug to my lips so I could drink.

As the sun's last glow dipped behind the mountains, my waters broke, and it became clear, even to me, that I had begun to labour. Hilda had no idea what to do. She cursed my parents for leaving us isolated and alone and for burdening her with this responsibility. And she cursed me for sending the 'Black' away.

Nonetheless, hours later, it became apparent that babies birth themselves, regardless of how little those present know of the process.

I writhed in pain while Hilda kept an eye on progress. In the end, I managed to force the child into the world. Hilda dealt with the cord as she would a baby lamb. She placed the creature by my side, and I lay back in the bed with my eyes closed.

'It's a little boy,' Hilda whispered close to my face. I wouldn't open my eyes. Hilda held my wrist and felt the blood pulsing. She must've feared I was dead.

She told me I would need to nurse the child.

'I will not be nursing it,' I told her emphatically.

Hilda waited for a few minutes, just hovering over me. I suppose she was watching it. It was pressed up against my arm and I could feel the rhythm of its chest moving up and down. *What would life be like for a child born of shame?* I thought. If it were allowed to develop into a child. What possible good could come of such a life?

Hilda was clearly exhausted. As she left me for her own bed in the back of the hut, she passed a wooden fruit box on the sideboard. It was lined with an old pillowcase. She touched the box lightly and looked back at me. I closed my eyes, and she took herself to bed. When she woke in the morning, I was sitting up.

'I'm glad you are awake,' she said. 'I heard the door close early this morning. I assume it was Jimbo come early with the provisions.'

I didn't answer her.

Hilda scanned the disturbed bed clothes. 'Where is the baby?' she asked.

'We'll be returning home in a few days,' I told her. 'As soon as I am well enough to travel.'

Hilda's eyes shifted to the sideboard. The box was no longer there.

She threw open the front door. I heard the silence as she stood there. I imagined her view across the endless paddocks with the endless sheep.

The next day, when Jimbo came with supplies, he was less cheery than usual. 'Did you take him?' I heard her ask.

Jimbo silently stocked the fireplace.

'Where is the child?' Hilda demanded.

I saw him look her in the eye on his way out and for a moment he hesitated. Then he put his head down and left.

Hilda knew he had taken the child, and she also knew none of us would ever speak of it. If no one spoke of it, it ceased to exist.

On the evening of our arrival back at Southport, my mother summoned Hilda to the library and informed her that her services were no longer required. She was provided a month's pay in lieu of notice and asked to leave first thing in the morning. There was no need for Mother to warn Hilda against speaking about our awful secret because Hilda knew that without a reference, she would not acquire another position in a comfortable house."

When Glenda stopped talking, her eyes were dry and Bellamy, Hamish and Rita were silent.

"Your husband knows nothing of this?" said Bellamy at last.

"He does not." She let the handkerchief drop. Hamish plucked it from the floor with the tips of two fingers and placed it gingerly back in his pocket.

"You must know that what you have told us makes you a suspect in the murder of Hilda Jenkins," said Bellamy. "Not to mention the fact that you may be complicit in infanticide."

Glenda's eyes widened and darkened. She took on the appearance of a startled cat.

"I don't understand," she murmured.

"Hilda knew something that threatened your marriage, your reputation and potentially your life," said Bellamy. "You may well have killed her to stop her from talking."

"But I didn't," said Glenda, quietly. "Why now? Why kill her now when she could have spoken the truth and destroyed me at any time in the last twelve years?"

"Perhaps your paths had not crossed," said the sergeant. "I'll notify the authorities of what you have told us, and it will be up to the local constabulary to investigate what happened to the child. But you remain the primary suspect in this murder."

Glenda was silent while she pondered that. She seemed confused, disoriented. Bellamy nodded to Rita and made a gesture toward the door.

Rita gently encouraged the woman to stand and she led her from the room. The woman who left the room was frail and broken. It seemed that her secret had sustained her. She was in no sense the same woman who had entered almost an hour earlier.

CHAPTER EIGHTEEN

The inhabitants of this charming watering place are to be congratulated upon the success that has been attended efforts to provide entertainment for visitors during the Easter holidays. A regatta and race meeting, well organised and successfully carried out are no light undertakings for a small community of little more than five hundred people with the preparations for the sport both by sea and land.

Southport is crowded with visitors from the metropolis, who have turned up for their holidays at the hotels and lodging houses. In the matter of catering and table attendance, Southport hotel keepers will hold their own in any place, and the example set by them in this respect might well be copied by some metropolitan hotels.

The Regatta, the eight that has been held, took place on Saturday and was full of pleasurable interest. The steamer, Natone, the flagship of the aquatic tournament, arrived in Southport on Friday afternoon bringing upwards of one hundred people from Brisbane. The boats entered for competition reached Southport between noon and ten o'clock on Friday evening. Most of them started from Brisbane on Thursday night. They were picked up at Bulimba and at the headquarters of the Brisbane Sailing Club in Hamilton Beach. A nice light westerly breeze sprang up on Thursday evening as the fleet of little craft proceeded down the Brisbane River. The moon was bright and clear. The scenery from the shore was impressive and beautiful in the pale moonlight. After arrival at Southport, camp was pitched at Porpoise Point on Stradbroke Island, and in the evening the boating men congregated around two or three tents, where a gathering took place, songs, recitals and a theatrical performance.

The Brisbane Courier. Tuesday 27 April, 1886.

The following morning, Hamish checked the sherry bottle in the reading room. It was still empty from the night before. "That's not like Campbell."

"Don't you think it's a bit early?" asked Rita.

"Probably."

"I'll let Campbell know," said Bellamy, getting up.

They had all slept restlessly after the revelations from Glenda Hembrow. They had no doubt Glenda slept least of all. Breakfast was quiet, as no one was willing to say anything that may be overheard in the dining room, and they were each rolling their thoughts over in their minds. Mr and Mrs Hembrow did not come down to breakfast.

Once they were back in the privacy of the reading room, Hamish was the first to speak. "I'm sure we have the full truth about those missing few months now," he said.

Rita nodded in agreement. "It's a powerful secret to hold."

"I wonder what James will say?"

"It's not certain that he didn't know," said Rita.

Bellamy returned with teacups on a silver tray and Campbell followed with a fresh jug of tea. "More suitable for morning," he told them as he poured, after which he left silently.

"Who didn't know what?" asked Bellamy.

"James Hembrow. I was saying he may have already known his wife's secret. That would give him a reason to kill Hilda Jenkins to stop it from getting out."

"That's true," said Bellamy, "but what evidence do we have that he knew?"

"None," said Rita.

"He says he didn't know," said Hamish.

"The obvious conclusion is that Glenda Hembrow killed Hilda to shut her up. The simplest solution is usually the correct one."

"Hilda may have been blackmailing her," suggested Hamish.

"Now what evidence do we have of that?" said Bellamy.

"None," said Hamish, sipping his tea.

Rita put her cup down. "I can't help thinking about the child. I shiver when I think what may have become of him, poor little thing."

"How old would he be now?" said Hamish.

"Fourteen, according to the timing," Bellamy said, swallowing his tea, "if he survived."

Rita looked ill.

They were all silent for a few moments while they considered the fate of Glenda's child.

"She was so cold before the story was revealed," said Hamish. "She only became emotional once she knew the secret was coming out. She had no emotional connection to that baby at all."

"Some women don't connect with their children," said Rita. "I've seen it many times at the Lying-in Hospital. Consider her circumstances. Her parents sent her away with an inexperienced young woman to accompany her. She was consumed with shame. They probably told her not to return with the child. Where could she have gone? We don't even know the circumstances of the pregnancy. She might have been raped by someone in authority. It might even have been her father." Rita had become quite impassioned by the end of her speech.

"Now wait a minute," said Hamish, "that seems a leap."

"Don't pretend it doesn't happen," snapped Rita.

Bellamy intervened before a full-blown argument started. "The point is that either Glenda or her husband might have killed Hilda Jenkins. We need to know whether James Hembrow was aware of the secret. If he genuinely wasn't, he would have had no motive for the murder."

"They speak for one another when they say they were in bed when the attack occurred," said Rita. "That makes it difficult to be sure of either one of them."

"I can't get past the problem of the key," said Hamish. "Campbell swears there are only two keys and we are missing one of them. Perhaps we should search the Hembrows' room for the missing key? Who knows where this key we do have comes from?"

"I would be surprised if either of them would leave it around in their room to be discovered," said Bellamy. "That key will be hidden somewhere safe, somewhere that can't be connected to the killer."

"I think we should consider possibilities other than the Hembrows," said Rita. "Who else has secrets that Hilda might have known?"

Hamish tilted his head to one side to think. His fringe fell over his face, and he smoothed it back slowly with one hand.

"There is also Murdo Black's secret to consider. Was he telling the whole truth about his childhood friend Donald and the Chinese fugitive?"

Bellamy laughed. "Sounded more like a sailor's tale than the truth to me."

"I've seen him talking to a Chinese man," said Hamish. "Here at the hotel. The same man was here when we arrived. Do you remember?"

Rita thought for a moment. "Yes, I remember," she said. "A Chinese fellow was talking to Campbell. He scurried away when we approached."

"That's him. I saw him again the morning of the balloon exhibition. He was with Captain Black. I saw him exchange money for a package." Hamish hesitated, deciding whether to go further. "I think Murdo Black takes opium."

Rita and Bellamy stared at him. "He is edgy, he can't sleep. I think it's an addiction."

"Do you think that has something to do with the murder?" asked Bellamy.

"Not necessarily," said Hamish, "but it could. He has a short fuse and Hilda did seem to upset him."

"So, if his tale is true, then the Chinese man you have seen selling him opium could be this fellow he saved," suggested Bellamy.

Just then Wallace walked in with Red tucked under his arm. He put the terrier on the floor where he curled up under the table. It teetered as Red pulled his legs under and the teapot and cups threatened to tip. Hamish and Bellamy held each side of the tabletop while Red found his comfort spot.

"If you're talking about Murdo Black, his tale is true enough," Wallace said, pulling a small silver flask and a whiskey glass out of his coat pocket.

Hamish stared at him.

"What?" he said. "I picked it up from the kitchen on the way through."

"We're not bothered about the glass," said "Bellamy. "How do you know Murdo Black is telling the truth?"

"Because I met Wei Sing, this morning," said Wallace casually.

They all stared at him now.

"I accompanied Captain Black to Southport town, where he had an arrangement to meet with Wei Sing. The Chinaman was in town picking up supplies. Wei Sing confirmed every part of the story. He clearly appreciated what the captain had done for him."

"That also confirms the reason Murdo Black gives for staying in Southport rather than travelling to Brisbane with the rest of the passengers on the Scottish Prince," said Bellamy.

"I think Wei Sing is supplying his cocaine," said Hamish.

"He probably is, but using cocaine doesn't make him a murderer. It isn't even illegal if the supplier has a license. How do we know Wei Sing didn't bring it from the pharmacy for him?"

Hamish didn't look convinced.

"He could have added cocaine to the sleeping draught Hilda took. To stop her from waking up."

"I'm not sure when he would have done that," said Bellamy, giving it some thought, "but it's possible. The question is why? What reason would Captain Black have to murder Hilda?"

"I can't help thinking there are more mysteries in the captain's past," said Hamish. "What about Hilda's quip, about his responsibility for the deaths of others?"

"Ask him," said Wallace.

Hamish blinked.

"He strikes me as an open man," said Wallace, "I imagine if you ask him what the nurse was referring to, he'll tell you."

"I agree," said Bellamy. "We'll speak with him. Although at this stage, I'm inclined to put my money on Glenda Hembrow. She remains our primary suspect."

"What about Celestine?" asked Rita.

"She did lie about her whereabouts on the night of the murder," agreed Hamish, "but I can't see her suffocating anyone."

Rita raised both eyebrows. "Is that a personal assessment?" she asked.

"Yes, as it happens, it is."

"You do seem to be more intimately acquainted with Mademoiselle

Dupont than the rest of us," she said, sipping her tea slowly.

Hamish put down his cup. "What do you mean by that?"

"I wonder whether you might be too close to make a sound judgement."

"I'm not close to Mademoiselle Dupont. And I believe you're jealous, though I wouldn't have expected it."

"I'm not jealous," laughed Rita, a little too loudly. "I'm simply stating what any reasonable person might assume – that you have become emotionally involved with a suspect in this murder case."

"I'm not emotionally *involved*."

Rita put down her cup. "Really, Hamish," she said. "You do this. You become infatuated with a pretty woman, and you can't see objectively. Remember Charlotte at Cloverton?"

Hamish was silenced. He poured whiskey from Wallace's flask into his empty teacup and swallowed it in one mouthful.

"We don't yet know the full story about Celestine's father," Rita said as if putting a full-stop to the argument.

CHAPTER NINETEEN

This salubrious spot, which but a few years ago was very little frequented, is now the resort of the invalid, the convalescent and the pleasure-seeker. The means of access are by steamer and coach. The former was chosen by several of us who had been longing to have a glance at this much talked about township. Accordingly, we gathered unto us our belongings and made in the direction of Hart's Wharf where the President and the Natone, the steamers that ply between Brisbane and Southport, were lying. A tremendous rivalry exists between. The two boats. Some look upon the Natone as having more accommodation and more speed, but the result of our trip did not prove the latter.

On nearing Southport, the eye is met by a palatial structure which upon enquiry we learned was the Grand Hotel. This is really a splendid building and much too good, one would think, for a watering place which can only be said to be in its infancy, although the infant is unquestionably exhibiting signs of health and vigour.

Southport has undergone many improvements during the past five or six years. Then it was a wild and uninviting place, with a score of houses. There were two hotels then, but now there are six or seven, all commodious and reflective of enterprise and the general belief in the prosperity of this much frequented sanitorium.

Facilities for bathing are everywhere met. This can be done at any time with safety, an ample shelter is provided by Stradbroke Island on the one hand and the mainland on the other. Fish are also caught in abundance, the facilities for which are unbounded. Southport can boast of three churches and another is in contemplation. There are many places of interest here, which cannot be seen in a day.

Warwick Examiner. Wednesday 1 September, 1886

Hamish decided to go to his room, wash his face and collect his thoughts. His irritability was tugging at him, but he couldn't put his finger on what was making him feel that way. He splashed his face with water from the jug on the washstand in his room. Rita's comments about his objectivity toward Celestine were unwarranted. Yes, he may have been enchanted by her at first, but that didn't mean he was incapable of objectivity in her regard. He simply couldn't see her suffocating Hilda. Why would she? Hilda was insignificant to someone like Celestine Dupont, surely? Still, she did infer that Celestine's father might be alive. Hamish rubbed his face hard with the towel. There were too many stories in this case, and too many levels to the stories. He was pulling a comb through his unruly hair when a knock on the door surprised him. He had barely called "come in" when Wallace peered around the opening.

"Is everything alright?" asked Hamish.

Wallace looked surprised at the question. "Fine. Murdo Black has returned and says he's happy to answer questions about the event alluded to by Hilda."

"Good," said Hamish, "after lunch then."

Wallace nodded but continued peering in through the opening.

"Anything else?" asked Hamish.

"There is something he'd like to share," Wallace said. "There's some urgency."

Hamish raised one eyebrow. "You've been spending some time with Murdo Black, then… for him to feel comfortable sharing secrets?"

Hamish wondered at the pace at which his friend could gain the trust of strangers. Wallace's skill in this regard had been useful to him before. But then it was hardly surprising that Wallace and Black would get along, given their shared experience of life at sea.

Wallace coughed sheepishly. "Should I bring him in here?" he asked.

"Where is he?" Hamish said, trying to see past Wallace into the corridor.

"His room," said Wallace as he stepped aside.

Hamish slapped him lightly on the shoulder. "You didn't come down here to make friends with the suspects," he whispered, but he couldn't hide a small smile as he did so. Truth be told, that is exactly why he came along.

When Hamish entered Murdo Black's room, he saw the man sitting in an armchair staring through the window out to sea, smoking a pipe and looking every bit the image of a sea captain from one of Robert Louis Stevenson's stories. Hamish could see how Wallace was drawn to him.

The captain did not acknowledge Hamish as he dragged over a chair to sit next to him.

Hamish looked at Wallace. "Well?" he said.

"It's best if he tells it himself."

Black slowly turned to Hamish and took a long draw on his pipe.

"Glenda Hembrow and Hilda Jenkins were having an argument in the Hembrows' room two days before Miss Jenkins was killed," he began. "The argument was carried out in hushed tones, but I could hear them right enough. I couldn't hear what it was about, but it was clear they had known each other before meeting at the Grand."

Hamish blinked slowly. "Why didn't you tell us this sooner?"

"I keep my own counsel," he said. "I'll talk freely about my own life, but I don't bother myself with what others are doing. I mentioned it to Wallace just now because it occurred to me it might be important to the case."

Hamish thought of a lot of things he could say, but he settled with, "Thank-you."

It didn't add much to what they already knew. Unless Hilda was attempting to blackmail Glenda. Or unless James overheard the conversation. If Black heard, James could have heard also. James seemed convincing when Hamish asked him about it, but there was no way to know for sure.

He returned to his room and stood before his open window, staring out at the Scottish Prince twisted and contorted after the storms, no longer comfortable on the sand, but rather trapped by it. It occurred to him that pride had given way to hubris, the ship's shame on display for all to see.

The water was bright this morning, light danced on the surface and a soft breeze tipped the waves near the shore with white. It struck Hamish that a swim might clear his mind. He had been at the hotel for three days and had been too busy to take a swim in the famously clear waters. Once his mind was made up, he wasted no time. He took the stairs two at a time, hoping not to meet anyone.

After crossing the street, he stood on the promenade, his shoes touching the edge of the cement that made up the top step. Directly in front of the hotel, the sea came up to the bottom step at high tide, creating perfect swimming conditions. Further down, past the pier, there was a sandy beach with bathing huts. Only a king tide could eliminate the white sand on the little beach. Women were more inclined to enter the shallow water there, but Hamish slipped into the water from the steps and fully submerged himself, letting the cool water shock the fogginess from his mind.

Swimming from north to south and back again in the deep water in front of the hotel, he was able to restrict his focus to his breathing and the pull of his arms through the water. All thoughts of secrets and murder were held at bay. Hamish swam until his body was tired, glad of the respite it afforded his mind. The water tugged at his arms and legs as he propelled himself forward. He was aware of the rotation of his shoulders and the flick of his ankles. It felt good to be aware of his body; he spent so much of his time caught in his mind. He took one last opportunity to duck into a rolling swell and he rose again on the other side, facing the Grand. He was admiring the panoramic view of the sweeping verandas when something caught his eye. A face looked out of a ground-floor window. A quick calculation told him it was the colonel's suite and it looked like a man's face. *The colonel's suite is locked up*, he thought. No one is allowed to go in there. He was troubled by the image, to the extent that he decided to cut his swim short. He took strong strokes toward the steps, but by the time he reached the promenade, the face had disappeared, and he could no longer be sure it was even the colonel's window. He put it from his mind.

Further up the beach, past the pier and the beach huts, he noticed a small fishing boat on the sand. He hadn't seen it there the day before and he wondered briefly who it might belong to.

After dressing, Hamish returned to the dining room to have lunch with Rita, Bellamy, and Wallace. Red was in his position under the table nearby Rita, who was the most likely to supply him with snacks. They were enjoying the first course when James Hembrow joined them.

"Try the sea mullet," said Wallace, "my latest catch."

"Yes," agreed Bellamy. "I recommend it. The fish is superb."

James Hembrow sat down and placed his napkin on his knees without acknowledging them. His hands were trembling.

Hamish leaned across the table to touch his sleeve. "Is anything wrong?" he asked.

Hembrow looked startled. He rearranged his napkin before he spoke.

"Yes, actually." He looked up. "I'm rather anxious about Mrs Hembrow… Glenda. She went out for a walk early this morning, at dawn. Couldn't sleep, she said. She's not back…"

Hamish and Bellamy stopped eating to give him their full attention. "Does she normally go walking in the early hours?" asked Bellamy.

"No. But she has been troubled since she spoke with you yesterday. Crying. It's like she's been holding onto something for a long time, pretending. Now it's been let out, she's not herself. Her confidence has shifted. Caved, you might say. She won't talk to me."

His eyes were a moist mixture of confusion and fear.

Then he passed Bellamy a crumpled piece of quality paper.

Bellamy took the paper and smoothed it out. The letterhead belonged to a prominent family in Beaudesert. Bellamy read the letter out loud for the benefit of Hamish and Rita.

Miss Jenkins,

We can see no good that will come from your enquiries, however since you seem insistent and the tone of your correspondence implies wrongdoing on the part of this household, I have decided to provide you with what little information I have on this matter, in the expectation that this will prevent you from taking it any further.

The infant to which you refer was taken by Jim Hawker, the caretaker you would no doubt have known as 'Jimbo'. The child was taken to his wife and raised as their own. Since that time, the wife has born six more children and the brood could not be accommodated in their small cottage. The eldest then, was sent to work at one of the mills on the Upper Nerang River.

I implore you to let this information set your mind at rest that no ill fate befell the child and do not pursue this matter any further.

Their mouths dropped.

"Where did you find this?" asked Bellamy.

"It was in my wife's writing bureau. I confess I looked in there for something that might explain her disappearance."

"You were searching for a suicide note?" cried Hamish.

Mr Hembrow expressed shock, but it was clear to Hamish he had guessed correctly.

"We'll help you search for your wife," said Hamish. "I'm sure she is along the beach somewhere, coming to terms with the revelations of the last couple of days. She'll talk to you when she is ready."

Bellamy seemed more deeply concerned. "Do you think she might have set off toward Nerang in search of this child?"

"I don't understand the relationship between this child and my wife," said James.

Hamish stared at the letter. "There's too little to go on, but I don't think she's looking for the child. I don't think she wanted the subject raised at all."

"What subject raised?" cried James. "Why won't anyone tell me what's going on?"

"We should start now," Bellamy said, taking one last draught of tea from his cup and ignoring James. He stood up and Hamish followed. "If you walk north, I'll walk south," he said to Wallace. "Hamish, you go into town. Check if anyone has seen her there. If she did go to Nerang, she would have had to hire a cab to get there. We'll meet back here in two hours."

"What about me?" asked James.

"You look around here, on the hotel grounds," said Bellamy.

James looked dismayed at the idea of a fruitless search close to the hotel, but he remained where he was seated. Rita stayed with him.

"Take some food," she said, "it won't do your wife any good to have you weakened by hunger."

These were the last words Hamish heard spoken as he stepped out of the reading room into the great hall and strode out into the sunlight. He still thought Glenda would be found sitting alone in a quiet retreat somewhere, reflecting on her past and working out how to tell her husband about it. He felt no urgency as he started toward the Southport township, walking down Marine Parade before turning into Government Road and on toward town. The entire area was divided into five perch allotments. Hamish understood they had all been sold and building was in progress on a few. The area would soon be densely populated. As he came closer to the township, he passed established homes of the usual worker's cottage style low set, symmetrical with a central entrance and a window either side, timber walls, corrugated iron roof and a veranda along the front. Many had picket fences. The houses projected working class respectability. Hamish noted an Aboriginal girl in a white dress working in the garden of one of the houses. She looked up as he passed and he would have asked if she had seen a woman go that way that morning, but she shifted her eyes downward immediately, without acknowledging him and continued with her digging. It was obvious she didn't wish to speak to him. A pang of shame caught his breath for a moment as he realised it was a high probability that she would be chastised, or even beaten, for speaking to him. He rushed past the house.

The telegraph station and post office were close by, and he asked a boy leaning on the veranda rail if he had seen a woman matching Glenda's description, but he said he had not. He went inside and asked if such a woman had called in to arrange a telegraph communication that morning. But the telegraph operator, eyeing him suspiciously, assured him no stranger had been in prior to himself. The next sign of life was at The School of Arts Building, an impressive, two-storey timber structure with arched windows, where two women were making their way down the stairs. He stopped to address them, and they paused to stare.

"Fine morning," he said cheerfully.

They continued to stare. The larger of the two, and they were both of a healthy size, looked threatening. She grabbed her companion's arm and dragged her forward.

"Impertinence," she said as she guided the other woman around Hamish.

"I apologise for my lack of manners," said Hamish quickly, "but I'm looking for someone. A woman is missing. I was hoping you might have seen her this morning?"

The women hesitated and looked back. The larger woman appeared to be taking into consideration the idea of calling for police protection.

"We have seen no one," she said at last. She tightened her grip on her companion's arm and pulled her away from the intolerable stranger.

As Hamish approached the police depot, he considered entering but decided that any decision to report Glenda officially missing should come from James, so he kept walking.

Two hours later, Hamish, Bellamy, Wallace and James Hembrow converged at the seat on the promenade in front of the Grand Hotel. Bellamy looked at Hamish first and he shook his head.

James Hembrow let out a breath and his chin dropped to his chest.

"I haven't found any sign of her either," said Bellamy. "Do you think she would travel to Nerang? Or head towards Brisbane, by coach?"

James raised his head. "Why would she do that?"

Hamish hesitated before answering. "Perhaps so she can avoid facing you with her secrets."

James threw his arms into the air and turned away from them. Hamish and Bellamy were left staring at one another.

At last, he turned back. "I'm worried about her state of mind." James' face was contorted with such deep concern it was impossible not to believe his anguish was real.

"I'll go to Southport Police Station and inform Sergeant Cooper," said Bellamy. "Do you have any objection, James?"

James Hembrow looked to the sky for an answer. He pressed his lips together. The lump in his throat shifted and he shook his head.

"It's too early to think the worst," Bellamy assured him. "She'll probably wander back into the Grand later today, ready to talk to you. Still, I think it's important we check all possibilities."

As Bellamy left, the freckled-faced boy who had checked the keys against every lock in the hotel appeared with another lad in tow. The second lad was tall and strong, and older by at least two or three years. It was clear he had led a life of hard work, but he looked healthy for it. His clothes were those of a labourer. He removed his cap when he entered and held it between his hands nervously.

"This is Samuel," said the freckle-faced boy. "I'll leave him to explain his business here." The younger boy appeared to be in a hurry to leave them to it.

"Good morning, Samuel," said Hamish. "What can we do for you?"

Samuel hesitated. He appeared to be carefully considering each word and how he might string them together. His lips parted and closed again several times before an identifiable sound escaped.

"I've come to meet my mother." It came in a single rush as though it were one word.

"Your mother?" repeated Hamish.

"Oh dear," whispered Rita.

James Hembrow went pale.

"My mother's name is Glenda Hembrow."

Hamish felt his throat go dry. He didn't dare look at James.

The boy hurried to explain himself. "A woman came to tell me. She said my mother was staying here at the hotel. I always knew I was adopted. My parents, the ones who raised me, they never kept it a secret. They were black for a start, and I weren't. All my younger brothers and sisters were Aboriginal. I knew I wasn't one of them. But I was loved. I had a great run, never wanted for *nothin'*. I never knew my mother's name – I didn't want to know. I never asked. But then this woman came and says she was there when I was born. *Who cares?* I thought. My mother didn't want me then, so why should I care now? But then this weird feeling came over me and I couldn't shake it. I needed to meet her. Just to see her. I don't mean no harm. And I don't want nothing."

James was speechless. He was staring at the boy as though he couldn't understand what manner of creature he was looking at.

"I'm afraid Glenda Hembrow is missing," Hamish said.

"Missing?"

"Yes, she left the hotel for a walk early this morning and hasn't returned."

The boy's face was pale, but beyond that there was no noticeable sign of reaction.

"We've been looking for her," Hamish went on.

"I'd like to look with you," the boy said.

James Hembrow put his hand to his temple. "I don't understand any of this," he moaned. "Glenda told me last night that the interview with you and Bellamy had upset her terribly, but she wouldn't say why. Now, this boy, raised by natives, is saying he is her child?"

The lad stood nervously, waiting to find out what would happen next.

"There'll be time enough for sharing stories when we find Glenda," said Hamish. "I think we should let the boy join the search. The problem is," he said, "we have nowhere else to look."

CHAPTER TWENTY

The Minister for Lands and several officials from the Land's Department, and a number of friends of the Minister, proceeded on Friday afternoon in the Kate to the southern end of the bay, for the purpose of selecting a site on the south end of Stradbroke Island for a township. A suitable site was fixed upon extending from the extreme point of the Island three or four miles immediately facing both the Pacific on one side and the Bay on the other. Most importantly, there was plenty of water found and everyone was delighted with the grand view afforded from the new township, embracing as it does, glimpses of mountain, sea and Island. Pleasure was largely combined with business and boating, bathing, fishing and shooting were all entered into, the last thoroughly satisfying those who entered upon them.

The Telegraph. Monday 25 October, 1880

Hamish stood silently alongside James and Samuel, desperately trying to imagine where Glenda might have gone. The beautiful white beach set against the fern green foliage of Stradbroke Island floated in the mid-range of his vision, a marker between sea and sky.

"What if she went there?"

Hamish turned to James. "She's been wanting to visit the island since you came to Southport."

"Where? To Stradbroke?" cried James.

"Yes. Stradbroke would be the perfect place for someone wanting to get away for a few hours."

James nodded slightly as if it were, at best, a slim possibility.

"If she did go over to the island, she'll be back on the afternoon ferry, I should think," said Hamish.

Then, as soon as he had spoken, he noticed the small fishing boat on the beach about twenty yards to the left of where they were standing. "That boat was there earlier this morning," he said, as much to himself as anyone.

James turned toward the boat. "Yes, I think it was. What does it matter?"

"I don't know," Hamish said. But he kept wondering about the boat.

James began to sway. "I think I need to lie down," he said.

Hamish saw the man's body turn to jelly in the next instant. Samuel tucked himself under one arm, only just in time to stop James Hembrow from falling to the ground. He was a strong lad, but he was teetering under the weight of the man who was married to his mother. Hamish tucked himself under the other arm and together they managed to drag James back to the hotel. By the time they had crossed the street, he was sufficiently conscious to assist using legs that would only partially take his weight. Once they were inside, Campbell Charles and one of the waiters took over and assisted him up the stairs to his room.

James Hembrow had not spoken to Samuel during their encounter.

"Hembrow is suffering from shock, I should think," said Hamish when he and Samuel were alone. "He's had a lot to take in during the last 24 hours."

Samuel blinked. "Oh, it don't worry me," he said. "That man doesn't know me from Adam. I'm just some boy who turns up and claims his wife gave birth to me. I'm relieved he didn't beat me and throw me into a ditch or something."

"Are you sure you want to stay until we find Glenda? Sometimes people's reactions don't match our hopes. What I mean is, it doesn't always turn out the way you imagine it…"

"I've come this far," said Samuel. "I'll see it through."

Hamish took a deep breath. He felt anxious for the boy, but he had no right to keep him from meeting his mother.

When Bellamy returned from town, Hamish and Samuel were again seated on the promenade outside the hotel.

"Sergeant Cooper telegraphed the railway, Cobb and Co and the steamer companies," Bellamy said. "Glenda hasn't turned up on any of those."

"What about Stradbroke Island?" asked Hamish.

Bellamy stared at the island. "It's a possibility," he said.

"That fishing boat," Hamish nodded toward the beach, "Who do you think owns it?"

"Why?"

"It wasn't there yesterday."

A much larger vessel was docking at the pier. A burly man with arms like tree trunks began throwing a rope over a wooden pylon. "Why don't we ask him?" said Samuel.

Hamish and Bellamy hesitated while making up their minds whether the man was a local or a visitor to Southport. Samuel didn't wait for them to decide. He strode onto the pier. Both Hamish and Bellamy lurched out after him. They were less concerned about whether the man was local to Southport than they were worried about how he might react to impertinent questions from a youngster.

"We were hoping to ask you who owns the small craft on the sand there," said Bellamy over the boy's head.

The fisherman, too weathered for Hamish to judge his age, looked up.

"Who wants to know?"

"Sergeant Bellamy, Brisbane Police."

"Brisbane Police? You're away from home." He continued rolling thick rope into heavy coils.

"Do you know who owns the craft?" asked Bellamy.

The old man nodded toward the road. "Lives up there," he said. "Small house, one room. Lives alone."

"Has he got a name?"

The fisherman shrugged.

"Thanks," said Bellamy, turning away. Just as Hamish was about to turn around as well, the man spoke again.

"Not like him to leave it on the sand like that, though. He does hire it out to visitors like yourselves from time to time. But it would be in the boathouse up yonder, as a rule." He was gesturing toward a corrugated iron shed further along.

Hamish, Bellamy and Samuel left the man to his ropes and walked across the road to the house where the boat owner was said to live. The place was square and squat, on wooden stumps about three feet from the ground. The windows were few and small, which was just as well because they had no shutters or glass. Bellamy peered in one window at head height. Hamish stood beside him, unable to see anything but the back of the sergeant's head. Samuel stayed on the road.

"*Summit* I can do for *yer?*" said a voice behind them.

They all turned to see an elderly man as weathered as the fisherman. Two tiny pin-pointed eyes peeked out from folds of leathery skin.

"We were wondering about the boat on the beach," said Bellamy. "We're told it belongs to you."

"It's mine, all right," said the man. "What's it doing on the beach?"

Bellamy looked at Hamish. "We wanted to know the same thing," said Hamish.

"I been in town with me sister," said the man. "I got home ten minutes ago to find me boat there on the beach. I left it in the boathouse last night. Locked it in there just after dark."

Bellamy looked toward the boathouse. "So, sometime between dark last night and this morning, someone took the boat from the shed and left it on the beach," he said.

"I'll be eager to find out who," said the fisherman. "No one local would touch me boat. It must've been one of you visitors."

"Could we pay you for the use of your boat for a few hours?" asked Bellamy.

The man's eyes wrinkled. "It won't be cheap, mind," he said.

Bellamy settled on a price and they headed back to the promenade.

"Where are we going?" asked Hamish.

"Stradbroke," Bellamy said.

Hamish stopped walking. "Do you think we're going to row that boat across the bar?" he demanded.

"That's my intention," said Bellamy.

Hamish headed for the hotel.

"Where are you going now?" called Bellamy.

"To get Wallace."

"What for?"

"To row the bloody boat," came back the reply on the wind.

Ten minutes later, the four of them were rowing towards Stradbroke Island. They could see the Scottish Prince to their right past the spit. The sea was relatively calm in the passage and a strong current was behind them. With Wallace doing the heavy work, and Samuel taking his turn, Hamish found the trip pleasant. Within thirty minutes, they were on the beach at Stradbroke. Hamish looked up and down at the row of tents to the left of where they landed. He tried to reconcile what he saw with the northern end of the island where Dunwich was situated. The land here seemed wild and unfettered compared to the township. The two ends of the island were joined by a narrow land bridge, but to Hamish it felt like two separate islands. There was a small settlement not far from the beach with a dozen houses, flimsy structures, mostly fishing shacks without permanent residents. Around Christmas, campers would be set up along the beach for a mile. Wallace stayed with the boat while Hamish and Bellamy picked their way through the grass to the permanent settlement. Most of the shacks were empty, but in one they found a woman out back scrubbing clothes in a tub. There was an open fire with a kettle hanging from an iron tripod. The woman wasn't friendly, but she answered their questions. No one had been seen wandering through the settlement that morning, woman or otherwise. They walked toward the tents and found a woman watching over her children as they splashed in the shallow water. She smiled. But she hadn't seen anyone unusual that morning either. Her husband was on the surf side, fishing. He had been there since before sun up, so there is no way he could have seen anyone.

Hamish and Bellamy found the ferry pilot sitting with a small group of men at the jetty. The pilot assured them he had not brought a woman of Glenda's description across to the island that morning and none of them had seen anyone come across in a small dinghy.

They returned to their boat, deflated.

"It was always a long shot," said Bellamy.

They were rowing back against the current and the small craft kept pulling toward the opening into the broad water. The veins in Wallace's forearms stood out as he drew the oars through the sea while it fought against him. They were being dragged toward the sandbank that gripped the bow of the Scottish Prince. Wallace fought against the current for ten minutes before he rested the oars on the side and leant back into the boat.

"It's no use," he said, catching his breath. "The best option is to let the boat go toward the entrance and we can rest at the wreck until the tide changes."

The sheer size of the trapped schooner, held tight as it was by the sandbank, was alluring. One side loomed tall and black over their little boat.

They drifted easily until they were alongside her.

"We might as well board her," said Hamish. "Take a quick look, since we're here."

"I'm not sure about the legality of that," said Bellamy.

But by that time, Wallace was beaming from ear to ear. He drew the oars deep into the water and made two strong movements. The small craft swooped up onto the sand and came to a halt. Samuel was trembling with excitement. Hamish realised the boy had probably never seen a ship as large, let alone board one.

The front end of the ship sat high on the sand, while the back end was dragged down into deep water. It was low tide, so they had no trouble climbing out of their boat and onto the sandbar. The sand had shifted and built up around the vessel along one side through the recent storms. There was quite a bit of damage to the hull, and they saw that much of the cargo hold would be open to the water at high tide, hence the proliferation of booty washing up on the beaches. They took turns climbing the forestays that dangled into the sand from the bottom of the broken mast and clambered onto the deck. Hamish shuffled on his backside, his arms and legs propelling him forward toward the stern, which was submerged in about six feet of water, even at this low point of the tide. Samuel followed his lead and slid the last few feet, crashing into him near the side of the boat where the sea met what was once the upper deck banister.

The ship that had seemed so imposing from water level appeared smaller from this vantage point. The broken mast and the great hole in the hull made it feel vulnerable. Hamish looked out to the open sea where the waves rose and fell in relentless lines to the horizon.

"It makes you feel small," he said to Samuel, who was still tucked up against him where he had landed. "I have always felt small," said the boy. Hamish blinked.

He leant over the edge of the vessel and peered into the green depths. "Falls off quickly," he said. The lad tried to lean across him to see.

"What's down there?" The boy pointed into the water. Hamish followed his finger and made out a strange shape about two feet under the surface. A lot of rope was tangled around the anchor chain, and a cluster of fabric spread outward, taking on a strangely ethereal form. It didn't appear to be heavy canvas, as would be expected. It was a softer fabric, difficult to make out. Hamish called Wallace over to look. After a lifetime working as a ship's cook, Wallace would know what a submerged anchor should look like.

Wallace leaned over both Hamish and Samuel to peer into the sea. He pursed his lips. "Something caught around the anchor chain," he said.

"It looks like cloth," said Hamish.

Bellamy saw them staring into the water and joined them.

"That looks like clothing," said Samuel.

Suddenly, without saying a word to the others, Hamish jumped feet first into the water.

Samuel tried to stand up and slipped, Wallace catching him a second before he fell into the sea.

"What the hell?" cried Wallace.

They could see Hamish moving beneath the shape. Then he was pushing it upward. He struggled because the weight of the chain was holding the mass down. Slowly, it began to take shape, and Wallace slipped into the water to help. Between the two of them, they managed to raise the mass to the surface. Bellamy passed down a fishing knife and they cut away the rigging that had entangled the mass.

Hamish, Bellamy and Samuel stared. Hamish experienced a chill through his body that touched his bones. They had found Glenda Hembrow. Her body was entangled in rope attached to the chain, part of the rigging being washed back and forth with the tides. At high tide, the body would not have been seen at all. Bellamy lowered a fishing net and Hamish and Wallace placed it below Glenda's body. They brought the net up over her and tied it to form a bag. They then climbed back up onto the ship and helped Bellamy haul the catch onto the deck. The pile of fabric and hair landed with a surprising thud. Hamish untangled the rope and the fishing net and rolled Glenda over, so she was face up. He wiped away the tangled hair and seaweed. Her face was grey, her lips blue, and her eyes were wide and staring upward. There was a small round hole in the centre of her skull.

Glenda had been shot from close range.

CHAPTER TWENTY-ONE

The Board having heard the evidence of the Master, the First Mate and Second Mates and the man on the lookout, find the Scottish Prince was being navigated much too close to the shore, that if this was being done in order to avoid as far as possible the coast current, additional precautions were necessary to keep the vessel's position accurately laid down upon the chart, and the lead should have been kept going, especially at night when heading in towards the land. None of these precautions appear to have been adopted. The discrepancies between the chart, the log slate and the logbook cannot be explained. The Board can only come to the conclusion that an attempt has been made to make the logbook and chart show the vessel ought to have been in some other position than that in which she really was when she grounded on the bar. The logbook is most carelessly kept and the entries on the log-slate are not correct. The position of the vessel, as marked on the chart, shows similar carelessness and inaccuracy, and off Burleigh Heads they notice two positions, one laid down at eight o'clock and one at ten o'clock placed within half a mile of one another. The board consider that the boat was lost through gross carelessness and most slovenly navigation; and that the certificate of the Master, John Little, should be cancelled.

The Queenslander. Saturday February 12, 1887.

Samuel contemplated the blue-ish skin of his birth mother. Her eyes stared cold and empty past him. "I wanted her to see me," he said. "Most of all, I wanted her to see I grew up strong and smart without her. That's why I came looking for her. She can't see me now, can she? She's not even looking at me. Not even now." Tears began to fall.

Hamish put one arm around the boy's shoulders. With the other hand, he gently held Glenda Hembrow's fingers. "I'm sorry lad," he said. "I'm sorry you didn't have the chance to show her how strong you grew."

"Wallace and I will go back to the mainland," said Bellamy. "I'll bring back the water police to pick up the body. Samuel, you come with us."

Samuel kept his eyes locked on his mother.

"Samuel," prompted Bellamy.

"Leave him with me," Hamish said. "Let him grieve."

Bellamy nodded and he and Wallace climbed down to the sandbank and pushed their boat into the water. Wallace held the craft steady while Bellamy climbed in, then leapt in himself, as easily as would be expected of someone who'd been doing so all his life.

Hamish and Samuel were alone on the wreck, with the sea lapping at three sides and a large sea hawk circling above. The hawk flew in circles that came lower with every circuit, leading Hamish to wonder how long the bird had been aware of the tangled body tantalisingly close to the surface.

"What happened to her?" The boy sniffed back his tears.

"We'll find out. I promise you that."

While Samuel cried out emotions that had taken his short lifetime to build, Hamish had time to contemplate Glenda Hembrow's death, as the sun beat down on them with a sting.

Why had she been so coldly killed, and her body tossed into the sea? This was a calculated assassination, not a murder of spontaneous passion. Her body might never have been found if it hadn't been washed into the rigging of the Scottish Prince. And if they hadn't climbed aboard when they did.

Her eyes continued to stare upward. She would have seen her killer. What must she have thought in that last moment? Some scientists were saying you could see the killer reflected in the person's eyes after death. Hamish looked in her eyes for clues of what she might have seen, or how she might have felt. There were none. The woman, Glenda Hembrow, with her secrets, her anguish and her shame, was missing. She was gone. There was little left behind. The sea hawk continued to circle, and Hamish contemplated how long it would have been until Glenda became a meal for the bird if they hadn't discovered her body.

Samuel was left behind. The one aspect of her that would live on was her son. What would she have said to the boy had she lived to meet him? A pain in his chest told Hamish it was probably for the best that the boy would never know the answer to that question. He couldn't imagine Glenda embracing the child's existence or finding any pleasure in meeting him. She had denied him for so long, convinced herself that his birth had nothing to do with her. If he had been packed in a wooden crate and buried on that vast landscape of his birth, she would not have known or cared.

Hamish shook himself. An hour was a long time to spend with a body, unless one was in a laboratory studying it. In an attempt to turn his mind to practical thoughts, it occurred to him that it might have been prudent to leave the body in the water where it was cooler, but that was no longer an option, so he lay her on a canvas sheet and he and Samuel dragged her into the shade of the wrecked wheelhouse.

When Bellamy returned, it was in a large vessel belonging to the water police, with Sergeant Cooper and two police constables aboard. Two more were rowing out in the smaller boat that belonged to the fisherman. The four constables must have constituted the whole constabulary of Southport, but how often did they have two murders within a week?

"Leave her with Cooper," said Bellamy as he helped Hamish up. "We need to go back and inform Mr Hembrow."

Hamish, Bellamy and Samuel climbed into the smaller boat and one of the constables rowed them back to Deepwater Point.

They were entering the hotel feeling anxious when Rita darted out of the reading room and latched onto Hamish.

"Wallace told me you had gone out to the Scottish Prince, but he would tell me no more. What has happened?"

Hamish took her hands in his. "We'll talk soon," he said. "Wait for me in my room and take Samuel with you. He might need something to eat and drink. He's had a big morning."

Rita put her hand on the lad's shoulder and felt the muscle born of hard work.

"Shall we visit the kitchen first?" she said. The boy seemed numb, but he followed her silently.

Hamish and Bellamy knocked on James Hembrow's door and he opened it almost immediately, his hair sticking out and his clothes dishevelled.

"Have you found her?" he said.

"Can we come in?" said Bellamy.

Hembrow stood aside and they both entered. The three of them stood staring at one another for a moment.

"What's happened?" cried James Hembrow.

"We found your wife," began Bellamy, "I'm afraid she's dead."

Hamish thought the words sounded cold. Dead. But what other way was there to say it?

Hembrow crashed onto the bed and was sitting upright at the edge of the springs. "Dead?" he repeated. He shook his head slowly in disbelief. "She only went for a walk."

"She was found in the water next to the Scottish Prince," said Bellamy.

"Why would she be there? Did she drown?" His brow furrowed as an horrific thought gripped him. "Did she drown herself?" he croaked.

He stood up and grabbed the sergeant by the shoulders. His grip was tight, and he shook him hard. "Did my wife commit suicide?" he demanded.

"No," said Hamish gently as he carefully removed the man's hands from Bellamy's shoulders. Hamish guided him to sit back down.

"She was murdered," said Bellamy. "Shot in the head. We think her body was dumped into the deep waters off the point, but it was washed toward the sand bank and caught in the rigging of the Scottish Prince."

James Hembrow's head was in his hands now as he made strange mournful sounds. He looked up at Hamish with a face twisted by grief and confusion. "I don't understand any of this," he said.

"We don't either," said Hamish.

"I want to see her."

"Sergeant Cooper and his team are bringing her in," said Bellamy. "As soon as she is ashore, someone will come for you."

"I'm going out there to wait," said Hembrow. "I'm not waiting here." He pushed past Hamish and Bellamy for the door.

"As you wish," said Bellamy. "I'll make sure he's all right," he said to Hamish.

"You go to Rita."

Hamish watched the sergeant follow Hembrow down the corridor, then he entered the open door to his own room. Rita was seated at a small desk at the window, the boy perched on the edge of her bed with an empty plate swinging loosely from his fingers. His features were blank.

Hamish quickly caught Rita up to date on the events relating to Glenda Hembrow.

"Shot?" Rita cried when he finished. "I would never have guessed. Though I confess, I did assume the worst when Wallace wouldn't tell me anything."

"Wallace wouldn't want anyone to know until James Hembrow was told," said Hamish.

"How did he take the news?" asked Rita.

"He was distraught, obviously. But there was something else. He was… confused."

"Both Glenda and her husband had reason to kill Hilda if James knew about the confinement," said Rita. "He might have wanted Hilda silenced before anyone else found out. He might have also silenced his wife. He didn't tell anyone she was missing for hours, and no one saw him in the meantime."

Hamish's brow furrowed. "We can't be sure that he did know. He looked confused rather than guilty."

Samuel interjected, reminding them that he was still present. "Who is Hilda?" he asked.

Rita winced and Hamish felt a tingling sensation sweep up the back of his neck and across his face.

"Hilda is the woman who came to find you," he said quietly.

"And she's dead as well?" asked the lad.

Rita nodded slightly.

Samuel dropped the plate. He slipped off the bed to pick it up and placed it on the desk. He turned his back to them and stared out the window.

"We will find out who killed both Hilda and your mother," said Hamish.

"Do you think this is about me?" Samuel said, without turning back to face them.

"No!" said Hamish, too quickly.

"It may be," said Rita.

Hamish looked daggers at her.

"With Glenda out of the picture, James is the prime suspect," said Rita. "No good will come of misleading the boy."

Samuel looked from one to the other. "I think you should both tell me what's going on," he said.

The three of them sat on the bed, Samuel in the centre, and they told him of Hilda's body being discovered in her bed. They explained how Hilda had come to be present at his birth.

Then Rita shook her head slowly. "I feel sorry for Hilda, if she was killed to keep Glenda's secret safe, it has had the opposite effect. The secret is out now, and she died for nothing."

"I just don't believe Glenda's death is tied to her secret pregnancy and birth. It doesn't make sense," said Hamish. "Why would James kill her once the secret was out? We all knew. What good would it do? And Samuel is here now, in the flesh."

"Anger, frustration, shame?" suggested Rita.

Hamish shook his head. "I could accept that if he lured her into an early morning walk on the beach, for example, and strangled her in a fit of rage. But this was a cold and calculated shot to the middle of the forehead. It isn't consistent with that distraught man back in his room, struggling for days to understand what was going on with his wife."

Samuel was looking down at his hands throughout the conversation.

"I don't think James Hembrow killed Hilda or my mother," he said. "He doesn't look like he's got it in him, to me."

Hamish and Rita both looked at him in surprise.

"I don't think so either," said Hamish.

As Hamish spoke, Bellamy walked in with news that Glenda's body had been taken by the authorities. "You will be relieved to know," he said to Hamish, "you will not be required to conduct an autopsy. The cause of death is evident."

Hamish blinked in surprise. "Clearly, she died from a gunshot wound. But I would like to examine the body. There may be some clue as to the killer."

Bellamy rolled his eyes. "Hamish," he said, "Scratchley is adamant on this. He thinks that whenever there is a straightforward death, you are determined to paint it as something else. He doesn't want you examining the body. Anyway, you sat with the body for hours earlier today. Did you not get a good enough look, then?"

Bellamy walked away to avoid any further argument.

CHAPTER TWENTY-TWO

Emily Dickson 1830 - 1886

Samuel declined the invitation to join them for lunch and set off back to Nerang to join his workmates. Hamish accompanied him to the door and watched him as he strode down the street with the confidence of a man. He was sorry the encounter with his mother had not been anything like what the boy had imagined, but he supposed there was, at least, some closure to it.

As he turned back toward the staircase, Campbell almost fell over him, then handed him another telegram.

Hamish groaned loudly and climbed the stairs to read it in the privacy of his room.

Incident at Epsom Racetrack. Father bounded over fence and onto track. Threw betting tickets in the air to watch them fall about him, singing Beauties of Melbourne. In his undergarments. Police brought him home. Albert talked them out of pressing charges, even though he held up Race Six while they cleared the track. Albert has arranged for one of the staff to pick him up and take him to the racetrack each day, remaining with him until they return in the evening. All is manageable now. Don't worry.

Don't worry, thought Hamish. How could he not worry? He had to admire the way everyone seemed to be rearranging their lives around his father's illness. He wondered how long they could continue to sustain this approach. But he couldn't leave Deepwater Point yet. He needed to find out who killed Hilda and Glenda, and he needed to do it quickly. For one thing, there could be another death, and for another, the situation with his father might grow out of hand.

After lunch, Hamish, Bellamy and Wallace sat in the reading room with two full bottles of sherry and the entire afternoon to kill. Murdo Black came in and settled opposite them. Rita dragged in a chair for herself and sat beside the captain. While the room was crowded, it wasn't uncomfortable. There was an energy that suggested trust. Nonetheless, Hamish was eager to hear about the incident that caused Hilda to draw attention to the captain during her final meal. He didn't think Murdo Black was a murderer, at least he hoped he wasn't, but there could be something in the story that triggered the nurse's death.

"Why do you think Hilda made the comment about you being responsible for a person's death?" asked Hamish as he poured Murdo a sherry and handed him the glass.

"I imagine she overheard a conversation I had with Colonel Winter," he said. "I told the colonel there was one death in my career for which I feel responsible, and I will never forgive myself."

"Did you tell the colonel the circumstances of this death?" asked Bellamy.

"No. That's all I said. I *dennae ken* why the nurse made the comment she did."

"Could she have known the circumstances by some other means?" asked Hamish.

"I *dennae ken* how. I've not told a soul the details. Those on the ship at the time knew, but *t'were* thirty years ago."

Bellamy leant toward him. "It's best you tell us what happened now," he said. "It may provide some clue as to why Hilda was killed. If not, the story will never leave this room."

"It's not that I object to the telling," said Black. "Though it is not an episode of my life of which I'm proud. It happened and that's that."

They all stared at him, waiting.

"It was three decades ago," he began. "I was appointed captain in Her Majesty's Navy and it was my first voyage in that capacity. I was terrified most of the time, overwhelmed by the weight of responsibility. And when I wasn't terrified, I was arrogant, too sure of myself. Anyway, we were preparing the ship in Glasgow to carry cargo to Bombay. I had trouble recruiting a full crew. You couldn't trust seamen in those days to return to the ship from port. You had to recruit constantly. They used to press-gang men into service, but on this occasion even that failed. We were preparing to sail short, when two young fellows decently clad in navy blue walked aboard and announced they were available for service if required. They were engaged at once. In all the confusion of getting ready to sail, I soon forgot about the newcomers. A few days later, I began to hear talk among the men about the young ones being strange in their manners. I asked the chief mate about their work, but he could find no fault with it. He did notice they did everything together. Any task one had to do, the other would assist. Whenever they were called to perform a duty near my station, I observed them carefully and was convinced they were no ordinary seamen. For one thing, they weren't rough and uncouth like sailors – on the contrary, there was a mildness of manner about them. But no man complained of their work, and they seemed to be well-liked. Not only that - the language of the whole crew was modified by their presence. It must have been the most politely spoken ship in Her Majesty's service. Most of us decided they must have been young men who run away from a wealthy home to test their mettle at sea.

And test it was – on the sea thirty years ago. Everyone had their work to do. There was no standing idle, no skulking below, no shirking when all hands were called. Any deviation from roles or orders would bring a man's back to the cat. Breach of discipline was visited with a flogging.

Tom and Ned, as the newcomers were called, seemed to be universally liked. But the amicable crew and the favourable weather were not to continue for the entire voyage. From Cape Verde onward, strong winds and high seas prevailed and hands were kept busy furling and unfurling night and day. It was evident that the nautical knowledge of the two young men was limited, but with all that, they worked as hard as any men. And they maintained their devotion to one another, no matter how rough the weather, or how arduous the task for one, the other assisted.

One day, it had been blowing great guns from westward and a couple of sails had been carried away. The chief mate ordered a number of hands aloft. Tom and Ned were on deck at the time the call went out, and both sprang forward to execute the order. But six men were already on their way to the main-top, and the chief mate called the two back. He didn't want the lads with least experience up the masts in a gale. But within a flash, Ned had made it first to the main-top and was climbing like a cat to the scene of the damage. Tom, heedless of the calls to return, was close behind him.

"Come down at once! Or by the Lord God, I'll bring you to your senses," bellowed the chief mate.

His voice thundered across the deck in the wind and brought me to the scene.

I shouted as well. "This is your captain. Come down at once!"

Neither of the boys responded. They continued with their ascent.

The ship was pitching violently, and it was all those on deck could do to hold on. It flashed across my mind that they had some strange suicide pact in mind. Regardless of repeated orders to come down, Ned and Tom persisted.

The chief mate was furious. Ned seemed at home among the ropes, and he soon released the tangled sail. Nonetheless, when they finally returned to the deck, I knew I had to punish them. Without discipline, all lives on board are at risk. The chief mate was muttering something about flogging and glaring hard at me.

I stood musing for some minutes. Then I made the decision.

"Bosun, muster the hands!" I shouted.

The bosun blew a long shrill blast on the whistle and screamed, "All hands on deck."

There were one hundred and fifty men in that crew and every one of them gathered on the deck that day. A murmur went through the crowd that Tom and Ned were to be flogged.

As the culprits stood forth, with eyes cast downwards, it was clear they were aware of the gravity of their circumstances.

"You have disobeyed an order from your chief officer and your captain. It devolves upon me to administer punishment. I could not avoid doing so, if you were my brothers, or my own sons. You should both be flogged.' I told them. 'However, I admit the wind was high and you may have heard the order imperfectly, therefore I'm modifying the sentence,' I said, 'Only one of you will be flogged. The other will be sent to the mast head. Which is it to be?'

The youths said not a word. The wind had dropped significantly by this time.

'Men,' I repeated. 'I have asked you a question. Who will be flogged? And who will go to the masthead? Time flies. Speak now!'

Blow me down if Tom didn't rush forward then and fall down at my knees. 'Sir,' he exclaimed, 'Use your whip on me and spare my brother.'

I was relieved that it was Ned who would go to the mast head as he was the best able to climb. And Tom was the larger of the two and I assumed he would be able to take the flogging.

'Up with you, then,' I commanded Ned.

He stood stupefied. The boatswain grabbed him and dragged him toward the masthead. He struggled, constantly looking back at his brother. When they reached the spot where he was to begin his ascent, the boatswain forced him upwards.

'You are fond of heights. You can watch your brother's punishment from above,' I cried.

A hum of satisfaction reverberated through the crowd. Justice was being seen to be done. I felt it essential that I restore discipline before the voyage continued any further into the treacherous waters I knew to be ahead.

At length all the preparations were completed. Tom was stripped to the waist and tied up ready. Fifty lashes were to be administered. The ship's flogger approached and raised the cat to strike.

'One!' cried the man whose job it was to keep tally.

Not a sound from Tom's lips.

'Two!'

Blood appeared on his white skin in ribbons.

'Three!'

The blood began to run in streams downward. The wounds told plainly the cat had struck home.

Above him, bending over, eyes filled with burning tears, was his companion, watching each stroke descend, and feeling the agony with each lash of his skin. His brain must have been overwhelmed with horror because he lifted one hand to place across his mouth to stifle a scream, and a moment later he lost his hold and fell hurtling through the air. I could see his fall was going to land him on the boom. Out of sheer instinct, I ran toward it and caught him by the shoulders, pulled him clear of the boom and we both landed with a thud on the deck. The lad on top of me. It was the stupidest thing I've ever done at sea. Every seaman knows not to stop something falling. I broke my shoulder in the incident. Still, I dragged myself up from under his body as a shriek burst from Tom, and the captain, officers and crew all crowded around the unconscious body on the deck. Kneeling beside him, the doctor felt his pulse but found it dull. In a few seconds, it was over.

'Dead,' said the doctor.

He unbuttoned the boy's shirt to examine the injuries. 'What have we here?' he cried. 'A woman?'

'Hold sir,' exclaimed Tom, struggling to free himself, 'that is my wife.'

'Wife?' declared the doctor. 'By all that's good.' He shook his head.

'Bear this body away, men. He or she, whichever it is, is dead.'

I couldn't believe my eyes. Ned was a woman, true enough!

The crew, shocked by the turn of events, appealed to me to release poor Tom. I have to admit I was shaken myself, and in a world of pain. I no longer had the heart for punishment. So, for the first time in my life, I consented to forgo the punishment and had Tom taken care of until his wounds were healed. The doctor strapped up my own shoulder but it hasn't been good since. I've spent twenty years at sea with that damned shoulder paining me the whole time - just in case I forget for a moment what I'd done. I take opium for the pain, but it's the opium that's done for me. I fear I'm not long for this world, and the end comes none too soon if it ends me pain.

Anyway, to return to the story, it was soon revealed that Tom was the son of an English gentleman. He became amoured of a beautiful young star of an acrobatic company travelling the provinces. His father was displeased and forbade the union, so they ran away together. But when he was unable to find employment, he suggested to his wife that he should go to sea. She would not allow him to go unless she accompanied him. That's when they devised their plan. Her skills as a trapeze artist prepared her well for the part of a seaman, and no one would ever have known if it were not for my punishment. In my arrogance and fear, I sent a woman to her death."

Black had not drunk since beginning his story, so he opened the second bottle of sherry and poured himself a glass. He swallowed all of it without taking a breath.

"That's an amazing story," said Hamish.

"Romantic," said Rita.

"Not likely to help with the murder," said Bellamy.

"What happened to Tom?" asked Hamish.

"He left the ship healthy, at Bombay. I have not heard of him since."

Hamish tipped his head back. "Even if he is still alive and by some coincidence in Southport, he would have no motive to silence Hilda," he mused.

"Well, now you have it all," said Captain Black. "I'm off to my room. While I enjoy your company more than that of most people, I prefer my own company above all." He strode out of the room, the black wool of his long coat flapping behind him.

Hamish glanced at Wallace and thought for a moment he was going to follow him. But he remained in his chair, restless but resigned.

"He's quite the storyteller, as we have said." Bellamy refilled his glass. Just then, Campbell appeared with a fresh bottle. It was as though he was lurking outside the room monitoring, not the conversation, but the consumption.

"Thank you," said Hamish, "no point decanting it."

"I realise that, sir," said Campbell without judgement.

Once he left, Hamish said, "I can't for the life of me see how it can relate to the murder."

CHAPTER TWENTY-THREE

At Deepwater Point we came to the Palace of the mosquito swamp. A magnificent hotel, equal to any in Australia. It was built by a transcendent syndicate who have spared no expense and have built this mansion out of the immense profits from their speculations in Southport alone. The different suites of first-class furniture must have loaded several ships from America. Everything from the most expensive mirror down to the humbler door mats bids you welcome and is of the best description. To feed well and sleep warm is the acme of idledom. On returning homewards I cast my face on the short expanse of water between Deepwater Point and Stradbroke Island, when 22 years ago I assisted Jesse Barker to paddle a big team of bullocks over to draw Cypress Pine, then plentiful on the Island. What changes have come in those years! Then, there was no hotel and no Southport. A few timber getters were camped near Worongary Swamp and the peep O'day boys were just felling their first clearing. What grand days they were, and what grand chances we missed. To think we could have bought the whole lot at five shillings an acre – if only we had known.

Logan Witness. Saturday 21 August, 1886.

Just as Hamish spoke, the housekeeper, Beryl, appeared at the door, nervously rubbing a small square of cardboard the size of a calling card. She handed it to Hamish without lifting her eyes. On one side it said *Celestine Dupont, Aeronaut,* and an address in Paris. On the other a few words were written in a fluent hand. *"Join me for dinner,"* Hamish read aloud, *"please."* In smaller letters, it said, *Colonel Winter will be in attendance.*

"Miss asked me to tell you she means tonight at seven o'clock," said Beryl, "in the colonel's private dining room."

Hamish stared at the card for a moment then nodded. "Thank Mademoiselle Dupont, and tell her I will be delighted to attend," said Hamish.

Beryl scurried away.

"What do you think that's about?" Hamish asked the others.

"I'd say she doesn't want to dine alone with the colonel," said Bellamy.

"Then why accept his invitation to dinner in the private dining room at all?"

"Perhaps she didn't feel she could refuse."

Wallace shook his head. "There's something dark in all this. This mystery goes deeper than we have been supposing."

Hamish brushed his hair back from his face, noticing as he did so that his hands were trembling. He bit his lip, then made a conscious decision to set his anxiety aside. Despite an underlying sense of foreboding, he was happy to be dining with Celestine that evening.

He had drunk two glasses of sherry, more than was his custom in the afternoon, but far less than Bellamy and Wallace, and they had drunk less than Murdo Black. Nonetheless, his head was a little foggy. Why had Celestine invited him to join her and the colonel for dinner? Was there something sinister behind the invitation, as Wallace seemed to imply? Or did Celestine simply wish to engage his company? He still felt the thrill of her kiss on his cheek, though the sensation was fading. Did the colonel think that as he had paid for Celestine's presence, he had the right to monopolise her time? Even if for only one meal?

If that were the case, he might not appreciate the intrusion of another guest.

Hamish dozed off with thoughts of how he might manage any awkwardness. It was half past six when he woke, annoyed at himself for sleeping so long. He rushed to dress and arrived at the colonel's door at exactly seven o'clock.

Colonel Otis Winter answered the door with a glass of whiskey in one hand. He was wearing a deep red brocade smoking jacket and his smile seemed genuine, but Hamish was uncomfortable.

"Come in," he said with slightly yellowing teeth on display. "Drinks on *der* sideboard. *Bedienen sie sich… er…* help yourself." His German accent making a casual gesture sound like a directive.

Hamish saw that Celestine was already there. She was lounged along an embroidered settee, one slim arm across the top, her chocolate curls bobbing on her shoulders. The gossamer light lace of her gown barely kissed her collarbone before floating half-way down her arms. Her dress followed her form as she moved her hand to dangle a cigarette loosely between two exquisite fingers. Her curls framed a face as pale as porcelain. Celestine didn't seem at all uncomfortable at first glance – on the contrary, she appeared as at home as if she were with family. Suddenly, Hamish felt trapped. What was he doing here? Was this the same woman who had told him she distrusted the colonel?

The colonel nodded toward the sideboard. "Pour yourself a drink," he said. Hamish went to the sideboard immediately and poured himself a whiskey on ice.

"The girl will be here with the first course, directly," said the colonel. "Would you care for a cigarette while we wait?"

Celestine hadn't looked at Hamish, or at least he hadn't caught her looking his way. Why did she appear so relaxed? Then it occurred to him that every movement Celestine made was as though it had been rehearsed. She wasn't relaxed. She was striking a pose that gave the impression of being at ease.

"You look enchanting, Mademoiselle," he said.

Celestine took a long, casual draw on her cigarette. "Thank you," she said slowly, "and thank you for coming."

Her voice was warm, but her eyes remained cold. Was she frightened under that confident exterior? There was something strange about the energy in the room. He expected the evening to be awkward, but this was not what he had anticipated. He was relieved that at least the colonel appeared to be unperturbed by his presence.

After an excruciating fifteen minutes of small talk, Beryl entered with plates of crumbed whiting and lemon sauce. Hamish, Celestine and Colonel Winter settled at the dining table and tucked into the delicious entrée.

The colonel then turned his attention to Celestine. "Thank you for coming to our insignificant part of the world," he said, holding up a glass of white wine. Hamish raised his glass also.

"Yes," he said, "it has been an incredible honour to see your exhibition." Hamish decided to pretend innocence in the hope of extracting some explanation for his presence at this dinner. Since everyone else appeared to be playing a role, he would play his own.

"What brought you to our humble shores?"

Celestine nodded and her curls bobbed.

"Colonel Winter, in fact," she said. "He and his syndicate invited me."

Hamish raised his eyebrows in feigned surprise. "Really?" He looked at the colonel for more information.

"It was the pleasure of my syndicate to invite Mademoiselle to our hotel," he said with a small smile and a certainty of tone that indicated he would offer no more in explanation.

"To you as well, then sir," said Hamish, raising his glass one more time. "Since we have you to thank for the presence of this enchantress."

Beryl brought in the main course and the conversation turned to the meal: How tender was the lamb, the smell of the herbed potatoes and the fresh creaminess of the butter.

"They produce a lot of their own food here, on the grounds," said the colonel. "There's a large vegetable plot, even a few cows for milk and butter."

"Splendid," said Hamish, taking a small portion of lamb from his fork and savouring the juices.

"Tell me a little about yourself," said the colonel, glancing at Celestine between mouthfuls.

"What would you like to know?" asked Celestine. Her response was elegant, but she seemed on guard for the first time in the evening.

"Where did you grow up?" asked the colonel.

"I was born in the Alsace region," she began, "but my mother and father moved to Paris when I was two. My mother contracted scarlet fever and passed away during that first year in Paris."

Both men let out a sympathetic groan. "I'm sorry," mumbled Hamish.

"It's all right," said Celestine. "I don't remember her at all. There has only ever been my father and me. He was always obsessed with aeronautics. We moved quite a lot. He would work with one famous aeronaut or another, one scientist or another. I was with him always. The balloon is as familiar to me as the kitchen stove might be to another woman. Flight as familiar as a horse and carriage."

"The loss of your father must have been very hard," said the colonel, leaning close and placing his hand over hers. His voice was gentle and his manner kind, but Hamish noticed Celestine's body stiffen a little at his touch. It was almost imperceptible. Celestine soon pulled her hand away and took a forkful of herbed potato to her mouth. Hamish wanted to comfort her. But what could he say that wouldn't be superfluous? She was no longer the enchantress lounged on the settee, nor was she the vulnerable girl who had tragically lost her father. She was poised, wary, almost like a beautiful snake ready to strike.

"Did you lose a lot of equipment?" asked the colonel.

"Equipment?" said Hamish. "She lost her father..."

Celestine spoke over him. She spoke with confidence. Hamish thought there was even a note of defiance.

"Oh yes," she said, "hundreds of pounds' worth. Father had other balloons and cars, but it was the photographic equipment he would have missed if he had lived."

"Photographic equipment?" asked the colonel.

"Father loved aerial photography. We were on a photographic mission when the accident occurred." Her eyes lingered on the colonel as though measuring his response.

"Tell us about this aerial photography," said Colonel Winter.

Celestine appeared happy to explain aerial photography and the unique perspective of the landscape from the air. Her description had fluidity, a beauty that was enticing. She intentionally lured her audience in. By the time Beryl returned with pudding and filled his glass with sweet, syrupy dessert wine, Hamish, for one, was convinced. Celestine's voice had come to sound like angels singing.

"I would love to see some of these aerial photographs," said the colonel, breaking the spell. "Do you have any with you?"

"One or two," cooed Celestine. "They are precious to me." Her eyes were watching him closely.

The colonel smiled as though he were indulging a child. "I would treat it as an incredible honour, to see such a precious thing as these photographs, some perhaps taken by your father during the last hours of his life."

The smile disappeared from Celestine's lips. Her eyes grew wary.

The colonel continued, as though he hadn't noticed her discomfort. "And you haven't heard from your father since the accident?" he said.

Celestine put down her spoon. "*Non.*" Her face was flushed. Hamish wondered if her pink cheeks were the result of the champagne, or whether it was the colonel's insensitivity that had excited her. Celestine drank her coffee in one swift mouthful, then announced she must go. She stood and Hamish took her shawl from the back of the chair and placed it around her shoulders.

"I apologise if I have upset you, dear," said the colonel, standing.

"Not at all," said Celestine. "I am tired."

Hamish noticed the coldness in her eyes. "I'll take you back to your room."

Celestine rejected the offer of his arm, ducking around him for the door. "Don't be ridiculous, I can find my own room," she said.

Before following her, Hamish thanked the colonel for a wonderful dinner and for inviting him.

"I didn't," he murmured.

Hamish stopped for a moment and caught the stony glint in the colonel's eye.

"I apologise if I seem rude, but I sense some tension between yourself and Mademoiselle Dupont," he said quietly.

Colonel Winter's eyes flickered. "She is influenced by the French blood of her father. In fact, she was born in Alsace. She believes herself to be French, but these people are German by tradition, by language and by conquest. It is out of sheer perversity they call themselves French."

Hamish wasn't sure how to respond. "Mademoiselle strikes me as deeply... French," said Hamish.

"Oh, that is the French influence on the woman's mind. Every outfit must froth like champagne, changing a mere dress into a poem. Women like her will be replaced soon enough through German education. Our education program in the region is second to none in the world. In a single generation, the population will remember only their Germanic roots, our language, and our customs. They will be fully germanised."

Hamish left the colonel wondering at the contradiction inherent in his reasoning. If the people of the Alsace were so thoroughly German, why did they need 'germanising'?

Once back in his room, Hamish tried to relax, but his clothes were itchy against his skin. He couldn't decide if the awkwardness of the evening was causing his discomfort or if it was the salt from his swim earlier. He decided to visit the washroom and refresh himself properly before attempting sleep. On his way back from the washroom, he was surprised to almost bump into Celestine outside his room.

"My goodness, not again!" he said.

Her long eyelashes fluttered exactly as they had done the first time he ran into her in the corridor.

"Thank you for coming this evening," she whispered, her lips like berries, in his mind.

"My pleasure," he whispered back, wondering why they were whispering.

"I'm not sure why I was invited, but it was a pleasure to be there with you," repeated Hamish.

Celestine hesitated, then kissed him lightly on the lips.

Hamish felt his heart pounding in his chest and a familiar tingling travel through his body. The moment during which she hesitated, her lips so close to his, her eyes almost closed and her long lashes resting on her cheekbones, seemed to swell to hours and allow a lifetime of emotions to pass. His longing for intimacy felt as though it might consume him, but somehow, underneath it all, he knew his longing was not for this woman. It seemed, then, that everything that passed between them had happened within a heartbeat and she transformed suddenly into a ball of buzzing energy. She drew away from Hamish, darted down the corridor and disappeared into her own room as quickly as possible.

Hamish was left wondering if he had imagined the encounter again. He went to bed and slept fitfully, elements of the dinner conversation and the meeting in the corridor reeling in his mind. At some point, a sharp repetitive sound punctuated his sleep. He rolled the sound about in his mind a few times as his brain tried to identify it, even while he wasn't fully awake. The sound became sharper and louder until it felt like someone hitting him on the head. Suddenly, a high-pitched call was added. "Doctor, doctor… Doctor Hart!" Hamish rolled off the bed and managed to find his feet. Someone was banging at his door. He grabbed his housecoat, stumbled to the door and opened it, at which moment Celestine Dupont fell into his arms.

"Someone has been in my room," she cried.

"What? What time is it?" Hamish looked around for his carriage clock. It was still dark and with his curtains drawn, it could have been the middle of the night.

"It's dawn," Celestine informed him, "but come, come and see what they've done."

Hamish followed in his bare feet and housecoat. When they entered the open door of Celestine's room, he surveyed the space. Her travel trunk was overturned, and all her clothes were strewn across the floor, as were her books and papers.

Hamish looked properly at Celestine for the first time since she had woken him. She was fully clothed. "Where were you when this happened?" he asked.

"Overseeing the men packing the equipment," she said. "The equipment is heading to Brisbane on the steamer today, and from there on the schooner to Sydney, ready for my next exhibition."

"Are you leaving so soon?" Hamish asked, unable to keep the dismay from his voice.

Celestine smiled. "I will be around for a few days," she said. "Sergeant Bellamy has asked that I stay until the murder is resolved, but I can only stay until Friday. I must meet the Saturday departure from Brisbane to Sydney for my exhibition the following weekend."

She looked around at the mess in her room.

"Who did this, Hamish?" she said quietly.

"What were they looking for?" Hamish searched the room for some idea.

Together, they picked up one item at a time. Celestine folded her clothes and undergarments while Hamish avoided them and set his attention on the books and papers strewn across the floor. There were several books on aeronautics and one on aerial photography. He placed everything neatly on the small desk in the corner.

"Is anything missing?" he asked.

Celestine shuffled through the documents on the desk. "I don't believe so," she said.

"So, whatever it was they were looking for, they didn't find it," said Hamish.

Celestine sat on the edge of her bed and took a few deep breaths. She shook her head and her upper body slumped.

"I'm sorry to have woken you for this," she said. "It is nothing." She waved her hands around the room dismissively.

"It's not nothing," said Hamish. "Someone has come into your room and gone through your personal belongings. We need to notify the local police… and Campbell Charles."

"Please don't bother," she said. "As the intruder has taken nothing, I would rather not have the fuss." She was staring out the window at the sea. The Scottish Prince still perched on the sand in the distance, was just within view. "I'm sorry. I shouldn't have disturbed you," she said again. "Please go and give it no more attention."

Hamish realised he was still in bare feet and housecoat as he stepped out into the corridor to return to his room. As he closed the door to Celestine's room behind him, Rita came down the corridor, heading towards the amenities wing. Rita's eyes went to Celestine's door and back to Hamish, standing there in his sleep attire and his bare feet. Her eyebrows arched so high they threatened to touch her hairline. Rita stood still to fully take in the scene.

"She called on me," Hamish stammered, "to help… earlier."

Rita walked on with a half-smile. Hamish watched her, feeling strangely frustrated at her enjoyment of the moment.

CHAPTER TWENTY-FOUR

Count Von Maltke, speaking in the Reichstag yesterday, stated that an alliance with France and a consequent ensuring of the peace of Europe was impossible so long as demands were put forward for the surrender of the confiscated provinces of Alsace and Lorraine, which Germany would never renounce possession of. He said that Germany disclaimed all idea of conquest, but was determined to keep all the territory of which she was already in possession.

The Ballarat Star. Wednesday 28 July, 1880.

"Let's look at it logically," said Rita. "If we begin with Captain Murdo Black, what do we know so far?"

Hamish, Rita, Bellamy and Wallace were walking toward the pier. Tired of the reading room, they felt they needed air after breakfast. Red was scampering ahead, stopping frequently to sniff at traces of those who had already passed the same way.

"He was awake with his light on at around the time Hilda must have been killed," said Hamish.

"Yes, but you were up and about yourself at that time. It doesn't mean much," said Rita.

"He's been open with us," said Wallace. "He gladly tells us his stories, even when they are less than flattering."

"Oh, he's ready with a story all right. But are they true?" asked Hamish.

"I think his stories are true," said Bellamy. "The question is, which story is he telling?"

"What do you mean?" asked Rita.

"As I said, the captain is full of stories and they are probably all true, at least in part. But how do we know the story he told us yesterday is the one Hilda was referring to?"

They crossed the road to the promenade and turned left towards the pier.

"We don't," agreed Hamish.

"We're no further along with a motive for Murdo Black," said Rita.

"I have a feeling about this murder," said Wallace. "I think it is more complex than Glenda Hembrow having a secret child, or Murdo Black having a violent career. We haven't talked about Celestine, for instance."

Hamish felt the hairs on the back of his neck rise. "What would Celestine have to do with Hilda's murder, or that of Glenda Hembrow, for that matter?"

"Don't be a fool, Hamish," said Rita. "She is as likely as anyone else to be a suspect.

She was out and about around the time of the murder," she said, "and she lied about it."

Wallace went on. "Hilda hinted that she had knowledge Celestine's father was alive. That might have been a secret worth keeping, if he faked his own death, for example."

Bellamy was warming to the idea. "Do you think Celestine's father faked his own death and she has knowledge of it?" he asked. "Perhaps she helped him?"

"He may have been avoiding debtors," suggested Rita. "Disappeared, so he didn't have to pay up. Or his debtors might have been threatening him, so he faked his own death."

"I think we may be wandering into the territory of assumption now," said Hamish with some annoyance.

"Or he might be avoiding other criminals," cut in Rita.

Hamish raised an eyebrow as he stared. "What criminals?" he demanded.

Rita stared back. "Blackmailers," she suggested.

Bellamy drew his brows together and spoke seriously. "What makes you think Celestine's father was being blackmailed?"

"Nothing," said Hamish defiantly, though the question was aimed at Rita.

"There is nothing to suggest such a thing." He sighed heavily and theatrically. "We are making up stories about the poor girl in her absence. We don't have any evidence of these things."

Wallace sensed the seeds of an argument developing, so he broke into the conversation. "Hamish is right," he said. "We have no idea whether Celestine's father is alive or not, whether he faked his own death, or if he did, why he might have done so. All we know is that Hilda hinted at his being alive. Then she was killed. The two events are not necessarily linked."

"Exactly," said Hamish emphatically.

"And still…" began Wallace.

"And still what?" said Hamish.

The four of them had reached the rotunda at the beginning of the pier. Red, who had been skipping happily along beside Wallace, suddenly darted onto the pier after a seagull. Hamish strode after him. "Red, heel," he cried. But Red ignored him and ran further along the pier. "The sky has come over dull again," said Rita, catching up to Hamish. He gave up on the terrier and stopped. He felt the wind blow a light sprinkle of sea spray across his face and he brushed his hair back.

"It's not what you think," he said.

Rita looked at him with mock surprise. "What is not what I think?" she asked.

Hamish shifted uncomfortably in his skin, then moved to lean across the rail facing the water.

Rita leant beside him.

"The thing with Celestine," he said. "Miss, I mean Mademoiselle Dupont."

Rita raised an amused brow. "Are you telling me you are involved in a 'thing' with Celestine Dupont?" she asked.

Hamish swung his head toward her. "No," he said. "There is no 'thing.'"

"Then what are we talking about?" said Rita. "You raised the possibility of a 'thing.'"

Wallace was standing a few yards from them, still calling his dog. When he had Red safely bundled in his arms, albeit wriggling to escape, he joined Hamish and Rita at the railing.

"Hamish was just telling me about the 'thing' he is currently involved in with Mademoiselle Dupont," she said.

Hamish dropped his head with a loud sigh.

Wallace looked mildly amused at his discomfort.

"Celestine was in the dining hall just now," he said. "Regardless of the 'thing' I think you need to talk to her about her father."

Bellamy joined them then. "You're right, we need to talk seriously with Celestine," he said. "Was there anyone else in the dining room with her?"

"There wasn't when I passed through," said Wallace. "I'm going back to my room," he added. "There's no need for all of us to confront her. Fewer people questioning her will be less intimidating." He put Red down and strode back along the promenade, with the terrier following.

Rita showed no sign of excusing herself from the interview. Hamish knew she would be determined to hear Celestine's responses first-hand.

When Hamish, Bellamy and Rita returned to the Grand and joined Celestine at her table, she was enjoying tea and sponge cake. She greeted them warmly. "How is the investigation going?" she asked. "Do you yet know who killed the poor nurse?"

"The investigation progresses well," said Bellamy.

"We acknowledge the difficult morning you've had, but we were wondering if we could ask you a few more questions?"

"*Moi, Monsieur?* I don't know what else I could tell you."

"Can you tell us exactly what happened at the time your father went missing?" asked Bellamy.

Celestine put down her teacup. To Hamish, she looked sad rather than nervous.

"If you think it will help," she said, "but I cannot imagine what it has to do with the unfortunate Hilda's death… or with who came into my room this morning."

"Humour us," said Bellamy.

Celestine began. "We left from Montbeliard that morning," she said. "Papa was interested in this new aerial photography. He took magical pictures of the countryside from a bird's-eye view. People were willing to pay a lot of money for these photographs."

Celestine used a fork to separate a small piece of cake from the slice on her plate. She seemed to take a moment to find the words she needed.

"It was a grey sky, but what day doesn't have a grey sky in that part of France?" She smiled and glanced at Hamish. Hamish couldn't stop the smile that crept across his lips in return.

"We weren't aiming to go high. We went up to about 800 feet easily, then we travelled slowly over Montbeliard and Papa took photographs of the Saint Martin Church. The breeze took us toward Mullhouse. After that, the wind began to build and we were swept south over Lorrach. The wind became gusty, unpredictable and we were blown into German territory, so Papa lightened the load. In the end, a terrific gust caught us, lifted us and then dropped us suddenly."

Celestine stopped to take a deep breath.

"There must have been a fault in the canvas stitching on the balloon, because there was a tremendous noise when the canvas tore and we found ourselves plummeting toward the ground. I recall seeing the ground coming closer and closer and wondering what it was going to feel like having my body smashed into it. Then I saw water. Suddenly it was the Rhine rushing toward us. An instant later, the car made contact with the river and there was a ghastly sucking sound as the water engulfed us. Instruments floated upward all around us. I could see light directly above, but mostly there was the dark underside of the canvas floating on the surface. There was a sensation of weightlessness and I recall thinking I ought to be terrified. But I wasn't. I looked around for Papa and briefly saw his limbs against the light, frog-kicking his way upward. This spurred me to do the same. I swam towards the light but it seemed to take forever. My chest felt as though it would burst by the time I broke the surface. I couldn't see papa anywhere. I hoped my view of him was obscured by the mass of canvas."

Celestine took another breath while twisting her fork in the cake. She didn't lift it to her lips but held it in mid-air and stared at it.

"I didn't have the strength to swim any further," she went on, "so I kept myself afloat, clinging to debris from the car. Then I heard voices. Swiss,

I thought. I realised we must have landed in the part of the Rhine that borders Germany and Switzerland. It came about that the voices belonged to fishermen from a village in the outskirts of Basel. They scooped me into their boat and took me home with them. The balloon and most of our equipment was lost. The fishermen retrieved my father's camera and a few slides survived, but that is all. I tried several times to ask about my father and though I couldn't speak the language, I think they understood me. They certainly understood that someone else had been on board when we crashed. They sent out people to search, but they found no one. Papa had vanished."

Celestine placed the cake back on the plate while maintaining her grip on the fork. Hamish wanted to reach out and touch her hand, release the tension. But his wariness stopped him. He wasn't sure how she could be both vulnerable and dangerous in his mind.

Celestine peered under her eyelashes at him as though she'd read his thoughts, then she went on, "I stayed in Basel a few days, hoping my father would somehow turn up, perhaps on the other side of the river, the German side. But he didn't."

There was a pause. Hamish watched her scan her listeners before continuing,

"I gradually came to terms with the fact that he was gone. In legal terms, he was listed as missing, and then later presumed dead. The newspapers were full of speculative stories, some arguing he was alive. But I know, if he was alive, he would have contacted me. He wouldn't leave me to grieve. We only had each other. He would contact me."

No one spoke for a few seconds. Hamish felt it was more out of respect than any real empathy. It was difficult to doubt the story, but he couldn't help feeling the emotion seemed contrived. *Or was that unfair?*

"Do you have any idea what someone might have been looking for in your room?" asked Bellamy.

Celestine picked up her cloak from the chair beside her and stood up. "I do not," she said emphatically. "Am I free to go?"

"Of course," said Bellamy, sitting back in his chair as the tiny woman glided towards the stairs.

Hamish, Rita and Bellamy were left once again, with one another.

"She certainly has a convincing story," said Bellamy. "It's difficult to believe she is lying about her father's disappearance."

"Just as I said," agreed Hamish.

Bellamy sat back in his chair and leant against the panelled wall. "Difficult, but not impossible," he said.

"But what possible reason could she have for killing both Hilda Jenkins and Glenda Hembrow?" cried Hamish.

Wallace joined them and they caught him up to date on what they had learned.

"We have more detail," said Hamish, "but we really don't know any more that helps us with the murders."

"Why did the balloonist come to Southport?" he said. "It's a long way, just for an exhibition. The thousand or so people on the beach yesterday must be nothing compared to the tens of thousands who turn up in Europe."

"Colonel Winter requested the hotel invite her," said Hamish. "He said so last night."

Campbell, who truly must have been lurking at the door, appeared at that moment.

"It is true," he said. "He and some of his wealthy friends in Southport funded her trip. Exposure for the region, they said. Sunny Queensland. Many of the colonel's friends have large developments in this region, including this hotel. They hope to attract the rich and beautiful."

Campbell removed the dirty glasses from the table and left.

CHAPTER TWENTY-FIVE

The declaration of the German Government that it will never restore Alsace and Lorraine to France affects the interests of every country in Europe and Australia also. France, as everyone knows, is simply waiting for an opportunity for recovering the lost territory and has largely increased her army for the purpose. Not satisfied with being able to put into the field at short notice a force which the Germans assert to be greater than their own, the Chiefs of the French War Office now demand about twenty million sterling to augment the offensive of the Republic. The preparations that France has made for revenge has not only entailed on the conquerors the necessity of keeping an immense body of combatants permanently under arms, but has prompted the German Chancellery to ask for an addition of 40,000 men. Russia, owing to the vast body of troops which her neighbour has to maintain constantly on the watch against all advances toward the Rhenish provinces by her late enemy, is likewise compelled to keep a proportionate mass of soldiers ready for any quarrel with Germany. With the present resources for attack which France possesses, we too, are obliged to be on our guard against the results of any difficulty between Great Britain and herself.

Mount Alexander Mail. Saturday 18 December, 1886.

"Reports," declared Bellamy with extra emphasis to overcome his reluctance. He stood up and left for his room.

Wallace also stood. "I'm joining Captain Black for cards before lunch," he said. "Red." He called the terrier to heel, and they left in search of the captain.

Hamish hoped Wallace's friend didn't turn out to be a killer. But he couldn't think of a single reason why he should.

Hamish and Rita were left alone in the dining hall. Hamish tugged a crumpled sheet of paper from his pocket and flattened it out on the table.

"What is it?" asked Rita.

"It's a telegram. It arrived yesterday, but there has been too much going on to talk to you about it."

Rita leaned over the flimsy sheet of paper to discern the text. "Is there something wrong?" she asked. Warmth spread through Hamish at the concern evident in her voice. "It's Father. He's ill. Not ill exactly. He has senile dementia."

Rita's hands shot to her face. She covered her mouth as a tiny gasp escaped.

"Everyone is running around compensating for him so they can avoid telling the doctor. But it's only a matter of time."

Rita let out a low, protracted whistle. "If he's referred to a doctor, they'll have no choice but to notify the asylum," she said.

"I know. Mother knows also. She thinks they can avoid it. But the symptoms are only going to worsen. I don't think she understands that part. She can't hide it forever. Especially as he refuses to stay at home. He's already made a spectacle at the racetrack."

"I'm sure the patrons thoroughly appreciated a spectacle," smiled Rita.

Hamish rolled his eyes at her. "This is serious. I'm worried about him, and mother."

Rita took his hand. "It will get worse," she said. "Do you need to go home and help sort things out?"

Hamish was surprised by the word 'home'. "Melbourne is not my home," he said. "What could I do if I went down there? I'm not leaving the murder of two women unsolved."

Hamish knew he was arguing with himself. And he knew Rita knew it as well. The best thing about her was that she knew him so thoroughly.

"You just have to hope that the murders are solved before your father's condition worsens," she said.

Hamish refolded the telegram and placed it back in his pocket. He took a deep breath and refocussed his mind on the task before him.

Rita was still thinking about Glenda Hembrow's death. "Who would have a gun here?" she said out of the blue.

Hamish avoided her eye and stared at his hands. For too long.

"No!" she cried.

He looked at the ceiling.

"You didn't?"

One side of his mouth dropped.

"You did?"

She was furious.

"Why would you bring your gun on a holiday weekend at the seaside?"

"It's not my gun, as you know very well. It's my father's gun."

"The gun your father gave you when you left for the 'frontier', as he calls it?"

"Yes. I didn't expect to have to use it, but as you recall, it came in quite useful last year when a crowd was ready to lynch our friend."

"But why did you bring it *here*?"

"I didn't bring it on purpose. It was in my long coat pocket, where it's been for months. I just packed the coat."

"Is it still there?" she cried.

Hamish hesitated. "I'm scared to look."

Rita raised her eyebrows. They went upstairs to his room together. The suitcase was on the bench crafted from mahogany for the purpose. He opened the lid gingerly and felt around in the coat's long pockets until he made out the bulk of the gun. He lifted out the small colt. The gun was cold and had not been touched.

Hamish and Rita breathed a collective sigh of relief.

Hamish refolded the coat and returned it to his suitcase. As he did so, he felt something odd crackle under his shirts. Paper. He dug out a corner to reveal a large brown envelope. He turned it over and scanned it from one side to the other. There was nothing written on it. He noticed it was unsealed, so he slipped his hand inside and removed the contents. Five photographic images about ten by eight inches were revealed; aerial images of buildings in a forest.

Rita shut the door to his bedroom. "What are they?" she whispered.

Hamish stared at the photographs. He turned them over and back again in his hands. Then he looked at Rita with a combination of shock and confusion.

"I think they're Celestine's aerial photographs," he said quietly. "Taken by her father."

"Why do you have them?"

"I don't know," said Hamish, looking around the room, as though the person who left them there might magically reappear. He recalled Colonel Winter asking about them the night before. He told Rita about the conversation.

"When Celestine's room was ransacked this morning, she called me for help. That's why I was coming out of her room when you saw me," he added.

Rita laughed. "I thought…"

"I know what you thought," cut in Hamish.

Rita suppressed a laugh.

"But she said nothing was taken," said Hamish.

"Perhaps she didn't notice they were missing."

"She would notice," said Hamish, "I'm certain of it. These photographs were important to her."

He recalled meeting Celestine near his room.

"I think she placed them here herself," he said. "She must have hidden them in here to keep them safe."

"So, you think she knew someone was going to ransack her room?"

"No, not that. But she was afraid someone would try to steal the photographs."

Rita thought for a moment. "You say Colonel Winter asked about them at dinner?"

Hamish looked up. "Yes. He did. He asked if she had them with her and she told him she did."

"We need to talk to the colonel about the mess in Celestine's room," said Rita.

"What does this have to do with Glenda's murder, do you think?" asked Hamish.

"I don't know. But we need to show these photographs to Bellamy."

"Where is Wallace?" asked Hamish.

"Playing cards with Captain Black."

"Of course he is."

"Let Bellamy and Wallace know we need to meet in the reading room," said Hamish. "I'll tell Campbell to bring us some sustenance there."

As Bellamy joined Hamish and Rita in the reading room, Campbell arrived with sandwiches and sherry.

Wallace came in last. "Have any of you seen Red?" he asked.

They all looked under the table and around their feet.

"No," was the consensus.

"He ran out of the room as I was leaving to join you," said Wallace. "I didn't see whether he ran down the stairs or along the hall."

"He'll be somewhere," said Rita.

"Probably at the kitchen door, begging for scraps," said Bellamy.

Wallace sat down and nodded. "He'll not be far," he said.

"These latest developments, I can't help but think they're related," said Hamish.

"First, the death of Glenda Hembrow and second, Celestine Dupont's room being ransacked in the early hours of the morning."

"Do you think Glenda found something in Celestine's room and was killed for it?" suggested Bellamy.

"I might think that," said Hamish, "if I wasn't reasonably sure I know what they were looking for."

"What?" cried Bellamy.

Hamish took the envelope out and tipped the contents onto the side table. They each picked up an image examined it. "They don't look like much," said Bellamy, tipping the photograph sideways to see if he'd missed something. "Where did you get them?"

"They were tucked into my suitcase," said Hamish. "I think by Celestine herself.

I think she slipped into my room last night after we had dinner with the colonel."

"Why would she do that?" asked Bellamy, putting down the first image and picking up a second.

"This perspective can be beautiful when it's looking down on churches and palaces," said Rita, "but these images are of ordinary buildings in a forest."

Wallace picked up a second image. "It looks like a factory," he said. "A large manufacturing plant, I'd say. Or a warehouse."

They all agreed.

"Where did Celestine say the balloon came down?"

"The Rhine somewhere," said Hamish. "She mentioned a Swiss town. It was near where the borders of France, Germany and Switzerland meet."

"They were flying across the Alsace-Lorraine region?" asked Wallace.

"I suppose so," said Hamish. "It's interesting. She told Colonel Winter and I that she was born in Alsace."

"These images may have been taken in German territory then. At least in the contested territory," said Wallace. "I think Celestine's father might have been taking photographs of installations in German territory to pass on to the French."

Everyone stared at him.

"That's a leap, isn't it?" said Bellamy.

"I don't think so," said Hamish. "Look at these, it makes sense. Dupont could sail above the disputed territory, taking photographs of armaments and fortifications. The French government would probably pay a fortune for these photographs."

"Do you think Celestine knows her father might have been spying on the Germans?" asked Bellamy.

"No," said Hamish emphatically, "she thought he was selling the images for art."

Rita rolled her eyes. "This is not art," she said, holding up one of the images.

Hamish gave a sigh of resignation. "All right. Let's assume Celestine's father was taking photographs for the French Government and she knew about it. How does that help us with the murders of Hilda Jenkins and Glenda Hembrow?"

Bellamy was leaning back in his chair, thinking.

"Someone who knew about the photographs and their value might have aimed to sell them to the highest bidder," he said.

"Glenda Hembrow?" asked Rita.

"Possibly," said Bellamy. "I can't see Celestine telling her about the photographs, though. That's the only thing. They weren't friends."

"Could the colonel have told her?" asked Rita.

"He couldn't," said Hamish. "The colonel heard that she had them with her last night at dinner."

"Not unless they were all working together," suggested Rita. "The colonel couldn't ransack Celestine's room from his wheelchair. He might have had James do it for a share in the profit."

They took a moment to consider this option.

"What about Hilda?" asked Hamish. "How does her murder fit into this theory?"

"Maybe..." began Rita, excited about the story that was unravelling now, "Glenda Hembrow did kill Hilda, for all the reasons we already know about, and the colonel knew – he was in the next room after all. Maybe he was blackmailing Glenda and James and forced him to get the photographs for him."

"Then who killed Glenda?" said Hamish.

Rita looked disappointed. "I don't know," she said.

"The point is," began Bellamy, thinking as he spoke, "whoever was after the photographs didn't get them. Hamish has them. I think we need to talk to Celestine and ask her why she hid them in Hamish's suitcase. She must have suspected someone."

Hamish noticed Campbell striding past the reading room on his way to the dining hall.

He called out to him.

"Could you ask Celestine Dupont to join us, please? Let her know it's important."

Campbell bowed and changed direction, heading back toward the main entrance and the staircase. A few minutes later, he returned. "Mademoiselle Dupont is not in the building," he said. "She was seen by the staff rushing out about thirty minutes ago. She seemed to be in a great hurry," he said.

"Can you bring Colonel Otis Winter, then?" asked Bellamy.

"No, Sir. He left about ten minutes prior to Mademoiselle Dupont. The staff saw him wheeling himself toward the pier. He often had Hilda take him there to watch the steamers come and go."

Campbell checked the watch hanging on a chain from his waistcoat. "He should be back by now, though. The steamer is long out of sight." He looked out the window to confirm his assumption.

"Has everyone gone missing this morning?" asked Bellamy, out of frustration.

"Mr Hembrow is in his room where he has been since his wife was found, and Captain Black is in the games room, reading,"

"Let Captain Black know we would like a word with him, then," said Bellamy.

They waited nervously for Black to join them. "Both Colonel Winter and Celestine Dupont are missing," said Hamish. "They were both seen heading for the pier about half an hour ago."

"And Red is missing," added Wallace.

"That doesn't sound like they're missing," said Murdo Black. "We'll catch up with them at the pier. Red has probably followed them."

They all walked along the road, scanning the beach as they went. There wasn't another soul anywhere. When they reached the pier, they could see that the steamer had long gone, and the lengthy stretch of jetty was empty. Hamish peeked into the rotunda at the start of the pier. It was dark and cool inside. He was about to return to the others when he noticed a small glint reflecting a shaft of sunlight coming in under the rotunda roof. He made out the outline of something at the back of the rotunda. Hamish explored further and found Colonel Winter's wheelchair pushed back against the wall in the shadows.

"Rita, Bellamy," he called. They all crammed into the dark space of the rotunda and stared at the wheelchair.

Hamish felt a cold stone in the pit of his stomach. They looked up and down the beach, but there was no sign of anyone. The tide had come in and the water lapped lazily at the feet of the beach houses that lined the shore.

A small shape was moving in front of one of the beach houses. The shape melted into the shadow at the corner of the building, but it was moving. It was digging.

"Red!" cried Wallace at the same time as Hamish registered what he was seeing. "There he is." Wallace ran toward the huts to retrieve his dog.

"Thank goodness for that," said Hamish. "I thought we might have to mount a search for that dog, as well as for Celestine and the colonel."

"Celestine may have gone on the vessel with her equipment," suggested Bellamy. "No one could blame her after Glenda was murdered."

Hamish considered the possibility. "Would she go without her images?" he said.

"She'll know they're safe with you," said Bellamy. "She's had enough of the cloak and dagger here at the Grand Hotel and is already on her way to her next engagement. Doubtless, you'll hear from her in a month's time wanting the images returned."

Rita's loud laughter caught the attention of both Hamish and Bellamy. Wallace was climbing onto the jetty with Red firmly in his grasp. Sand was stuck to the terrier's whiskers and his feet were wet. He had thrown two sticky paws across his master's shoulder and rested his sandy nose against his neck.

"Let's walk back toward the hotel. The colonel can't have travelled far without his wheelchair," said Bellamy.

As they approached the Grand, Wallace said, "You go up, the captain and I will check the boathouse further on."

"Good idea. I'll call in to see the boat's owner. The old man is usually sitting at the window sketching that shipwreck when he's not out at sea. He might have seen something," said Bellamy.

Hamish and Rita continued up to Hamish's room. "I need to find somewhere safe to keep these images," he said, slipping the envelope from his coat pocket. When they opened the door, they both stood in shock. The room was a mess. Everything Hamish owned was strewn about the floor.

"Someone has been looking for the photographs," said Rita. "But who knew you had them? Other than Celestine?"

Hamish shook his head. "Fortunately, I've had them on me," he said. "Perhaps Colonel Winter guessed they might be in my room."

"I'm worried about Colonel Winter," Rita said. "He and Celestine being missing..."

Wallace swung through the door, interrupting them. "Is Red here with you?"

"You had him a moment ago," said Hamish, looking past Wallace into the corridor.

"As soon as I put him down, he charged off again."

Rita frowned. "He's not with us. Do you think he scarpered back to the beach?"

Wallace rushed out of the room and down the corridor to the stairs. He took the stairs two at a time, his feet barely touching the polished wood.

Hamish and Rita ran after him. There was no sign of Red on the beach in front of the hotel. The tide was receding and there was plenty of wet sand between the wall and the water. There were seagulls, but no terrier.

Wallace stood on the sea wall, gazing first one way and then the other. "Red. Red. Come, you bloody dog!"

Hamish and Rita stood beside him, also looking to the left and the right and back again.

"He'll come back when he's ready," said Hamish. "He's a stubborn little…"

"He could be back at the pier," suggested Rita. "He seemed excited about something along there earlier."

They only had to walk a few yards before they saw the terrier in the distance, running back and forth in front of the beach houses below the pier. His yapping pierced the air. Gulls squawked at the intrusion on their territory.

"What's got him worked up?" said Hamish.

"I think there's someone in one of those beach houses," said Wallace.

Rita's eyes opened wide. "Aren't they locked?"

"That wouldn't stop anyone," said Hamish. "Someone could drag the colonel that far, I imagine."

"You don't think Celestine could have taken the colonel captive?" said Rita.

"I don't know what to think. But they're both missing… and we have two murders already."

Red was barking hysterically at the door of the hut closest to the pier when they caught up with him. Wallace tried to scoop him up, but he side-stepped, ran around his master's ankles and arrived back at the door, scraping and yapping. The last beach house door had a shining new padlock. There was a row of similarly coloured huts, but locks on the others were rusted and discoloured from the weather.

Rita tucked her hand under her vest and produced a narrow iron pin. She placed it in the lock mechanism and jiggled it until she heard the click.

"What are you doing?" asked Hamish. "How'd do you know how to do that?"

"A friend in London taught me to pick locks," she said over her shoulder. "It wasn't just a medical education I gained while I was over there."

Within seconds, the door was opened.

At first, the space inside was too dark to see anything. But they heard a muffled whining sound. As their eyes grew accustomed to the low light, they were able to make out a figure in the far corner. A woman was lying in an awkward position against the wall. She was kicking and writhing, attempting to wriggle free of the restraints on her wrists and ankles. A gag was stuffed in her mouth and wrapped tightly around her head.

"Celestine," breathed Hamish, as Red shot past them all to greet her. She screwed up her face and tried to turn toward the wall to avoid his enthusiasm. Hamish and Bellamy stood just inside the door, staring in disbelief, while Rita slipped past them, leant down and gently removed the gag.

Celestine let out a loud, deep breath. "Thank you," she coughed.

"Who did this?" cried Hamish.

Celestine didn't answer. Her eyes stared straight past Hamish and over his shoulder. He turned to see what had terrified her and saw a large shadow against the sun. It took the shape of a man. It was a second later that he distinguished the shape of a gun, and he realised it was pointing towards him.

Hamish struggled for a moment to gain his focus. With the sun behind the figure, he could make out little more than a silhouette.

"Now you can give me *der* photographs," the figure said.

There was no mistaking the accent, but Hamish was confused by the fact that the man was standing rather than seated in his wheelchair.

"Go ahead and shoot me, Colonel," said Hamish. He instantly regretted calling the man's bluff. This man, who had lied to them from the start and had probably already killed two people. But in the moment, there was nothing he could do to take it back.

The colonel shifted his aim. "I'm not going to shoot you, Doctor. I'm going to shoot her. He took a step forward to hold the gun at Rita's temple.

She stood deathly still. Her hazel eyes shining in the dark. There was no fear, only defiance.

"You will hand over the photographs and the little French aeronaut will tell me *der* name of her contact in Paris," demanded the colonel.

"Why the masquerade?" asked Hamish, buying time.

The colonel shrugged his shoulders. "Who would be suspicious of an old man in a wheelchair? *Der* only lie is the wheelchair. I really did come to Queensland to be with my daughter. After her death I stayed for the agreeable climate. But a spy never retires. I took on the wheelchair so I could carry out the small assignments here in the colony without suspicion."

"A spy?" said Bellamy.

Colonel Winter smiled. A cold, mocking smile.

"Yes. A German spy, here in the remotest corner of the British Colonies. Who would guess? But then that's the point, isn't it?"

The only thing Hamish could think of to do was to keep the colonel talking while he tried to figure out a way for them to escape.

"What threat could Hilda possibly pose to a German nationalist?" he asked.

"Hilda was a necessary evil. It was both a risk to have someone living in such close proximity and an advantage in completing the cover. Unfortunately, I was too arrogant in thinking I could hide my mobility indefinitely. I was careless and Hilda saw me out of the chair. Of course, she had to go."

"What did Glenda do?" said Hamish.

"She saw me in my room, out of my chair. I was retrieving Hilda's letters from her mother. I was concerned she may have shared my secret with her. She hid all her letters under her mattress. You lot hadn't found them, so I knew they must still be there."

Hamish winced. *Why didn't we look there?* he thought.

"I actually thought for a moment that you had recognised me through the window," said the colonel. "That day when you were swimming. But on reflection, I decided you had not."

"I didn't," murmured Hamish. Suddenly, a thought came to him. "That was you following us the day we discovered Mrs Jenkin's body in Nerang!"

"Of course," he made a hollow sound that might have been laughter. "I was there looking for her letters. There were none."

"You didn't kill her as well?" Hamish breathed.

The colonel shrugged. "Perhaps," he said. "I think she might have died, anyway."

"You could have brought her help…" Hamish was indignant and forgotten for half a second that the man had a gun pointed at Rita.

The colonel shoved it toward her temple to remind him.

Hamish felt the cold metal as though it were his own skin it was touching.

"My mission was to retrieve the photographs from Mademoiselle Dupont and to ascertain the name of her contact," said Colonel Winter. "My superiors felt she would be off her guard out here in the antipodes."

"But there will be plates for the images," said Hamish. "The ones Celestine has are only prints."

"Oh, we have the plates, Doctor. We took them from Monsieur Dupont when we scooped him from the Rhine. Bad luck for him. He couldn't tell us the name of the contact. Only the Mademoiselle knows that. She has always done the exchange, you see."

His voice became low and certain. "The prints, doctor," he said, holding out the hand that wasn't balancing the gun at Rita's temple.

Hamish slipped the envelope out of his pocket and held it out. He was clearly going to kill them anyway, and he would simply take the photographs from his dead body.

Colonel Winter took the envelope and turned to Celestine. "Now you can tell me the name of your contact," he said. "Or I will shoot your boyfriend." He shifted the gun to point it at Hamish's forehead.

"He's not my boyfriend," she said. "Go ahead and shoot him."

The comment cut Hamish even though he knew it was true.

Just as Hamish was certain this was the end, and he could find no way out, he noticed Rita's eyes flicker slightly. Shifting his gaze back toward Winter, he saw another silhouette behind him that blacked out the doorway completely. Captain Murdo Black was carrying a long rifle and he had it pointed directly at the back of Colonel Winter's head. A shot was fired and for a short time Hamish was unaware which gun had discharged it. But Hamish remained standing, and the colonel fell to the ground with a look of shock on his face.

CHAPTER TWENTY-SIX

In some respects, the Brussels Conference displayed the vagueness of sentiment that prevails about the use of spies in war. It was agreed between all the powers that no one should be considered as a spy but one who secretly or under false pretences sought to obtain information for the enemy in occupied districts; that military men collecting such information within the zone of hostile operations should not be regarded as spies if it were possible to recognise their military character; and that military men and even civilians, if their proceedings were open, charges with despatches, should not, if captured, be treated as spies; nor individuals who carried despatches or kept up communications between different parts of an army through the air in balloons. The German delegation proposed with regard to balloons that those who sailed in them might be first of all summoned to descend, then fired at if they refused, and if captured, treated as prisoners, not as spies. The rejection of this proposal implies that by the laws of modern war, a balloonist is liable to be shot as a spy; so that, from the point of view of personal danger, the service of the balloon becomes doubly heroic.

Morning Bulletin. Monday 25 August, 1884

Hamish realised he had his eyes closed only when he felt Rita's arms around his neck. When he opened them, he saw Murdo Black, the rifle held loosely at his side with Wallace and Bellamy on either side of him. The colonel was dead on the timber floor and Celestine was still tied up in the corner.

Hamish returned Rita's hug for a moment, drinking in the comfort of her closeness, and thanking God they were both still alive. Then he released her, and while she set about freeing Celestine, Hamish retrieved the envelope.

"He would have killed me slowly," she said to no one in particular. "A German spy," she spat.

Wallace was unmoved. "And you and your father are French spies," he said.

"Not spies," she hissed. "We are part of the League of Alsace. We stand against the filthy German Imperialists and the Germanisation of Alsace."

"The Treaty of Frankfurt cannot make people who believe themselves to be French, German," said Wallace. "But there has been too much bloodshed."

Bellamy added, "And two innocent people who have nothing to do with this conflict over territories are dead."

"That is the doing of the filthy German," said Celestine. "Not mine."

Bellamy spoke directly to Celestine. "You placed Dr Hart in danger when you hid those images in his suitcase," he said. "You knew the colonel was prepared to kill for them."

"You placed us all in danger," said Rita.

Celestine remained where she was in the corner of the beach house, though fully untied, and looked defiant.

"Tell us," said Wallace, "is your father alive?"

"My father is dead. They took him from the Rhine when our balloon went down and tortured him until he was dead," said Celestine. "I have known since I received intelligence from the German territory less than a week after the crash. I agreed to the invitation to come to Australia because I thought it would be an opportunity to get away to safety for a while. I had no idea Colonel Winter was a German spy until I arrived here. Even then, I had only suspicions. My suspicions were confirmed by a French contact here. He came to see me early in the morning before the exhibition."

"That's why you lied about meeting me on the stairs?" said Hamish.

"It was a mistake to lie about it," she said. "I can see that I drew attention to myself unnecessarily, but I was shocked to find I was in danger, even here, at the edge of the world."

Hamish thought 'the edge of the world' an exaggeration.

"When the colonel insisted on a private dinner, I knew he was plotting something – and when he asked about the photographs, I knew what it was. I kept them on me. Then, after he searched my room, I realised I needed to hide them. I told you I trusted you, Hamish. You were always going to be my back-up plan."

Hamish realised the French aeronaut had been grooming him for his part in this intrigue. His face flushed.

Rita helped Celestine to her feet. "Can you walk?" she asked.

Celestine drew away from Rita. "Of course," she said, dusting down her dress.

As Rita and Celestine stood, Sergeant Cooper came into view, with three police constables behind him.

"What have we here?" he said, standing tall.

The sergeant was enjoying his moment. Here was Bellamy, trapped in the beach hut with a dead German and a Scottish Captain with a rifle by his side.

Bellamy explained.

"Two women murdered, and all this," Cooper made a theatrical gesture that included the scene in the beach hut, "for a few photographs?"

"It would seem so," said Bellamy. The two police constables put handcuffs around Captain Murdo Black's wrists and held him firmly in place between them. Bellamy tucked his hand into the colonel's pocket and lifted out a key. "To Hilda's door," he said.

"There's the damn key," said Hamish.

Sergeant Cooper took the key and placed it in his own pocket.

"Evidence," he said. "I'll see you all at the station to give sworn statements. You come with us now," he directed the captain.

Hamish watched the constables drag Black to the police carriage and tuck him away. Then he, Rita, Wallace, and Bellamy headed back along the promenade to the hotel. Red was slung across Wallace's shoulder.

Celestine hurried ahead of them.

"What's her hurry?" said Bellamy. "It's all over now. The colonel can't steal her precious photographs."

Nonetheless, Celestine reached the hotel several minutes before them and when Hamish went into his room, she was already in there.

He stopped, taken aback. "I suppose you want these?" He removed the envelope from his pocket and held it out to her. "I retrieved the photographs from the colonel's body."

She looked at the envelope greedily for a moment before taking it. She broke into an engaging smile. Hamish was not as moved as he might have been before she had almost got Rita killed. The thought of the gun at Rita's head made Hamish's blood boil. He did not return her smile. Celestine slipped past him and as she did so, she reached up to kiss his cheek. He pulled away, so that she stopped and skirted by him to the door. She stood and looked back. "I told you; I trusted you, *mon ami,*" she said. "I am an impeccable judge of character." Then she was gone.

Hamish used the washbasin in his room to freshen up his face before he joined the others. They were ready to walk to the police station together.

They all gave their statements and signed them, and Captain Black was allowed to leave with them. No charges were to be laid against him. Indeed, he was something of a hero, at least to his friends.

***

After a sound night's sleep, Hamish and Rita were sitting on the bench outside the hotel. The rough weather of the past few days was over. The sun was shining on the sea like a patchwork of diamonds shimmering in the light breeze.

"It's going to be a warm day," said Hamish, staring out at Stradbroke Island.

"It's a beautiful day," said Rita.

"I think I'd like to return home on the Natone this afternoon," said Hamish. "What do you think? If you'd rather stay, we can. I promised a holiday and we haven't really had one."

"I think I've had enough of paradise," said Rita, smiling at him. "Anyway, you need to arrange your passage to Melbourne."

Hamish stared out across the blue sky. "I think I do," he said.

"What about Wallace?" Rita asked. "He may want to stay with the captain for a while longer."

Hamish looked back toward the hotel to see Wallace walking toward them.

"We're boarding the Natone for the return journey to Brisbane this afternoon," said Hamish.

Wallace didn't seem surprised. "I'll return with you."

"We thought you might stay a little longer," said Rita with a twinkle in her eye.

"*Aye*, lassie, that would be nice, but Black has to travel to Sydney to meet his berth back to Glasgow and I have to return to Brisbane to keep an eye on you two. God knows you attract trouble."

Hamish and Rita ignored him.

"Where do you think Celestine is now?" asked Hamish.

"Who knows? She didn't turn up at the police station yesterday to give her statement and her luggage is gone. I imagine she's on her way to Sydney. I wonder if she'll meet her exhibition commitments for the rest of the tour."

Hamish looked thoughtful. "The Germans will still be looking for those photographs," he said, "and more importantly, they'll still want the names of her German and French contacts."

"I don't suppose she'll be safe anywhere," said Rita. "The world has become a much smaller place with the telegraph."

"Where's Bellamy?" asked Hamish as they shifted along the bench so Wallace could sit down. Red clambered up onto Wallace's lap and Rita reached over to smooth down the terrier's wiry hair.

"You tried to tell us Celestine was in the beach hut, didn't you?" she said.

Red shifted his head so her fingers could scratch behind his ears.

"Bellamy's already on his way back to Brisbane," said Wallace. "He left by police transport early this morning. Apparently, there's an incident that requires his immediate attention."

Intent on their conversation, they didn't hear James Hembrow behind them. He came into view without offering any greeting.

"Good morning," said Rita. "It's wonderful to see you outside."

He nodded and took up a stance at the end of the bench, staring out across the passage.

"Do you have any plans yet? I mean, for what you might do next?" said Hamish.

James Hembrow continued to stare.

"What do you think will happen to the Scottish Prince?" he said after a while.

Hamish was surprised by the question.

"They can't salvage it now," said Wallace. "It will stay where it is."

"I'm glad," said James. "I'll always think of it as Glenda's resting place."

Hamish raised his eyes to look at him.

"I know her body has been taken elsewhere," said James, "but in my mind she'll always be out there."

They all stared at the wreck of the Scottish Prince. There was something ethereal about the wreck and the image of Glenda forever tangled in the rigging below the surface.

"And I might write a letter to the lad," said James. "He's a decent young man, and a link to Glenda. He might agree to stay in touch."

"I hope he does," smiled Rita.

Hamish tilted his head toward Wallace. "Did Bellamy give any details about this mystery case that required his immediate presence?"

Wallace scratched the terrier's ears and shook his head. "Something about a strange case up north. Maryborough, I think he said."

EPILOGUE

The wind blew against his face as he disembarked. The chill wind in late January reminded him immediately of one of the reasons he'd left Melbourne. One week on the schooner had felt like a lifetime. He hoped the trip would be worth it. He needed to at least assess his father's condition and his mother's ability to cope firsthand. If his worst fears were confirmed, he could see his father settled into an asylum. If his mother was being truthful when she wrote that his condition was manageable, well and good. But he had to know for sure.

Hamish stood before his parents' house and stared. He'd never seen this house. They'd moved here while he was in Queensland. It seemed strange to imagine this as his parents' home. They had gradually become like strangers; people who had very little to do with him. He didn't know how to feel about that, but he couldn't avoid a certain sense of responsibility.

Up the stairs and a sharp, purposeful knock on the door. His mother appeared almost immediately and stood looking at him as though she didn't know who he was. Then, as if a light had come on, her face changed. "Hamish, what are you doing here?" She stood with her body guarding the door and made no move to invite him in.

"I've come to see Father. And you, of course. I'm worried about you both."

"There's no need. You shouldn't have come all this way."

"Are you going to let me in?"

The woman, five years older than when he'd last seen her, but looking significantly older than that, moved aside.

Hamish leant in and kissed her on the cheek as he passed and entered the house. There was a narrow hallway with rooms off each side. It was a great deal smaller than the house they lived in when they moved from the goldmines to the city. His mother made no further effort to greet him. Instead, she stood watching him nervously as he placed his bag on the hallstand. "Where is he?" Hamish asked.

"In his study. You're lucky because he goes to the racetrack at ten. Another half an hour and you would have missed him."

"Where's the study?" Hamish asked as he peered down the hall, trying to decide by supernatural means which door on either side might reveal his father.

His mother hesitated another minute before leading him to the last door on the right. She knocked lightly before opening, then she walked in gingerly, and Hamish followed. He saw an elderly man, barely recognisable as his father, sitting in a leather armchair by the window.

"Hamish is here, dear," said his mother. The old man registered her presence and looked at her. Then his eyes went to Hamish. Suddenly, the old man became red in the face and sat forward on the edge of his chair.

"You shot my horse, you mongrel!" he shouted.

Hamish took a step back.

"No dear. This is Hamish. Your son."

The old man eyed him suspiciously. "My son is in Queensland," he said.

"Yes. But he has come to visit…"

She hadn't completed the sentence when the old man leapt from the chair and came at Hamish with his fists up. "You shot my horse, you bloody mongrel," he shouted as he came.

Hamish's mother pushed her son backward through the door and slammed it shut behind them.

"Get him out of my house," the old man yelled from behind the door.

Hamish and his mother went into the garden. She was holding his arm, guiding him, though the touch felt less like affection than gentle manipulation.

"Is he like this all the time?" asked Hamish.

"Of course not," his mother said, "as long as we all stick to his routine, he is relatively normal. It's only when something out of the ordinary happens, he becomes unnerved. Like you turning up. It's a shock, that's all."

"Mother, you have to face the fact that this will get worse. He was aggressive just now. What if he turns on you?"

"Don't be ridiculous. Your father is fine. I'm fine. You shouldn't have come. You're not going to admit him to one of those places…" She began to cry.

Hamish put his arm around her shoulder. She tolerated it for a moment before shrugging him away.

"I'm just here to see for myself, that's all."

A carriage stopped in front of the house and a man in a smart suit stepped down.

"Mrs Hart," he nodded. Mrs Hart smiled.

The suited man went into the house and emerged some minutes later with the old man, the two of them chatting like friends all the way to the carriage. It rattled away.

"He'll stay with him all day and bring him home for his dinner at six."

Hamish's mother watched her son closely.

"I'll talk to him tonight then," said Hamish.

He settled into the guest room in his parent's home and slept off the week's journey at sea and the shock of the first encounter with his father's dementia. The changes in both his parents after only five years were overwhelming. When he left for Queensland, they were on the wrong side of middle-aged, but they were fit and healthy.

That evening, when Hamish entered the dining room for the evening meal, his father was dressed smartly and seated at the head of the table. His mother was bringing in a tureen of soup. Hamish pulled out a chair to the left of his father and sat.

"Hamish is joining us for dinner," announced his mother.

The old man studied him with curiosity. "Have you come to see the horse?" he said.

"It's me, Father," said Hamish.

"Yes. Yes. You might as well stay to tea. You can come back tomorrow and check on the horse again, then."

His mother ladled soup into Hamish's bowl and he ate.

"Good of you to join us," said his father.

"Father, It's Hamish," said Hamish.

"I have every faith you'll be able to put that leg right. Don't worry about it now. Just eat your soup."

It seemed fruitless to argue. His father was convinced he was the vet, but at least he was no longer trying to hit him. Hamish ate in the knowledge that tomorrow was another day and he would have another chance to connect with his father.

Hamish woke early and went for a walk to clear his head and prepare himself for the next encounter with his parents. Feeling rejuvenated and positive about the prospect of having a conversation with the man he knew as his father, he stepped into the dining room. His father was tucking into his porridge.

"Ah… back to see the horse. Good man," said his father cheerfully.

Hamish stood close to the old man. "Father, I am not the vet. I am your son, Hamish," he said as clearly as he could.

The old man furrowed his brow and concentrated for a moment. Then he called out, "Mother, the vet is here to see to the horse. He can go down himself. No need for you to worry."

Hamish's mother came in and glared at Hamish. There seemed to be a mixture of fear and defiance in her expression.

The old man nodded towards Hamish. "Off you go. You know where the stables are."

Hamish shrugged and moved to leave the room. His mother started to go after him, but she stopped when the old man called, "don't worry about him. He knows where to go. Sit down and eat your breakfast." She sat. Hamish left them.

Half an hour later, Hamish was sitting in the garden when his mother joined him. He saw panic in her eyes. She was terrified of what he might do. He didn't want his mother to be afraid of him. His heart felt as though it had swollen to fill his chest.

"Keep me updated, won't you?" he said.

"Thank you," whispered his mother.

Hamish took one long look at her and made his decision. He squeezed her hand and was surprised to feel the bones beneath the skin.

He walked as fast as he could to the tram stop and caught a tram to the wharves. The ship he had sailed on from Brisbane was getting ready to return. He paid for his passage and made himself comfortable to wait.

"What the dickens is Bellamy doing in Maryborough?" he thought.

AUTHOR'S NOTES

Death at Deepwater Point is about stories. Each of the main characters has a secret and their secret is revealed through the stories they tell. At first, they reveal only a little of themselves, and gradually they tell their stories in full. This is the way people reveal themselves to others – a little at a time as trust grows. The ways in which people create themselves through story has always fascinated me. We see ourselves in a certain way and we share as much of ourselves in the form of stories as we need to, in order to create an impression. We embellish parts of an experience and leave other parts out. The aim is to tell a story that builds on our identity. In the same way as we do this in real life, characters create themselves within stories. Hamish never tells us everything about his childhood. Rita presents herself as confident and sure of herself, but we know there must be insecurities because we all have them. And we are aware there is far more to Wallace than a life at sea as a ship's cook.

We only know others, whether fictional or real, through the stories they choose to tell us.

It's the same with the history of places. We only know about the past, and specific places, through the stories that are told by, and about, those places. A walk around Southport today provides very few clues of the town as it was during Hamish's time. There isn't much left to see, to excite imagination. But there are stories. And some old photographs.

The three physical features within this book that form a framework for the narrative are the Grand Hotel (also referred to as the Deepwater Point Hotel); The wreck of the Scottish Prince; and Burleigh Headland.

In the case of the Grand Hotel, the modern building, close to the original site, is replete with references to the first Grand Hotel's architecture. The grand façade, the columns, the shape of the roof, all bear witness to the hotel that was present in Hamish's day. The Grand Hotel, also known in 1887 as the Deepwater Point Hotel was built in 1886. At the time, it was isolated from the township of Southport by surrounding land that soon came under allotment. The site had magnificent views of the Broadwater and Stradbroke Island. The interior of the building and the furnishings are all carefully described by visitors and published in the local newspapers at the time.

When it was built, the Grand Hotel was celebrated as the most luxurious hotel in the southern hemisphere. Designed by architects John Hall and Sons, it was American in style and had a roof that replicated the mansard shape of Parliament House in Brisbane. Furniture and fittings were shipped from America to ensure the latest in style and opulence.

The upper middle-class residents of Brisbane flocked to the Grand Hotel for summer holidays on the beach.

There was a jetty in front of the hotel for guests to disembark from the two steamers, The Natone and The President, that ferried visitors from Brisbane daily. The two steamers had a friendly rivalry, just as is depicted in the story.

The wreck of the Scottish Prince sits jammed into a sandbank, where she has been since 1887, about 500 metres offshore in water at about ten metres in depth. It's a popular diving spot today. The iron hulled barque with three masts was a passenger and cargo ship working between Glasgow and Australia. On 2 February 1887, it ran aground near the southern tip of Stradbroke Island. The wreck could be seen by the people of Southport, and it caused quite a stir in the small community. A rescue mission was mounted to save the barque but before it could be dislodged, a series of terrible storms blew up, causing the ship to tilt to one side, the main mast split, and a great hole opened up in the hull. The cargo washed onto the shores of Southport and Stradbroke Island and people eagerly retrieved as many objects as they could. Some objects were declared but most were not, especially the large vats of whiskey. An investigation found the ship had been sailing too close to the shore and there were inconsistencies in the logbooks. Captain Little had his license revoked.

While the spit and the Broadwater looked very different in the 1880s, I did move the wreck of the Scottish Prince a little closer to Deepwater Point for the convenience of the story. That can be taken as artistic license, but it really emphasises my point – we tell the parts of the story that create the impression we hope to convey.

Burleigh Heads is an imposing basalt headland that has become a tourism mecca on the Gold Coast. The Burleigh Heads that Hamish visited with Celestine was a wild and remote place with a rugged windswept cliff facing the sea and heavy sub-tropical flora on the land side. There were no buildings beyond a small dwelling providing refreshments and a stable to freshen the horses. A company called Echlin did provide horse and carriage trips along the sand from Southport to Burleigh Heads. I have a wonderful photograph of a carriage and horse travelling along the sand, with the sea spray flying up from the horse's hooves.

The stories these places tell today to the millions of visitors who come to enjoy the sun and the surf are not the whole story. Places, and more importantly, people's perceptions of them build over time, and through the stories they tell. More than a century of stories have been told about the sun and the surf waiting to entice people to the area now known as the Gold Coast. It is interesting to know that the perceptions of late Victorian visitors are similar to those of tourists today. The area has always been known for its long stretches of white sand, clear waters and opportunities for fun. My representations of the area are based on descriptions told by people who visited in the 1880s. They are true only in the sense that they reflect the impressions shared by those visitors.

The stories told by Captain Murdo Black may also be true, if you accept them as told in the newspapers at the time. The story about Donald is adapted from a story that appeared in the Telegraph, Brisbane, Saturday 4 December 1886; the story of the two sailors named Tom and Ned appeared in the Port Adelaide News, Tuesday 6 January 1885. The stories were both told to the newspaper at some distance from the original experience and may already have been told and retold many times, so the "exactness" of the truth cannot be recovered. But this is how truth is; a slippery customer at best.

The story told by Glenda Hembrow is fiction in its entirety, but it has a ring of truth to it. The earliest draft of the story had infanticide at its heart. In the second half of the nineteenth century, in both England and Australia, the number of cases of infanticide reached epidemic proportions. The introduction of the *New Poor Law Act* in 1834 is believed to be a major cause of this increase. Prior to this law, a man accused of fathering an illegitimate child could be made to provide for the child. If paternity was not established, the mother and child could be provided charity. But the *New Poor Law Act, 1834* had a *Bastardy Clause* that placed sole responsibility for the illegitimate child on the mother and prohibited the child and mother from receiving charitable relief. Unmarried mothers, then, were left with limited options. The aim of the *Bastardy Clause* was to reduce promiscuity among women and therefore, reduce the number of illegitimate births. However, it missed the point that men also played a part in the process. Not all unmarried women who fell pregnant did so as a consequence of their own promiscuity. The unexpected result was an increase in the rate of infanticide. The unmarried woman who gave birth was a 'fallen woman' with few prospects for a future, and the child would carry the burden of illegitimacy throughout life, also limiting their prospects.

The issue of how we think about infants from conception to birth and beyond in contemporary society is topical. Lawmakers are debating issues relating to the point of gestation at which a foetus is considered an individual with its own human rights. In the late Victorian period in Australia, infanticide was common. In some ways, it was treated as a kind of 'abortion after birth'.

Glenda's story represents a story of 'potential'. This is largely what historical fiction is: stories made from 'potential truths'.

BIBLIOGRAPHY

Bates, Victoria. The Legacy of 1885: Girls and the age of sexual consent. *History and Policy*, 8 September 2015.

Butterworth, Lee Karen. What Good is a Coroner? The Transformation of the Queensland Office of the Coroner 1859-1959. Doctor of Philosophy Thesis. Griffith University 2012.

Eiler, Karen Lynn. *A Conflict of Cultures: Alsace-Lorraine 1871-1918*. Honours Thesis, Butler University Library Collection 22. 1979

Elliott, George. *Adam Bede*, Digireads, 2009.

Gardiner, Amanda. It is Almost as if There is a Written Script: Child murder, concealment of birth and the unmarried mother in Western Australia, *M/C Journal*, Vol 17. No.5, 2014.

Goc, Nicola. *Women, Infanticide, and the Press, 1822-1922: News Narratives in England and Australia*, Taylor and Francis Group, 2013

Pesk, Elizabeth. Feminist Responses to Crimes against Women 1868-1896. *Signs*. Vol.8.No.3

Women and Violence pp.451-470 University of Chicago Press, 1983.

Simons, Fraser. *The Early History of Ballooning – The Age of the Aeronaut*, Read Publishing Limited 2014.

Stuer, Anny The French in Australia 1788-1947. Doctor of Philosophy Thesis, Australian National University 1979.

Swain, Shurlee. Birth and Death in a New Land: attitudes to infant death in colonial Australia, *The History of Family*, Vol.15. No.1, p.25-33. 2010

Throsby, D. J, Zwar. C, Morgan. *Australian Book Readers: Survey Methods and Results*. Macquarie Research Papers, 2017.

Wilkie, Ben. Lairds of Suburbia: Scottish Migrant Settlement and Housing in Australian Cities 1880-1930. Journal of Scottish Historical Studies. Vol. 36, No. 1. pp81-102 2016.

New Generation Publishing Ltd

www.newgeneration-publishing.com

Shawline Publishing Group Pty Ltd
www.shawlinepublishing.com.au

More great Shawline titles can be found by scanning the QR code below.
New titles also available through Books@Home Pty Ltd.
Subscribe today at www.booksathome.com.au or scan the QR code below.